THE
UNVEILING

LAURIE HARRISON

ISBN-13: 978-1-7332859-0-2

Library of Congress Control Number: 2019913443

Emerald Rain Publishing LLC
7643 Gate Parkway, Ste. 104-156
Jacksonville, FL 32256

For my parents, Richard and Catherine Metzger.

PROLOGUE

I t was silent with the exception of the sound of my heart beating wildly in my chest. I was certain I'd heard footsteps just moments ago.

Sure, I could try to explain away the noises by rationalizing that it was just my older sister, Becca, getting up for a glass of water or her boyfriend, Seth, sneaking over to see her since our parents would be gone all night. I could easily explain it away if it wasn't for this feeling. This gnawing pit in the middle of my stomach that had awoken me from a deep sleep. Something wasn't right, and I *knew* it.

I grabbed my cell phone and contemplated calling the police, but what would I tell them? I knew there was an emergency, but I just didn't know what it was yet. Would they even believe me if I couldn't describe what was really going on? Would they think I was just a fourteen-year-old girl with a wild imagination?

A faint thud echoed from down the hall.

I carefully peeled back the covers and placed one foot on the floor, trying to delicately shift my weight. The bed creaked in response anyway.

When both feet were on the floor, I lightly tiptoed to my bedroom door. The socks on my feet helped keep my footsteps silent against the wood floor.

With my cell phone clutched in one hand, I slowly turned the doorknob with the other, leaving the safety of my bedroom to head into the dark unknown of the rest of the house. Although both of our bedrooms were on the second story of the house, Becca's was on the opposite end of the hallway.

The knot in my stomach tightened. *She's in trouble.*

I hurried down the hall to her room, unsure of what I would do once I got there. All I knew was that I needed to help her.

Becca's door was partially cracked open. Her room was quiet. Gently, I pushed the door open further. The moonlight beamed through the bay window in her room, casting a faint glow on my sister, who was sleeping soundly in her bed.

For a moment, I was tempted to wake Becca up but decided against it. She was the one person in the world who wouldn't think I was crazy for doing so, but she needed her rest for her calculus test tomorrow.

For the first time, my instinct had been wrong. Becca was safe. I must have just imagined the strange sounds. At least I hadn't called the police. My mother would've been furious with me for creating a story for the neighbors to gossip about.

I let out a small sigh of relief and turned to go back to my room. But instead of stepping back into the hallway, I hit a barrier. Something tall and unmovable was blocking my path. In the split second it took me to realize that the barrier was a person, they grabbed me by the head and slammed me into the wall.

ONE

A lthough the streets of St. Augustine were crowded with tourists, I was alone. And that was the way I preferred it.

I avoided eye contact with the people I passed as I made my way down St. George Street, one of the most popular destinations in the nation's oldest city. In the six months since moving to Florida, I'd become accustomed to diving in between groups of slow-moving sightseers as I made my way to work at the Cuna Café. I'd also perfected the art of passing by without being stopped for casual conversation.

Despite the crowds, I loved St. Augustine. The downtown area where St. George Street was located consisted of longstanding Spanish-style buildings that lined its cobblestone streets. The buildings, separated by narrow alleys, had been converted into various shops over the years, but during the process, the owners had been very careful to maintain the integrity of the city's history. Even when the city had finally put in a parking garage to accommodate the tourist population, they had taken great care to ensure that the architecture blended well with the neighboring buildings.

I stepped around two women who were speaking with very distinct British accents. They barely noticed me as I glanced down at my watch to confirm I was still on time. It had always been in my nature to be on time, especially for work. It was a quality that my father had instilled in me at a young age.

"If you're not ten minutes early, you're late," he would say.

The Cuna Café sat at the intersection of Cuna Street and St. George Street. Cuna Street was a convenient side street that led to Highway A1A, which ran parallel to the Matanzas River. My boss, Carl, had once told me that he chose the location because he believed it would draw both the tourists who were out shopping and those who wanted to view the water. Carl had been correct in his assumption; the Cuna Café rarely had a slow day and drew in not only tourists, but also a steady stream of local college students. Carl was considering opening a second location right across from St. Augustine College.

I turned down Cuna Street, and the café immediately came into sight. It was a relatively plain building that Carl had taken great care to make noticeable. Outside, in the bushes surrounding the entrance, were twinkle lights that sparkled even in the daytime. On the walls outside the front door were wrought iron sconces that added a warm, homey touch. The day's specials were advertised on a chalkboard sign that sat within a bright yellow frame, held in place by an old painter's easel.

As soon as I entered the café, my coworker Jen was at my side.

"Natalie, you are not going to believe this!" she said, her brown eyes wide with excitement.

I knew that she had some sort of juicy gossip for me. If there was one thing I could always count on with Jen, it was for her to be in the know about everything going on in St. Augustine.

"What happened?" I asked.

A mischievous grin spread across her face as she tugged my arm, pulling me into the corner. "I came in early today and guess who I caught making out!"

It took me only a split second to know exactly who she was talking about, but I just shook my head anyway. I could tell how excited she was to tell me, and I didn't want to ruin her fun.

"Carl and Jessica!" She bit her bottom lip and took a small step back.

My inkling had been right, but for Jen's benefit, I let my jaw drop in shock.

"I know," she agreed, pleased with my reaction. Then, she quickly added, "He'd just better not give her all the good shifts."

Out of the corner of my eye, I saw Carl eyeing us from the cash register. I grabbed Jen's hand and led her past the counter and into the back room that we used as the employee break area. The old metal door squeaked as it swung closed behind us.

I removed my jacket and crossbody purse and shoved them into my locker. "I hope it works out for them," I told her. "Jessica's a nice girl, and I know she's liked Carl for a long time now."

"How do you know that?" Jen asked, her brow raised.

I looked up at her and shrugged. I knew a lot of things that I couldn't explain. "Just a feeling, I guess," I replied, trying to sound nonchalant.

Jen casually sat on a large crate and stretched out her legs. "I always hoped you'd be the one to hook up with Carl." She shot me a careful glance.

I grabbed a hair tie from my bag and pulled my hair into a messy bun. "What are you talking about? I'm not interested in Carl." It was the truth even though that would be hard for someone to believe. No one could argue that Carl was a great catch—handsome, smart, and quite successful for someone in his mid-twenties—but I'd never had those feelings for him. And not that I thought badly of Jessica, but I would never date my boss.

"I just think it's time for you to date," she replied. "You haven't gone on one single date since you moved here. You're eighteen! These are your prime dating years!"

"Maybe I haven't found anyone I'm interested in yet," I defended myself as I closed the door to my locker.

Jen nodded thoughtfully, her blonde bob bouncing around her face. I could tell she already had a backup plan for my answer. "What about Michael?" she asked with fake innocence.

I almost laughed out loud. Michael was a customer who had started coming into the café about a month ago and now came in at least two or three times a week. He always sat at a small table in my section but never spoke to me, outside of necessity. The only reason I even knew his name was because Carl knew him. Apparently, Michael's family owned an antique furniture store called The Treasure Chest a few blocks away.

"Just think about it?" she asked as she stood back up.

I playfully rolled my eyes at her as I opened the door and stepped back into the dining area. Jen was a normal twenty-one-year-old girl. I was far from that.

I took two steps into the dining area and stopped short. Jen bumped into me from behind.

Michael was standing in the entrance to the café. He was alone, as usual, and I couldn't help but wonder why.

Don't good-looking people usually travel in packs, like wolves?

Jen peered from around my shoulder. "It's a sign. Maybe it's fate," she whispered in my ear.

Michael's eyes met mine as he took his seat. I quickly looked away.

I could feel his eyes still on me as I walked behind the counter and cut a slice of chocolate ganache cake. I didn't even have to ask Michael what he wanted; this was what he always ordered.

As I approached his table with the cake and a glass of water, I noticed how the sunlight came in through the window behind him, making his dark blond hair shine brilliantly. His blue eyes contrasted brightly against his healthy, glowing skin.

Seeing him made me recall how I'd hit the snooze button three times this morning before getting out of bed and how this caused me to rush to take a shower and leave before I could dry my hair all the way. My auburn hair usually hung in long, wavy ringlets halfway down my back. The lack of styling today, combined with the Florida humidity, was without a doubt causing some frizzing. I was glad I'd pulled it up at least.

I glanced at the other waitresses in the café. First, there was Jen, who was outgoing and confident—not to mention, gorgeous. I couldn't even count the number of times she'd received unsolicited phone numbers and date offers from customers she'd waited on.

Then, there was Jessica, who was flirting with Carl at the cash register. It was easy to see why he was attracted to her. She was tall, like a runway model, with light-brown hair that cascaded around her face in long layers. Her makeup was always perfect, as if it had been professionally applied.

Why would Michael sit in my section when he could very easily sit where there was more eye-candy for him? Perhaps he has a girlfriend and is afraid she would get jealous.

Michael watched silently as I placed the cake and water in front of him. I felt like he was always observing me, waiting for me to do something. I just had no idea what that something was.

"Can I get you anything else?" I asked, trying to break the awkwardness.

"No, thank you," he replied, now avoiding eye contact.

I nodded once. Then, I turned and walked away.

Jen watched expectantly from behind the counter but didn't say anything as I approached. I knew she would grill me about every detail later, not that there was anything to tell.

I tended to two other tables while Michael slowly ate his cake. Without trying to be obvious, I glanced over at him. He was already looking at me, his eyes immediately meeting mine. His gaze was intense, almost angry. I resisted the urge to look away.

Why is he looking at me like that?

Reading people had always been my gift, and it wasn't often that I found someone who was unreadable. Well, *gift* was being a bit generous. It was more of a curse, depending on how you looked at it.

I could easily tell when people were lying, if they were trying to fool someone, if they were falling in love, etcetera. This was how I'd known about the chemistry between Carl and Jessica, even before Jen had told me. The curse didn't sound so bad until you slipped up and freaked someone out. And believe me, it had happened more times than I could count despite my best attempts to stifle it.

Blood rushed to my cheeks as I realized I was still staring at Michael. As my eyes finally broke from his, I noticed that his water glass was empty. I almost laughed at myself as I understood that the intent behind his stare was probably irritation as to why I hadn't refilled his glass yet. Relief mixed with a small sense of embarrassment washed over me as I grabbed the water pitcher and headed back to his table.

When I reached his table, I saw that he had finished his last bite of cake. The cake plate was completely clean with the exception of one tiny crumb. There wasn't even a trace of frosting left.

"You missed a spot," I joked as I refilled his glass. I surprised myself in my attempt to kid with him.

He didn't respond, and just as I was beginning to wonder if he'd heard me, he replied, "It was good. Thank you."

He was always polite, and his words were always careful, deliberate. It was odd.

With the water pitcher in one hand, I reached with the other to pick up the plate. The side of my hand bumped his water glass, knocking it over.

"Oh!" I jumped back in surprise.

Water and ice flowed across the table and down the side. Luckily, I'd missed him, and it didn't land in his lap. I set the pitcher on the table, and we both instinctively reached for the napkin holder at the same time. My hand touched it first, and his hand landed on top of mine.

Michael reflexively jerked his hand back. He held it, as if burned by my touch. He blinked at me but said nothing.

Is he that offended by me that he can't bear the thought of even touching me?

I tightened my grasp on the napkins in my hand and frantically wiped up the mess I'd made. "Sorry," I mumbled, humiliated and unsure of what else to say. I could feel my cheeks getting hot.

He blinked again and then grabbed a handful of napkins to help me clean up. I noticed that he was very careful not to touch me as we blotted up the rest of the water from the table.

When the mess was cleaned up, I quickly refilled his glass and left his table as fast as I could.

"What was that?" Jen asked as I put the water pitcher on the counter.

"Not fate," I replied sourly.

I managed to convince Jen to deliver the bill to Michael while I hid behind the espresso machine. Within a few minutes, he was gone, but the embarrassment from the experience lingered.

"Don't worry about it," Jen said, trying to comfort me. "If it's any consolation to you, he looked disappointed when he saw me."

Jen seemed to believe it was true, but I also knew that she was optimistic beyond reason. He could have fallen asleep at the table, and she would've interpreted that as some sort of sign that he liked me. It didn't matter. I knew the truth. He thought I was a mess, and he was right.

Around eight o'clock, the café began to slow down, and Jen asked Carl if she could go home early. I managed to stay busy until eight thirty, but then Carl insisted that I leave as well.

"Go ahead," he told me. "You're not making any tips with it being this slow. Go out. Have some fun."

Yeah, right, I thought but appreciated his kindness.

I considered offering to let Jessica go early instead, but I caught them exchanging a flirtatious look and realized they would prefer to be alone.

I stepped outside and was surprised by how much the temperature had dropped. It was in the high fifties, which I'd heard was unusually cold for St. Augustine in October. I buried my hands in my jacket pockets and started my short walk home.

I couldn't help but notice everyone else was walking in pairs or groups, and for the first time since moving there, I felt a pang of loneliness. Even though I'd specifically chosen St. Augustine for the solitude and made the choice to leave home and move to a city where I didn't know anyone, I occasionally missed home. But I missed the home I'd once had, not the home I'd left behind. The home I'd left behind was one where I no longer belonged.

I turned down my street and could see my car parked in front of my apartment. My car—a 1991 silver Saturn SC, which I'd paid cash for—was really just a convenience for when I wanted to go somewhere that wasn't within a reasonable walking distance. I'd bought the car when I first moved to St. Augustine, and it had left my driveway maybe a dozen times since then. After an unfortunate incident between my car and a neighbor's mailbox that had resulted in a deep scratch on my back right bumper, I'd decided to try to walk whenever possible.

As I stepped inside my apartment, I instantly felt relieved to be home. My apartment wasn't elaborate, but it had become my safe haven over the past several months.

The building that occupied my apartment was actually an old house from the early 1900s that had been converted into two small apartments. I lived on the left side of the building, and the right side was currently unoccupied.

I loved the antiquity of the apartment and couldn't help but think that it would make my mother break out in hives if she ever came to visit. I kept it clean and tidy, but the apartment was very small. If she visited, I knew she would refuse to touch anything and would complain of how claustrophobic she felt.

My apartment, although advertised as a one-bedroom, more closely resembled a studio size. As soon as you entered the apartment, you were in the living room. It was the largest room in the apartment but was by no means spacious. I was proud, however, of my modern lime-green couch that I'd bought for seventy-five dollars from a recently graduated college student who was moving to Michigan. The couch was practically new, and after adding a few black-and-white pillows, it felt like it had been made for me.

To the right of the living room was a cramped kitchen with appliances that were at least fifteen years old. The hexagon tiles on the floor were black and white, and my landlord had attempted to update the cabinets by painting them white before I moved in. There was no telling what color they had been prior to that.

To the left of the living room was the area that I used as my bedroom. It didn't have a door, but there was an entryway leading into it. I'd put up a gray curtain to separate the two rooms. The bedroom had just enough space to house a queen-size bed, a nightstand, and a small four-drawer dresser. The room didn't have a closet, so I'd purchased a clothing rack to hold my hanging clothes.

To access the tiny bathroom, you had to walk through the makeshift bedroom. With the exception of Jen, who occasionally came over, I never had company, so this layout didn't bother me. The only grievance I had about the apartment was the lack of an actual bathtub. Every now and then, after a long shift, I would find myself longing for the comfort of a relaxing, hot bath. The bathroom did have a narrow stand-up shower, but it just wasn't the same.

I walked into the kitchen, flipping my purse onto the counter. My cell phone slid out, and I noticed it was lit up to let me know I had a voice mail. I picked it up. Maybe Carl had called to change my shift tomorrow.

I grabbed a glass out of the drainboard, poured myself some water, and hit play to listen to the voice mail.

"Hi. Uh, Nat, it's me."

I froze. I hadn't expected the voice I heard.

"It's Seth," he said. "I hope you're doing okay. I know it's been a long time."

The glass shook in my hand, and I carefully placed it on the counter.

"Look, I really need to see you," Seth continued. "I'm in Jacksonville, so give me a call if you can get together tomorrow. It's important."

When the voice mail ended, I just stood there, staring at the phone. I stared at it the same way I had the night Becca vanished, the night my entire life had changed.

Even though it was several years ago, I would never forget how I'd dialed Seth in the middle of the night from the darkness of the upstairs hallway of my parents' house.

When I came to, the house was silent, and I could see Becca's empty bed from the floor where I lay. My phone was on the floor beside me. It must have fallen out of my hand when I hit the wall. My first instinct probably should have been to call the police, but instead, I called the first person who had come to mind. Seth.

Seth answered the phone, half-asleep and innocently unaware of what had just occurred. I opened my mouth, but I couldn't say anything. A part of me was having trouble forming the words, and the other part of me couldn't bring myself to destroy his heart. Having known me my entire life, Seth quickly realized something was wrong.

"Natalie? Are you there? You okay?" he asked. I could hear the alarm in his voice as he asked each question and received no response in return.

My head had ached as I tried to lift it, and all I could muster was a moan. It was like a bad dream that I couldn't wake up from.

"I'll be right there," Seth told me before the phone went dead.

I lay there, unable and unwilling to move. I just stared at the phone in my hand, praying that he'd hurry.

Coming back to the present, I put the phone down on the counter and took a step back from it. With that single phone call, I realized that the sanctuary I'd worked so hard to create for myself was about to come to an end. My past, no matter how diligently I'd tried to hide from it, wouldn't allow me to hide forever.

TWO

I flopped onto my back, allowing the morning sunlight from the window to shine on my face. The decision of whether or not to call Seth back had weighed heavily on me all night.

Seth hadn't just been Becca's boyfriend; he was like a brother to me. Our fathers had grown up together and were business partners, so Seth was practically family. I'd known him my entire life, and I still cared for him, but allowing him back into my life was sure to bring up the very memories I had been trying to avoid.

The truth of the matter was, it was only within the past several months that I'd actually started feeling human again. I knew that my decision to move and to stay away from the things that reminded me of Becca was what was helping me survive. If I were to allow Seth back into my life, all of the things I'd been trying to escape would surely come back, and I wasn't sure I was ready to deal with them again. I wasn't sure I was capable of it.

On the other hand, it wasn't fair to Seth for me to avoid him. I'd already hurt him once by cutting him off after that fateful night. I recalled how he'd begged me not to shut him out, but I couldn't look at him without thinking about her. Seth without Becca was just unbearable despite the fact that he was my best friend.

"Ugh," I groaned to myself.

Calling him back was the right thing to do. Whatever he wanted had sounded important. He'd said it was. If he were in some sort of trouble, I needed to help him.

I peeled myself out of bed, got dressed, and headed to the café.

Seth was on my mind as I tended to customers. Halfway through my shift, I finally got the courage to call him back.

Once the breakfast crowd cleared out, I excused myself to the back room and grabbed my cell phone out of the locker. I quickly dialed Seth's number before I lost my nerve. Seth picked up on the second ring, as if waiting for my call.

"Hi, Nat," Seth answered. He sounded so normal, as if nothing had changed between us.

"Hey," I replied, unsure of what to say. I decided to just get straight to the point. "I got your voice mail. I can come up after work this evening. Where do you want to meet?"

Seth gave me directions to a restaurant in Jacksonville, which was about a thirty-minute drive from St. Augustine. I'd been to Jacksonville a handful of times with Jen but never to this particular area, although I'd heard Jen talk about the nightlife there.

"So, who is this guy again?" Jen asked when I told her of my plans. She made no attempt to hide her intrigue. "Is he hot?"

I'd never really given Jen much information on my family or my past. I'd told her that I had a sister who was missing, but that was it. Jen seemed to understand it wasn't something I wanted to talk about and never pushed the subject. It was one of the reasons I was friends with her.

"It's not like that," I replied.

Jen looked slightly disappointed but let it go. "Okay, okay. Just be careful, driving to Jacksonville though. You know driving isn't really your thing."

Jen scrunched her nose, no doubt recalling the one time she'd asked me to drive to Jacksonville with her. We'd almost gotten into three separate accidents before we even got on the interstate. In my defense, they hadn't really been my fault. It was more like plain bad luck when I got behind the wheel.

"Honestly, Natalie," she added, shaking her head, "I've never seen anything like it."

I was about to reassure her that I would be okay, but she seemed distracted. A huge smile spread across her face.

"What?" I followed her gaze.

I regretted asking when I noticed Michael sitting at his usual table, intently watching us. His right leg bounced beneath the table.

"He looks nervous," Jen said.

I lifted the glass lid from the stand that held the chocolate ganache cake. Jen handed me a plate.

"He's probably worried I'm going to pour water on him again," I said, not attempting to hide the bitterness in my voice.

She rolled her eyes at me and tried to hand me a glass of water.

"Will you wait on him?" I asked.

She gave me a disapproving look and tried again to hand me the water.

"Please," I begged, trying to keep my voice down.

"Nat—"

"*Please.*"

Jen took a deep breath, looked at Michael, and then looked back at me. "Fine," she replied, giving in, but I could tell that she was formulating another plan in her head. "But I do have one condition."

I braced myself. Although I wasn't one hundred percent sure what this condition was going to be, I would be willing to bet money that it wasn't going to be something I liked.

"You have to come to the masquerade ball with me," she said. "It's going to be so much fun!"

I groaned but weighed the options in my head. Option one was to go wait on Michael and risk having another awkward, humiliating moment in front of him. Option two was to go to the masquerade and risk having a different type of awkward, humiliating moment in front of everyone else in St. Augustine. After stealing a quick glance at Michael, I decided that I'd rather face humiliation in front of anyone as long as it wasn't him.

"Deal." I handed the cake plate to Jen.

It was a cowardly decision, not that I wouldn't have to put on a brave face to get through the masquerade ball. Jen had been trying to convince me to attend the ball with her for two months, and despite my best attempts at declining, I always knew deep down that I would cave and end up going.

I did my best to ignore Michael as he ate his cake. Several times, I was tempted to sneak a peek at him, but my will to salvage my dignity prevailed, and I managed to resist. Instead, I poured all of my energy and concentration into mopping every square inch of space behind the bar counter. Twice.

"He looked disappointed to see me again," Jen told me once Michael left. "I think he wanted you to wait on him. Especially since he sat in *your* section."

"I doubt that," I replied. "I appreciate you taking care of him though."

"Natalie Rose Clark!" Her frustrated tone reminded me of my mother. "He was watching you the entire time! He was so distracted that I had to ask him four times if he was ready for his check before he responded to me. How did you not notice that?"

I heard Carl call my name from the back room and was relieved to end the conversation and get back to work.

Once my shift was over, I hurried home to change. In less than thirty minutes, I was in my car, carefully merging onto the interstate.

My plan was to just stay in the right lane, go the speed limit, and focus on the road.

As I checked the rearview mirror, I noticed a red sports car flying down the far-left lane. The cars in the left lane were not going fast enough for it, so it swerved into the middle lane. A white van was blocking its path in the center lane, so the red car swerved into the far-right lane behind me to try to pass the van.

The red car quickly approached me from behind. Glancing in my side mirror, I could tell that the van was only a few feet away from my back left bumper. It would be nearly impossible for the car to pass.

The engine of the red car sped up as it raced toward me, obviously trying to gain enough momentum to squeeze in front of the van. I knew it wasn't going to make it. Terrified, I slammed on my gas. My old car reluctantly picked up speed as the red car grew closer and closer. Frantically, I glanced over at the van again. The red car wasn't going to make it.

I cringed as the red car slammed on its brakes, missing my rear bumper by mere inches. Luckily for me, the red car had sufficient brakes, and yet another accident was avoided. I brushed a bead of sweat from my forehead.

I continued to drive so slowly and so cautiously that it took me an additional fifteen minutes to reach the exit of the restaurant in Jacksonville.

The restaurant was located across the street from St. Johns River. As I walked to the entrance, I took notice of the old mansions lining the river, mixed in with trendy restaurants and art galleries.

As I stepped into the restaurant, I was greeted by a waitress close to my age with dark purple streaks in her hair. "Hi there! Table for how many?"

"I'm meeting someone," I replied as my eyes nervously searched the restaurant for Seth. It took only seconds to locate him.

Seth stood as I approached his table. He hadn't changed a bit. He was about five-ten with thick dark-brown hair and deep brown eyes that always twinkled as if he were keeping a secret. Although he was now twenty-one years old, he still had a mischievous, boyish quality about him.

I smiled tentatively, unsure of what his reaction would be toward me. The last time I'd spoken to Seth was before he left for college, and it wasn't a pleasant good-bye.

"Becca would have wanted you to be happy," Seth told me as he stood in the doorway of my bedroom.

He'd been trying to convince me for almost fifteen minutes to come to the going-away party his parents were throwing for him that night. I'd tried all of my usual excuses, so he was resorting to bringing Becca into it, which was guaranteed to send me into a rage.

"Don't tell me what Becca would have wanted," I spat back at him. "You barely even remember she existed." I knew the words would hurt Seth, but the fire in my chest was already burning out of control, and there was no taming it.

"You know that's not true," Seth replied. "I loved her."

"Please. You've had no trouble moving on," I said, throwing the dozens of girls he'd dated since Becca's disappearance in his face.

I could tell he didn't know what to say.

Back then, I'd thought he was trying to come up with an excuse, but after replaying the conversation in my head a million times since then, I realized he had been trying to figure out how to tell me how he was feeling in a way I'd understand. I was only fifteen. He had known I'd never had a boyfriend, much less been in love. He had known I couldn't relate.

"It's not that I don't miss her," Seth stammered. "Those girls are ... distractions."

"Just go," I told him. "Just go away to school. I don't ever want to see you again."

I thought I meant it. Being around Seth was just too painful. It was so hard to see him moving on with his life without Becca. I'd spent my entire life thinking that he and Becca would go off to college together, get married, and have kids. There he was, at this pivotal moment in his life, and he was willing to do it without her. He could move on, and I couldn't. It infuriated me to no end.

"I don't want to leave things with us this way. You're family to me," Seth said, trying to reason with me despite how hateful I was being.

"Go," I insisted.

With that, he turned and silently walked away.

I hadn't gone to his party or to his parents' house when he visited home for the holidays. I'd deliberately avoided him at all costs until now.

"Hey, Seth," I said cautiously as I returned to the present. I braced myself for the anger and resentment he must be feeling toward me.

Seth stared at me for a moment, and I fought the urge to run away. It was time to face him regardless of the consequences.

"Get over here," he finally said, holding his arms wide.

A large, familiar smile spread across his face. I'd missed that smile.

I closed the space between us and hugged him.

"Missed you, nerd," he said, giving me a tight squeeze.

I swallowed a lump in the back of my throat. "I missed you too."

Letting Seth back into my life would open up the door to my grief all over again. It would lead to endless nights of nightmares and guilty memories of things I couldn't change. But now that he was here, I believed it would be worth it. I had to at least try.

During dinner, I listened while Seth described Cornell business school, where he'd just graduated. He told me how he was interning at our fathers' pharmaceutical company, Clark and Weber, which did not come as a surprise at all. Our fathers had been plotting since we were kids to have Seth take over the business someday.

I did my best to keep the conversation on Seth and off myself. Every time I felt the conversation turning in my direction, I would find another question to ask Seth to put the focus back on him.

"Enough about me," Seth said, finally calling me out for my attempt at avoidance. He knew me too well. "I want to hear about you."

I frowned at him. "What do you want to know?"

He moved his napkin from his lap and folded it onto his plate, showing me that he was finished with dinner and his attention was fully on me. "What's your story? I've heard your father's version and your mother's version, but I would like to hear *your* version."

"There's not much to say," I told him as I opened the billfold that contained our check.

He immediately snatched it from my hand. "Oh no, you don't. This is on me. But once we get outside, you're talking."

He paid the bill and insisted we take a walk as we left the restaurant. We wandered toward a sidewalk that ran along St. Johns River. I stared out at the water as we walked, unwilling to start the conversation.

He shook his head. "You haven't changed a bit, just as stubborn as ever."

I wanted to say something, but the words weren't coming to me. Where would I even start?

Seth continued to wait for me to speak, and when I didn't, he decided to break the silence. "All right, let's start at the beginning. You decided not to go to college, and you're living off your trust fund."

He'd said it so matter-of-factly that it sent a heat wave straight to my face. He still knew how to press my buttons.

"Look, I'm not blowing off school completely," I replied defensively. "I'm just taking a little time off. It's not a crime. And I'm not living off my trust fund, thank you very much. I actually work for a living. It might not be much of a living and certainly not the standard that you're accustomed to, but I don't mind waiting tables." I was prepared to continue with my rant but stopped when I realized that Seth was smiling smugly at me. "What?"

"Gotcha talking." He playfully nudged me with his shoulder.

"Shut up." I couldn't help but smile back as I gently shoved him. I'd forgotten how aggravating he could be.

"Level with me, Natalie," he said, his face turning serious. "You didn't move to Florida to get away from your parents or to satisfy some rebellious teenage desire—which is your mother's theory, by the way. You moved to Florida to get away from … well, you know, what happened."

"Couldn't someone say the same thing about you, Mr. Cornell?" I asked.

He stopped walking and turned to face me. "I'm not the one who made straight As in school, only to turn around and wait tables at a tourist-trap café."

I contemplated my rebuttal, but Seth anticipated this.

He held up his hand to indicate that he wanted me to let him finish speaking. "I'm not saying there's anything wrong with your job." I gave him a doubtful look, but he continued, "I'm just saying that you have so much more potential than what you're doing."

I started walking again, more briskly this time. Seth followed.

"What's your point?" I asked.

I wanted to get this lecture over with as soon as possible. He was just as bad as my mother.

Seth kept up with my pace, insisting that I hear him out. "My point is, you moved here because you thought it would take the hurt away. I'm not sure why you chose Florida, but I know that's why you did it." I grimaced, but he pressed on. "You can't run away from it, Nat. Becca's gone, and she's not coming back. I know it hurts. It hurts me too, more than you probably know, but you can't hold up your entire life because of what happened to her. You have to move on."

I stopped walking and grabbed on to the cement railing that separated the walking path from the river. My breath began to feel tight, and if not for the railing, I would certainly melt into the ground.

Seth put his arms around me. "Hey, I'm sorry. I didn't mean for that to come out as harsh as it did." I could tell that he felt remorseful and that he probably thought I'd made a little more progress in my grief after all this time. "I just don't know how else to get through to you. Just like before, it's like you've shut down and you can't hear me."

"I don't want to talk about this anymore," I said as I desperately tried to pull myself together. I always hated getting emotional in front of people.

"Natalie, you have to," he insisted, trying to keep his voice as soft as possible despite his frustration. "Anyone can see how much this is haunting you. You've never dealt with it."

As his words sank in, I could clearly see the difference between us. Yes, we were both hurting, but Seth had found a way to move on, to salvage some sort of a productive life for himself. Me, on the other hand, I'd only been able to do the bare minimum to survive.

My body began to shake as sobs erupted from deep within my chest. This was *exactly* why I'd never dealt with it. I was incapable of it.

An elderly couple stared at me with concern as they passed by. They exchanged a worried look but continued to walk past us. I was mortified but unable to stop the emotions that were flooding out of me.

Seth pulled me from his chest to look at me. He gently squeezed my shoulders. "Please don't cry. I'm just trying to help you. Honest."

Deep down, I knew this was true. I knew Seth was sincere and was concerned about my well-being. Still, I didn't know if I had the will to change. Even as I stood there with my onetime best friend, a part of me yearned for the solitude of my little apartment. Once again, I longed to hide from the pain rather than face it.

After several minutes, I finally attempted to speak, so I could explain myself to him. I owed him that much. "I'm working through this the best way I can." My voice was hoarse but under control. "I know I've made some mistakes though. I'm really sorry for shutting you out the way that I did."

He looked at the ground. "It's okay. I mean, I understand why you did it."

"I hope that we can be friends again," I told him, wanting him to feel my sincerity.

He looked up and carefully eyed me for a second. It suddenly occurred to me that he might not want to open himself up for hurt again.

As I prepared myself for his rejection, he flashed me his carefree smile. "I knew you'd come around sooner or later."

He reached out and tousled my hair to break the tension. I couldn't help but smile back as I swatted his hand away.

We walked back toward the restaurant parking lot. It was starting to get late, and I had to be at work early the next morning for the breakfast shift. Even though I was glad to see Seth, the emotional turmoil of the evening had worn me out.

"Did you mean what you said about us being friends again?" he asked.

I turned and looked him in the eyes, understanding that it was only fair that he doubted me. "Of course I did."

There was something else though. I could sense that he had something he wanted to tell me, and whatever it was, he was worried that I wouldn't share his enthusiasm.

He nervously shifted his feet. "One of Clark and Weber's largest clients is right here in Jacksonville, so they've decided to open a satellite office. Guess where I am being transferred?"

Instinctually, I threw my arms around him. "That's fantastic!"

"Really?"

"Absolutely." I squeezed him one more time before releasing him. "I'm so proud of you."

"I really have missed you," he said.

"Me too." I put my arm through his.

Seth stopped behind a shiny, brand-new silver BMW. I released his arm.

"Seriously?" I asked, raising an eyebrow at him. "And I'm the one supposedly living off my trust fund?"

"Back off," he replied with a smile. "You have met my parents, haven't you? They love to throw around their money just as much as yours do."

I laughed and shook my head. He was right about that.

He opened the trunk of his BMW and began rummaging through a suitcase. His back stiffened, and the atmosphere of his mood changed slightly. I could sense his apprehension. Whatever he was looking for, he was worried it would upset me again. It must be something of Becca's.

He pulled an item from his suitcase but tucked it behind his back before facing me. "I have something for you," he said, confirming my suspicions. "But I am worried that I'll upset you more than I already have tonight."

My curiosity overpowered my instinct to run away. Maybe there was hope for me after all. I held out my hand and nodded my head to let him know it was okay to hand it over.

He hesitantly pulled a book from behind his back and placed in in my hand. I recognized it right away. It wasn't a book actually; it was Becca's journal.

Becca and I had shared the same sense of intuition, only hers was stronger. My intuition tended to be more real time, whereas Becca's was more focused on the future. Becca would use these journals to sketch out things she thought were going to happen. It was her way of tracking her accuracy. Most of the time, she had been spot-on. If only she could have predicted her own disappearance and avoided it.

I turned the journal over in my hand, running my fingers along the Celtic knot branded into the front of it. I remembered this particular journal, although I'd never read it.

"Did you read it?" I asked, not hiding the urgency in my voice.

Seth shook his head. "No, because I don't think it has the answers we're looking for." He knew what I was really asking. "I don't think she knew it was going to happen, or she would have said something to us. I still think you should read it though." He paused to gauge my reaction. When he saw that I was still composed, he continued, "I think it would be good for you, and I think Becca would have wanted you to read it."

I smiled grimly. Maybe he was right, and it was something to consider.

If Becca isn't coming back, would it make a big difference if I read her journal? Is it so wrong for me to want to hang on to her last thoughts, whatever they were?

"Thank you," I told him as I contemplated the possibilities. "Where did you find it anyway?"

"I found it at my parents' house when I went back for the summer. I was looking for a file in my dad's office and found it buried in a drawer. She must have left it, and I guess one of the housekeepers put it away, thinking it was his," Seth said with a shrug.

I tucked the journal into my purse as he walked me to my car. He laughed as I stopped by the driver's door.

"Is this thing safe?" he asked as the door whined when I opened it.

I rolled my eyes at him. "I couldn't let my parents waste their money on the Audi they really wanted to buy me. I barely drive this thing as it is."

"Your mom is still pretty bitter about that, just to let you know," he replied. "Does she know about this?" He pointed to my car.

I laughed and shook my head. "Are you kidding? She'd hire someone to steal it. She would be mortified if she knew."

My mother was famous in Richmond for keeping up appearances.

It began to drizzle, so I gave him a hug good-bye. He held my door for me as I climbed into the driver's seat.

"Hey," I called after Seth as he started to walk away.

He stopped and turned around, expectantly looking at me.

"I meant what I said. I've missed you."

He smiled again, and I knew I was truly forgiven. "Drive safe, nerd."

THREE

A s I headed back to the interstate, I felt a twinge of optimism that hadn't been present in years. I knew I wasn't ready to move on—not even close—but I was ready to rekindle my friendship with Seth, and that was something. Maybe if I could successfully do that, one day, I could repair the relationship with my parents as well.

The rain began to come down in steady streams as I got back on the interstate. I drove slowly for about fifteen minutes when traffic suddenly came to a stop. I glanced in the rearview mirror as headlights approached from the distance and finally stopped behind my car.

I started flipping stations on the radio, hoping to hear what the holdup was. I heard nothing about an accident or construction, so I settled on the most soothing song I could find and took a couple of deep breaths.

An hour later, going on ten o'clock, I had moved less than five miles.

Another thirty minutes later, I came up to an exit for US Route 1. If I recalled correctly, this ran parallel to the interstate and would take me back to St. Augustine. If I went this way, I could potentially make it home around eleven. I decided to go for it.

Checking my blind spot first, I carefully moved into the turn lane and got off the exit. I began to head south on my detour, feeling relieved to have found a way around the traffic jam.

Within minutes, I was past all of the strip malls and car dealerships that lined US Route 1 and was completely alone on the road. The next ten miles were nothing but trees and the occasional deserted motel. The absence of civilization put me a little more at ease. There was less chance of a disaster if I was the only vehicle on the road.

As I drove, I began to once again reflect on my evening with Seth and how seeing him made me feel a little homesick. I hadn't talked to my parents in months, and while I knew that wasn't right, I didn't know what to say to them. Things hadn't been good between us when I told them I was leaving.

It was two days after high school graduation, and I'd done everything I could up to that point to dodge questions about my future. The truth was, I didn't feel like I had much of a future.

It wasn't that I didn't think I was smart enough to go to college or that I didn't have good enough grades. In fact, after Becca had disappeared, I'd shut out everyone in my life, and the only thing I did was study. The problem was deeper than that. It was a feeling that when Becca had gone away, I had as well. She'd disappeared, and as a result, I'd wanted to disappear too.

"What do you mean, you're moving?" my mother demanded.

She looked expectantly at my father, but we both knew that wouldn't do her any good. Ever since Becca's disappearance, he had mastered the art of burying his head in the sand. He was even better at it than I was, and that was saying something.

"I-I need a change," I stammered, unsure of what to say to her to help her understand.

There was nothing I could say to make her feel better about this decision. I knew that no matter what I said, she was going to take the decision personally, as if I were trying to escape her specifically, but that wasn't true. I wanted to escape everything, my entire life.

Ever since the night Becca had been taken, I'd felt like I was gradually suffocating, and it was to the point I was waking up breathless every night. The weight of the guilt and grief had become too much to bear. I couldn't escape it. Her memory lived in every room in the house, in every photo hanging on the wall, in the dishes she used to help me wash when it wasn't her turn, in the garage where her bike still hung on the rack, and in the sorrow I saw every time I looked into my parents' eyes.

It wasn't that I didn't want to remember my sister. Of course I did. I loved her more than anyone in the world, but remembering her and feeling haunted by the ghost of her were very different things.

Every day when I got home from school and entered that house, I'd expect her to greet me. It didn't matter how much time had passed. I would get amnesia that she was gone and feel that deep pain in my heart all over again when I realized that she wasn't coming back.

Every time I passed by her room, I would imagine the terror she must have felt, being taken in the middle of the night by a stranger. When I walked by the spot where I'd lain unconscious, I would hate myself more and more for not stopping it, for being useless.

"You need a change?" my mother asked, smirking at my remark to hide her hurt. "How about going to Windsor College? That would be a better change for your future, and you can stay here at home. What exactly are you going to do in St. Augustine anyway?"

I sighed at the mention of Windsor College, as it was an argument we'd had countless times since my junior year. My mother had pressured me to apply, and when I'd refused, she'd literally filled out my application for me. She took an essay that I had written as part of a school assignment and mailed it in. My excellent grades, high SAT scores, and the fact that both of my parents were Windsor alumni had been enough to get me an acceptance letter. Since Becca's disappearance, I had become my mother's outlet, and it was smothering me. The more I withdrew, the more she chased me. It was a cycle we couldn't get out of.

"For the hundredth time, Mother, I am not going to Windsor!" I nearly shouted back at her. "And I don't know what I'll do in St. Augustine, but anything is better than being here!"

I felt guilty the second I said it, but the pressure was building in my chest, and it felt like someone was sitting on it. I wanted to take it back, but I was struggling to catch my breath. I'd had a doctor tell me once that it was a panic attack coming on, but whatever it was, I wanted it to go away, at any cost.

I could tell this hurt my mother, and she responded the only way she knew how—by lashing out.

"What did I do to deserve this?" she shouted back. Frustrated, she grabbed at her curly strawberry-blonde hair. She pulled at it with such intensity that I feared she would yank it straight from the roots. "Why are you punishing me? Why do you always have to be so difficult? Why—"

"Why wasn't it me?" I asked, starting to feel delirious. I'd often wondered why it wasn't me who'd disappeared and not Becca, so it was reasonable to assume she wondered the same thing.

I watched my mother's expression turn completely sober as she comprehended what I'd asked.

"I wasn't going to say that," she replied.

I shrugged. "But it's what you were thinking."

My mother shook her head. "That's not true—"

"I ask myself that same question every day," I said, cutting her off. "And that's why I have to go."

I calmly walked out of the room and packed my bags.

I'd gotten up the next morning before the sun came up and left for Florida. I hadn't been home since.

My heart began to ache as I thought about that fight. I felt guilty. Guilty for leaving, guilty for yelling at my grieving mother, and guilty for making the assumption that she would trade me for Becca. Deep down, I knew it wasn't true. Those feelings were more about my own insecurities than any evidence that my mother would choose Becca over me.

I'd been driving as if on autopilot, and as I came back to reality, I noticed that the rain was now coming down in thick, angry sheets. I turned the windshield wipers to full power, but they struggled to push water away fast enough.

I leaned forward and squinted to try to make out the white lines on the road. The street wasn't well lit, making it difficult to tell the asphalt from the grass. The heavy rain made it impossible to see the trees that lined each side of the road.

My right tire hit a pool of water, causing my car to skid. I tightly gripped the wheel and regained control. My heart pounded as a knot formed in my stomach.

Something appeared in the street ahead. At first, it just looked like a shadow, but within seconds, my headlights casted a glare on a pair of wide eyes staring back at me in shock. It was a deer.

Instinctively, my hands jerked the wheel to the right, and I slammed on the brakes. My car missed the deer by inches, but I hydroplaned off the road, sending my car soaring toward the tree line. I was helpless as my car uncontrollably careened into the woods.

I managed a single scream before the car crashed head-on against a tree. I closed my eyes but could hear the metal twisting and shrieking all around me. The windshield shattered, sending shards of broken glass into the front seat where I sat. Something pressed firmly into my lap, pinching into my abdomen and forcing the air from my lungs.

When the horrible sounds of screeching metal finally ended, the only sound that remained was the innocent tapping of rain on the roof. My conscious mind told me that I was still alive and that I should open my eyes to survey the damage. It also told me that maybe I didn't want to know.

I decided to force my eyes open, and it took me a minute to comprehend what I was seeing. I anticipated the car was damaged, but nothing could have prepared me for what I saw. The front left side of my car was shriveled up against the trunk of the tree. If I were to lean forward and stretch my arm up, I would be able to touch its bark.

I looked down and realized that the pressure I felt against my stomach was the remnants of what was left of my steering wheel. It was hard to tell what it was mixed with, but I assumed it was the rest of the crushed dashboard.

My mind raced as I tried to take it all in. There was nothing but silence all around me, and although I usually found solace in being alone, I was now terrified. No one knew I was here, and no one would be looking for me. I was now so far off the main road that even if a car were to drive by, I doubted they would see me through the rain.

I remembered that my purse had been in the passenger seat, and my cell phone was in my purse. I tried to lift my arm to search the rubble next to me, but I only cried out in pain. My arm was broken.

I stared into the darkness beside me and could barely see my purse under the glove box. From here, my bag and the glove box looked intact. The passenger side of the car was less damaged with the exception of the hood.

Once again, I tried for it. I attempted to move my body to the side, but it was completely pinned. The aching in my abdomen turned to a stabbing pain, making my breath catch in my throat.

This is bad.

As the initial shock wore off, the pain really began to set in. A scream escaped from my throat as the stabbing pain stretched from my stomach up to my rib cage. I couldn't feel my legs at all, which told me I'd damaged my spine.

My mouth felt wet and was filled with the distinct taste of iron. Blood. I was dying. I knew it. I could *feel* it.

Before this moment, I'd never been able to fully picture how I would die. Sure, the reality of inevitable death had become somewhat of a frequent thought in my mind since Becca's disappearance, but my own death had never been my concern. I was always more concerned about losing those around me, those I loved.

As I pondered this in the final moments of my life, I grew angry with myself. It was horrible to leave my parents this way. They'd already lost one child, and I was going to put them through the agony of losing the other. Tears stung my eyes as I thought of my mother receiving the news. Surely, they would eventually find my body here.

Then, I considered an even grimmer possibility. *What if they didn't? Would my parents have two missing children and once again be denied the closure they deserved?*

I shivered—not from the outside, but from the inside. My insides felt oddly cold.

My eyelids began to feel heavy, and although my thoughts were hazy, I recognized the end was very near. I knew within minutes that I would be past this life and on to the next. *Would Becca be there?*

Through the fog that clouded my mind, I heard a light tap. With my eyes half-open, I saw a bird—a raven—perched on the crushed pieces where the hood of my car used to be. It squawked at me and flitted its wings. It was watching me. I must be hallucinating.

I closed my eyes and heard the sound of crunching, tearing metal. A darkness began to settle behind my eyelids. It drew me in, sucking the life out of me. It didn't frighten me, but still, I pushed against it, stubbornly resisting it.

Through the cold darkness that filled my mind, I heard a frantic voice call out, "Natalie! Natalie, can you hear me?"

It was a voice that my drifting mind recognized.

I struggled to open my eyes and to keep them open long enough to focus.

I was face-to-face with blue eyes that I would recognize anywhere. It was Michael.

"Natalie?"

I wanted to say something to him, but all I could manage was a gurgle. I could barely breathe. Blood trickled from my mouth and dripped onto my lap.

The driver's door to the car was completely gone, and Michael was crouched beside me. His hand lightly touched the side of my head. When he removed his hand, it was coated with blood.

His eyes grew wider and wider as he surveyed the wreckage that had penetrated my body and pinned me to the seat.

Unwillingly, I drifted away into unconsciousness. I wasn't sure how long I was unconscious for, but I startled awake as the pain in my abdomen intensified. My insides felt like they were being ripped out.

I opened my eyes in shock, expecting to see something tearing apart my stomach. The ripping pain was gone, but I still anticipated seeing a wild animal, ready to finish clawing apart my body.

Instead, I found myself lying in the wet grass, outside the car. The pieces of the dashboard that had impaled my body were completely gone, as if they'd somehow disappeared into thin air.

Michael sat beside me on the ground, leaning over me. His shirt was covered in my blood.

How am I still alive?

"Look at me. Keep your eyes on me," he said. "You're going to be okay." Although he was right in front of me, he sounded so far away.

He reached a bloody, shaking hand out and stroked my cheek, trying to comfort me. He pressed his other hand to my stomach where I'd been impaled. My sluggish brain wasn't able to comprehend the reasoning behind it.

Is he trying to stop the bleeding? Or maybe he isn't really here at all.

The raven had been a hallucination, so maybe he was too.

Michael's deep blue eyes stared into mine with a concentrated intensity. Despite the heaviness of my eyelids, I wouldn't allow them to close. My will to hold his gaze was stronger than death's will to claim me.

I began to feel an odd sensation within my body—a slight tingling, a vibration. It was pleasant, warm, like a fresh blanket out of the dryer. My body welcomed it.

The sensation started in my cheek, beneath his hand, and quickly spread to my head and neck and into my chest. It traveled throughout the rest of my body, including my legs. I could feel my wounded abdomen vibrating and the pain beginning to subside.

31

The intensity of the vibrations began to multiply, and the coldness I felt was replaced by a heat wave. The vibrations became so intense that I could practically hear their soft hum in my ears.

A bright light flashed from within my mind. In reality, I knew that my eyes were still locked with Michael's, but I couldn't concentrate on anything, except the light. Through this strange light came a memory of Becca and me about six weeks before she'd disappeared.

"I don't understand why you keep fighting it," Becca said, crossing her arms in frustration.

"I'm not like you," I replied with a shrug. "I don't need to advertise this weird thing about me."

Becca was confronting me for the hundredth time about why I was suppressing my intuitive abilities. There was nothing I could tell her this time that I hadn't already tried to explain to her before.

She let out a frustrated groan and gathered her long mahogany hair up in a ponytail. I could tell I'd struck a nerve by telling her our abilities were weird. She released her hair, letting it cascade down her shoulders in soft waves.

"I didn't mean that you were weird," I apologetically told her.

"It's a gift, Natalie," she replied, her voice calmer, softer. "Who you are is a gift. I hope that, one day, you'll learn to appreciate it, to appreciate yourself."

The light subsided, and the memory faded along with it. I found myself once again lying on the wet ground, the raindrops tapping against my face.

Michael lifted me off the ground, cradling me in his arms as he walked through the woods. All of the panic that I'd felt before was completely gone, and I was overwhelmed with a sense of calmness. My eyelids were heavy and impossible to keep open. I leaned my head against his chest and allowed the peacefulness of sleep to overtake me.

FOUR

Ring. Ring. Ring.
    Groggy, I reached over and slapped the snooze button on the alarm clock.

Ring. Ring.

It confused me at first as to why the alarm clock was still going off, but as I became more conscious, I realized it wasn't the alarm clock. It was the phone. I pulled my comforter up over my ears, planning to ignore it.

Ring. Ring. Ring. Ring.

"Go away," I groaned.

Ring. Ring. Ring.

"Ugh!" I jumped out of bed, nearly falling over onto the floor. My balance was completely off, and my body was still heavy from sleep. I steadied myself and tried to follow the ringing with one eye open.

Finally, I found the phone lying on an end table in the living room. It was ringing when I picked it up.

"What?" I snapped into the phone, expecting it to be a telemarketer. No one ever called me on my landline. I only had it for emergencies.

"Natalie?" an unsure voice asked.

I quickly realized who it was and instantly felt guilty for snapping.

"Hey, Jen," I replied, softening my voice. "Sorry, I just woke up."

"Natalie?" she asked, sounding concerned. "Are you okay?"

I blinked my eyes a few more times in an attempt to fully wake up. I tried to process her question but couldn't understand her concern.

"Yeah," I replied cautiously. "Why wouldn't I be?"

There was a long pause, and just as I was about to ask if she was still there, she responded, "Because you haven't shown up for work in two days. I've tried calling you a hundred times, but your cell phone goes right to voice mail. I even knocked on your door yesterday, but you didn't answer. I was about to call the police!"

How can that be? I felt light-headed as I threw desperate glances around my apartment, looking for some clue as to what was going on. Everything looked exactly as I'd left it the afternoon I went to meet Seth. *Could I really have missed several days of work?*

A power surge went through the apartment, causing my TV to make a loud popping noise. I jumped.

I looked down at myself, unsure of what to expect. I was in my pajamas, but I didn't remember putting them on.

As I tried to recall what I had done last, images of being trapped in my car, all bloody and broken, came back to me. *Did that really happen?*

I rushed to the front window of my apartment. My car was parked in the driveway and was in perfect condition. If I had been in an accident, then the car wouldn't be there. I shuddered as I recalled it being broken almost in half. It must have been a dream, a horrible nightmare.

"Are you still there?" Jen asked. "Are you sick? Do you need me to come over?"

"Um, yeah," I replied without thinking. "I mean, no, you don't have to come over, but yes, I think I was sick or something." That was the only logical explanation.

"Natalie, what's going on?" she demanded, going into protective friend mode.

"I must have gotten sick after dinner with Seth the other night," I rationalized. "I guess I had a really high fever and just lost track of time."

"Okay," she said, but I could sense her hesitancy. "Are you coming to work today? You were supposed to be here an hour ago."

I hated missing work. In fact, I hadn't called out or been late once since getting the job.

"Yes. Please let Carl know that I'm sorry, and I'll be in as soon as possible."

Jen agreed to pass along an apology to Carl and offered once again to come over, but I insisted that I was okay.

But am I?

How was it possible that I'd slept for several days? I'd never done that before, no matter how sick I'd been.

I walked into the bathroom, flicked on the light, and took off my pajama top. I stared at myself in the mirror, unsure of what I was looking for. I ran my hand down my abdomen. The skin was smooth and perfect.

As I examined myself in the mirror, I noticed how healthy and well rested I appeared overall. There was an unusual, soft glow in my cheeks, and my skin tone looked even, without a trace of any type of blemish or imperfection. All of the rest must have rejuvenated my body.

Unable to find anything physically wrong with my body, I decided to hop in the shower and do my best to hurry to get to work. Although I tried to keep my mind off my car accident dream, it was hard not to dwell on it. As I got ready for work, the details of my dream kept coming back to me. Usually, dreams became muddled as time passed, not the other way around.

I could remember the accident and my blood soaking the front seat of the car. I remembered the excruciating pain of trying to move but being helplessly pinned to the seat. I remembered the raven appearing and realizing that I was going to die. And I remembered Michael.

I shook my head, trying to rid myself of the thought. I needed to focus on getting to work.

My stomach rumbled loudly, reminding me that I hadn't eaten in days. As I raced out the door to go to work, I grabbed an apple to eat on the way.

I contemplated driving to save time, but with the details of my dream still haunting me, I couldn't fathom getting behind the wheel.

As I briskly walked to work, I noticed it was particularly loud on St. George Street. I caught up to a group of teenage girls who were giggling and gossiping so frantically that it made me wonder how they could keep up with the conversation. As hard as I tried, I couldn't make out one single word. They were talking over each other, and their voices sounded jumbled. Feeling slightly annoyed by the chaos, I slipped between them and hurried to pass their group.

The noise on the street was almost unbearable, and when I finally made it to the café, I practically ran through the door, colliding into Carl. He looked stunned to see me as I apologized to him.

"Natalie! How are you feeling?" he asked, and I could tell his concern was genuine. "You could have taken another day if you needed it."

"I'm glad to be back at work," I replied honestly. "I'm sorry for being out the past few days without calling to check in. I think I was really out of it."

"She looks great. Really well rested. Maybe she should take days off more often," Carl said, but his lips didn't move.

I stood there, dumbfounded.

"It's not a problem. I'm glad you're better," he said. That time, his lips moved.

Did I just imagine the other comment?

A man and a woman walked into the café behind me, and Carl diverted his attention to greet them. I noticed that Carl was seating them in my section, so I hurried to the back room to throw my purse in the locker. Jen was quickly at my side.

"How are you feeling?" she asked.

"Has her hair always been that shiny? It looks gorgeous. I hate my hair." Jen's lips didn't move, but I was certain I'd heard it.

I just stared at her, unable to speak.

"What?" she asked self-consciously. "Does my hair look bad today?" She ran her fingers through her hair, making sure every strand was in place.

I forced myself to blink and breathe, and then I willed myself to remain calm. "Um, your hair looks fine."

"Uh-oh. She doesn't look so good. I hope she isn't still sick. I missed her so much. She's so much more fun to talk to than Jessica."

If I was crazy, at least I was imagining that people were saying nice things about me.

"Can someone please assist table nine?" Carl called from the dining room. "Where are all my waitresses?" It was unusual for Carl to get flustered in front of customers.

"Coming!" I called back. I turned back to Jen. "We'd better get out there. Carl sounds busy."

Jen gave me a funny look. *"What's the hurry?"*

As I walked into the dining room, I grabbed two glasses and began filling them with water for table nine. I needed to focus and get through the day. It was going to be hard to go through the motions, knowing there was a possibility that I had completely lost my mind. I'd always known that I was different from everyone else, but had I officially snapped?

I was almost to table nine when I heard the door chime. A strange feeling suddenly came over me, and instantly, I knew who'd entered the café before turning around to face him.

As Michael stood in the doorway, he glanced all around until his eyes met mine.

"What is wrong with her? I'm only dying of thirst over here!" The voice of the woman from table nine broke my gaze and pulled me back to reality.

As I continued back to table nine, I immediately noticed the blatant annoyance on her face.

The woman was skinny with badly bleached blonde hair and indigo-blue eye shadow. I had to stifle a smile as she pursed her ruby-red lips together with impatience. She looked like a band groupie from the 1980s.

"I apologize for your wait," I told her as I placed the glasses of water in front of her. "Are you ready to order?"

The man looked up from his menu for the first time. He smiled as his eyes searched me up and down. *"Helllooo, Red."*

"I will have the house salad, no onions, with the dressing on the side," the woman replied before cutting the man a dirty look. *"He'd better not even think about it. This stupid waitress ain't nobody."*

The woman slammed her menu on the table, trying to get his attention, but it didn't work. He was still eyeing me.

"I wonder how old she is. I hope she's over eighteen."

I shifted my feet, feeling uncomfortable by his attention. *This can't really be happening*, I lied to myself.

"I would like the cheeseburger," the man replied as he grabbed the woman's menu off the table, not taking his eyes off me. "Thanks, darlin'." He winked at me before running a hand through his greasy hair.

I could feel the woman's death glare on me as I turned and walked away. I began to feel panic-stricken as I wondered how I was going to get through this day. I was a person who had trouble handling a normal amount of attention. This was unfathomable.

Just when I thought it couldn't get any worse, I noticed Michael hadn't been waited on yet. He was sitting at his usual seat in my section, intently watching me. Out of the corner of my eye, I caught Carl gesturing toward Michael. He'd noticed it too.

I hesitated, not quite sure what to do. *If I'm hearing people's thoughts, what will I hear Michael say?* It would be unbearable to hear him think about what a mess I was.

I wanted to ask Jen to wait on him again, but I knew that would look bad, especially when I hadn't shown up for work twice this week. Although Carl seemed understanding of my situation, passing off my tables the first day back would be pushing it.

I mentally prepared myself for the worst as I approached Michael.

"Hi," he said, and all I could focus on was the fact that his lips moved. He'd actually said it aloud.

"Crap!" I blurted out.

Michael raised his eyebrows as a small smile spread across his lips.

"I forgot your cake," I explained.

I awkwardly stood there, waiting, listening for his thoughts but heard nothing. *How is that possible when I can clearly hear everyone else's thoughts around me?*

Jen was pretending to refill napkins at a nearby table, but she was really eavesdropping on us, looking for signs of romance. Carl was reliving details of his last date with Jessica in graphic detail. The jerk at table nine was still checking me out, and his girlfriend was contemplating storming out of the restaurant. I heard all of this going on right now, yet there was nothing but silence from Michael.

The noise level continued to increase inside the café as I turned and made my way behind the counter to get Michael's cake. I tried to tune out all the voices around me, but I couldn't. My hands began to shake as I lifted the glass lid covering the cake and attempted to carve out a slice.

"I bet she's something in bed. Redheads are always a little wild."

I dropped the slice of cake on the floor, tears stinging at my eyes.

"What the hell is he looking at? She's just a nobody waitress."

From the corner of my eye, I could see Michael watching me. He was leaning toward me, his palms pressed to the table. The lights began to flicker.

"Natalie doesn't look so good. Is she still sick?" Jen wondered.

My legs felt weak, and before I knew it, I was crouched on the floor behind the counter. I closed my eyes and put my hands over my ears, trying to tune out the voices as they grew louder and louder.

"Maybe I'll slip her my number when Wanda isn't looking. I could really sink my teeth into her juicy—"

The lights started to flicker violently, temporarily distracting me from the confusing thoughts of everyone around me. With a loud zapping sound, the lights completely went out. I stayed crouched on the floor, eyes still closed.

As I struggled to focus on my breathing and tried to force myself out of this weird, disillusioned state, I felt hands firmly grasping my wrists. I resisted against them, trying to keep my ears covered. When I finally gave in and opened my eyes, I saw Michael staring back at me with concern.

He gave my wrists another tug, and this time, I allowed my arms to fall to my sides. His hands rested on my arms, steadying me. Momentarily, the other voices faded away. The voices were jumbled, as if they were mixing with real conversations, but at least they sounded more like background noise.

"Are you all right?" Michael asked.

Unsure of how to answer his question, I shook my head. *No.*

"Let's get you out of here," he replied, helping me to my feet.

Jen spotted me on the floor and came over to see what was going on. "Oh gosh, Natalie! Are you all right? Did you faint?"

"Natalie isn't feeling well," Michael told her. "I'm going to take her home."

Jen nodded in approval, but her lips were tight. Her thoughts told me she was conflicted between being happy and being concerned for me.

"What the hell is going on in here? What kind of place is this? Can't even pay the dang light bill?"

I groaned and became unsteady as the flood of voices filled my mind again. With his arm securely around my waist, Michael led me out of the restaurant and onto the street.

As soon as the door to the restaurant shut, I instantly began to feel relief again. I was able to regain my balance, and Michael slowly released me. I glanced around and was pleased to see that the street was relatively empty, and the nearest tourists were still a good thirty feet away.

Jen brought me my purse and gave me a quick hug. "Call me if you need anything," she told me. "*Please get better soon.*"

"Thanks. I will," I assured her.

As Jen headed back into the restaurant, I realized how lucky I was to have her in my life. I hadn't allowed myself to get close to anyone else here, but I was glad that I was friends with her.

"I don't have my car," Michael said. "Are you okay to walk? I can call a taxi if you'd like."

I shook my head, definitely not ready to get in a car. "No. Walking sounds perfect. I think I need the air."

Michael and I walked in silence for several minutes, and I wondered what he must be thinking about me. I smiled to myself as I realized that he must think I was crazy.

He looked down at me with a puzzled expression on his face. "Feeling better?"

"Yes," I replied, grateful that the streets were still unoccupied for the most part. "Thank you for rescuing me." I was referring to how he'd helped me in the café, but my mind went back to my dream where he'd also rescued me from my accident.

"Glad to help," he replied, looking at the ground, his brows furrowed. "I haven't seen you in the café in a few days."

"It's all part of my secret life," I said jokingly, attempting to lighten the mood.

Michael's eyes shifted toward me, skeptically watching me. A small part of me wished I knew what he was thinking.

"Where are you from, Natalie?" He almost sounded angry.

"Richmond, Virginia," I replied, confused by the sudden change in mood.

"How long have you been here?"

"About six months. Why?" I responded, stiffening.

"Why did you choose St. Augustine?" His tone was urgent, and I started to feel like I was being interrogated.

I stopped walking and turned to face him. "Why do you want to know?"

Michael took a step closer, his eyes locked with mine. "Just answer the question." His jaw was tight.

He waited to see if I would answer the question, but I had no intention of budging. I couldn't answer that question honestly without telling him about Becca. Despite the fact that I felt like I knew him because of my dream and that he'd helped me today, I didn't *really* know him.

He let out a frustrated sigh and looked away, realizing I wasn't going to answer his question. "Let's just get you home."

Michael started walking but stopped when he realized I wasn't with him. He turned to look at me, and I decided to continue walking with him. Maybe I was just being defensive, overreacting due to everything that'd happened today. I knew I could be unreasonable when it came to talking about my past, especially if it was related to Becca.

We walked up the driveway to my apartment.

I pulled my keys out of my pocket and turned to him. "Thank you for walking me home," I said, conflicted between feelings of gratitude and annoyance.

"You should rest," he replied.

I got the sense he wanted to say more. I waited to see if he'd continue, but he just turned around and walked away.

I entered my apartment and flopped down on the couch, trying to make sense of everything that had happened today. As if finding out that I'd slept for two days straight wasn't strange enough, now, I was hearing voices. It dawned on me that those weren't the only strange things that had happened today. I recalled how the lights had gone out at the café when I got upset, and they'd also flickered this morning at home.

Is there any way possible that a power outage could be linked to me hearing voices?

Everyone had witnessed the lights going out; I hadn't imagined that. It had to be some strange coincidence.

I racked my brain, trying to figure out a logical explanation for all of this.

I pulled out my phone and opened up the web browser, ready to do some research on my symptoms. I typed out *hearing voices* and immediately erased it. I replaced it with *hallucinations*. That had to be closer to what was happening. The search results came back, and I clicked a link to a medical website. There were a list of potential matches, including brain tumor, migraine, and schizophrenia. I nervously read through the list of symptoms for each one, but none of them seemed like a match.

It dawned on me that maybe this was another symptom of post-traumatic stress disorder. I had been diagnosed with it after Becca was taken, and I'd been dealing with side effects of panic attacks, flashbacks, and nightmares ever since. Maybe this was a new symptom associated with that. I searched and read through the symptoms, but they didn't match.

Frustrated, I put my phone down. As much as it hurt to think about her, I began to wish Becca were here. Becca had known so many things, things no one else knew. She had known things before they happened, and when they were happening, she'd often known why and what the possible outcomes could be. If she were here, maybe she would be able to help me figure out what was wrong with me.

Just when I felt the tears stinging my eyes once again, I remembered something very important about the other night before all of this happened.

I opened my purse and pulled out Becca's journal. I hugged it to my chest, wishing it were her and hoping it would somehow make me feel closer to her.

For a moment, I considered opening it. The last time I'd read one of her journals was right after she disappeared. Seth and I pored through every one that we could find, desperately searching for clues. Every single one of them had turned up empty. I swallowed a lump in my throat and placed the journal next to me on the couch. Not tonight. Maybe I'd read it one day but not tonight.

FIVE

The next morning, I lay in bed for ten minutes after my alarm went off, trying to decide what to do. I needed to go to work, but I knew that I couldn't have another public meltdown. I also needed to figure out what to do about the fact that I might be crazy. *Do crazy people normally recognize and admit that they're crazy?*

I groaned, shoved off the covers, and sat up in bed. I'd slept hard last night, and I could feel my knotted hair sprawling out in every direction. My sheets were twisted and half off the bed despite the fact that I didn't recall turning even once.

My shift was going to start in less than an hour, so I needed to figure something out. I needed to find a way to test whether or not I could still hear people's thoughts. There was no way I could go to work and go through that again today.

Eager to get the test over with, I hurried to change out of my pajamas and into a pair of yoga pants, a sweatshirt, and sneakers. As I left the house, I put on a pair of sunglasses and a baseball cap so that I was less recognizable in the event I freaked out on the street. It would be my luck that I would bump into someone from work or one of our regular customers. Or worse, Michael.

I stepped onto the street, and all was quiet. None of my neighbors were outside, but since it was mid-morning on a weekday, most of them were already at work. Forcing one foot in front of the other, I made my way to one of the busier streets where I knew tourists were guaranteed to be.

Up ahead, I saw two women walking and taking pictures of one of the historic bed-and-breakfast hotels. One of the women reminded me of Seth's mother. She was around the same age with the same petite frame and curly dark-brown hair. Although I hadn't spoken to her in years, it was comforting that this stranger resembled her.

I calmly walked toward the women. Their conversation was just a little out of range, but I was positive their mouths were moving, so I didn't believe I was imagining the conversation. But I had to be sure.

"It's a beautiful house, isn't it?" I asked, trying to sound casual.

The woman who reminded me of Seth's mother turned to me. I could sense that she was a friendly, outgoing person who enjoyed small talk with strangers. She didn't find my presence odd at all.

"Why, yes, it is. We were just admiring it," she replied.

Then, silence. Sweet silence.

I felt almost giddy but managed to maintain my composure.

"We heard that there is a horse-drawn carriage tour that will take you around St. Augustine and show you the different historic homes," the other lady said. "Do you know where we can buy tickets for that?"

"Sure," I replied. "It's just right up the street."

I walked them to St. George Street and pointed them in the direction of a shop that sold tickets for the tour. The ladies thanked me before walking away, and I stood there on the busy street and sighed with relief. I heard nothing unusual. I practically skipped home, so I could get ready for work.

Later, when I got to work, Jen immediately noticed my good mood.

"You seem much better today," she said. "Could that have anything to do with Michael walking you home?"

I grabbed an empty napkin holder from the counter to replenish it and replied honestly, "I'm just happy things are back to normal today."

"Me too. I was worried about you yesterday. Now, tell me what happened. Did you invite Michael to the masquerade?"

I almost laughed at the thought. "No, of course not. Why on earth would I do that?"

"Well," she began, "he walked you home yesterday, and he comes into the café almost every day that you are here. We've been over this."

I stuffed the napkins into the napkin holder and placed it back on the counter. Just as I was about to accuse her of being ridiculous, the café door opened, and Michael entered. Jen raised her eyebrows at me as if to say, *I told you so*, and I was glad I couldn't hear her thoughts right now. I playfully rolled my eyes at her and grabbed the water pitcher.

I stopped in my tracks, however, when I realized that Michael wasn't alone. Right behind him as he walked to his usual table was a beautiful girl around the same age, in her early twenties, with shiny, dark-espresso-colored hair that hung straight just below her shoulders. She had striking hazel eyes, high cheekbones, and perfectly pouty lips. She wore a pair of ripped black skinny jeans with an olive-green shirt, a black leather jacket, and black ankle boots. As I gathered up the courage to approach their table, I noticed she had a small diamond stud in her nose and a tattoo on her wrist that said *free* with a tiny black bird next to it.

Michael smiled and looked happy to see me, a complete change from how he'd left me yesterday. I smiled back and tried to think of something to say as I poured his water.

I glanced at the girl and found her glaring at me. Her eyes dug into me as if she hated my existence, making me feel very small. I carefully poured her a glass of water and prayed that I didn't do anything clumsy.

"Um, do you want your usual cake today?" I asked Michael, trying not to look at the girl.

"Yes, please," he replied. "And she would like the same."

I dared to look at her again, and she pursed her glossy magenta lips. Without saying a word, I walked away to get their cake.

As I placed the slices of cake on plates, I noticed that Michael was leaning in toward the girl, intently talking to her. I desperately wanted to read the situation before going back over there, but for some reason, my intuition didn't seem to work well around him.

When I walked back to their table, Michael stopped talking and sat back in his chair. The girl sighed deeply. I placed the plates in front of them and asked if they needed anything else.

"No, you've done enough," the girl snapped, shooting me another hateful look.

"Raina!" Michael said. "That's enough."

He looked at me, apologetic, but I turned and walked away. I'd obviously done something to cause tension between the two of them, so I decided the best thing for me to do was leave them alone.

"Who's *that?*" Jen asked me when I joined her behind the counter.

I just shrugged and pretended not to be bothered by Raina.

"Are we still hanging out tonight?" I asked, trying to distract myself from Michael and Raina.

We'd had this planned for two weeks, and I hoped she hadn't forgotten and made other plans. It was rare for me to feel this way, but I needed a night out.

"Of course," Jen replied, biting her lip. She was hiding something.

"Uh-oh, what?" I asked, afraid of what she had in store.

"I hope you don't mind, but…"

"But what?"

"I ran into my friend Lance yesterday, and he wants to come with us," she replied.

I felt a little better. Lance was a guy that Jen was sort of interested in. She'd been on a few dates with him, but it wasn't anything serious.

"Oh," I replied with a laugh. "You scared me for a minute."

"And he's bringing his friend Ben who wants to meet you," she blurted out and then winced.

There it was.

"Jen," I whined. "I don't want to go on a blind date."

Jen took both of my hands to try to calm me down. "It's not a date. It's a non-date. It's just dinner and a movie with friends. If you happen to be attracted to each other, then you can decide to go on a real date."

"Ugh," I said and then softened. I couldn't stay mad at her. Her intentions were good. "Fine, I'll go."

Jen smiled and looked pleased with herself. "You're going to have fun. I promise."

Carl walked out of the back room, which reminded me to focus on work. I mustered up the courage to look over at Michael and Raina's table to see if they were ready for their check, but they were already gone. The cake was barely eaten, and there was a twenty-dollar bill on the table, which was twice as much as the bill. Michael had never left a slice of cake unfinished before.

When our shift was over, Jen practically dragged me out the door before I could change my mind about going out.

Jen had told Lance we would meet them at a casual but classy tapas restaurant around the corner from work. Even though I wasn't at all concerned about impressing Ben, I hoped that I wasn't underdressed for the restaurant in my jeans and sweater. I glanced at Jen, and even though she was also casual, she was well accessorized with a cute scarf and boots.

The hostess let us know that our party had already arrived, and as we approached the table, Lance and Ben stood up to greet us. Lance was about five-eight with light-brown hair that was growing out of a buzz cut. He was muscular and loved to show it off even though he would probably be more attractive if he didn't. His black shirt looked as though it were about two sizes too small for him.

I recalled how Lance had relentlessly dragged Jen to the gym with him the week after their first date. Although Jen enjoyed running, she wasn't one for heavy weight training. She limped from table to table at the café for an entire week afterward. Finally, she'd told him that she didn't want to work out with him anymore, so their number of dates had since tapered off.

Ben stood at the opposite side of the table. My first thought was that he was the definition of tall, dark, and handsome. He had perfectly gelled brown hair, dark eyes, and a golden tan. I didn't even have to look at Jen to tell she was mentally picking out *His* and *Hers* towels for us.

Ben and I exchanged an awkward handshake as Lance introduced us. Ben pulled out my chair for me, and I hesitated before sitting down. I wasn't used to dating—or even non-dating, for that matter.

We placed our order for a few tapas to share—a roasted olive and cheese plate, grilled chicken kabobs, tomato crostini, and hummus. Lance ordered a bottle of merlot for the table, and I clarified to the waitress that I would have water before she had a chance to ask for my ID.

"She's not twenty-one yet," Jen explained when she noticed Ben and Lance exchange a confused look.

"I'll give you some of mine," Ben whispered as he winked at me.

I smiled politely but still planned on sticking with water.

"So, did you grow up around here?" Ben asked a few minutes later, trying to make conversation with me.

"No," I replied. "I grew up in Richmond. How about you?"

"Born and raised here," he replied proudly. "My sisters couldn't wait to leave and go to college. In fact, my oldest sister moved to Denver and is begging me to move there." He took a sip of his wine. "What brought you to St. Augustine?"

I glanced over at Jen, who was trying her best to listen to Lance recount his latest bench press success.

I turned back to Ben and replied, "I needed a change. I guess I'm like your sisters in wanting to see something outside of my hometown." For some reason, it was easier for me to lie to him than to Michael. Although I wasn't sure if getting mad at the question and completely refusing to answer was much better than lying.

Ben nodded in agreement. I could sense this was the same story his sisters had told him when they left. "I think my sisters would like you," he said and then paused. "I know I do."

Ben winked at me again, and I realized that he was used to girls swooning over him. He didn't even notice that I wasn't.

Luckily for me, the waitress arrived with our food. Ben was annoyed with the waitress's timing but was quickly distracted when the plate of grilled chicken kabobs was placed in front of him.

I was enjoying a piece of pita bread and hummus when Jen announced that she had to go to the ladies' room. I didn't think anything of it until she gave me a wide-eyed stare. She wanted to talk.

"Oh, uh, I'll go with you," I said, hoping that was the right answer.

Jen smiled, and her eyes returned to their normal size, so I knew she wanted to speak with me privately.

"Girls always go in pairs," Ben joked, and I resisted the temptation to roll my eyes.

I obediently followed Jen to the restroom. As soon as the door closed behind us, she turned to me and squealed. I jumped, startled.

"Ben's so cute!" she said. "How's it going? Do you like him?"

I didn't say anything, and I could sense her frustration.

"What?" she asked, clearly disappointed.

"He's cute," I replied, agreeing with her. "But he's just not my type."

48

"Really?" she asked. "Are you sure? Because I think he's everyone's type."

"Yes, I'm sure."

Jen eyed me, trying to decide if there was any way to persuade me. When she realized that I was confident in my decision, she appeared defeated.

"Darn, I thought this might work out," she said. "Oh well. At least you're getting a free dinner out of it."

I laughed and made a mental note to ask the waitress for my check to be separated. I didn't want there to be any confusion. After all, this was a *non-date*.

Thirty minutes later and after a small argument, Ben insisted on paying for my dinner, and we headed to the theater. The theater wasn't within walking distance, so Lance offered to drive.

I climbed into the back of the car and realized this was the first time I'd been in a car since I drove to Jacksonville to meet Seth. Ben climbed into the seat beside me, and I focused on taking deep breaths, trying to ward off the anxiety of being in a car again. Luckily, Ben was too self-absorbed to notice.

As we drove to the theater, I replayed the dream of the car accident in my head. It wasn't just the memory of dying in my dream that haunted me; it was also the feeling of dying and of Michael bringing me back to life. It felt so real.

In the background, I could hear Ben talking about school. He was studying finance at St. Augustine College. Even though I managed a few polite smiles and nods, I was unable to completely focus on him. All I could think about was my dream.

"So, what do you think?" Ben asked a few minutes later.

I blinked, completely oblivious to the question he'd just asked me.

"Should I choose accounting or business as my minor?" he asked expectantly.

"Oh, uh," I stammered, trying to catch up with the conversation. "Business."

That was what Seth and Carl had majored in, and they seemed to be doing well.

Ben nodded in agreement.

I was relieved when we finally arrived at the theater, grateful to be out of the car. As we walked to the ticket booth, Jen and Lance argued on which movie we should see. Jen was adamant that we should see the new romantic comedy *The Love Effect*, and Lance wanted to see a thriller called *Dead Gorgeous*. I interrupted, voting for *Dead Gorgeous*. It was bad enough that I was going to get stuck, sitting next to Ben. There was no way I was also going to sit through a *romantic* movie with him.

After getting our tickets, Ben and I followed Lance and Jen to the concession stand. Jen pursed her lips as Lance ordered popcorn without any salt or butter, but she didn't say anything.

When it was our turn, I ordered a popcorn with extra butter and a soda. I threw a twenty-dollar bill on the counter before Ben could offer to pay.

Ben sulked as we went into the theater to get our seats. As I predicted, Jen and I sat next to each other with the guys sitting on each side of us. I offered her some of my popcorn, and she smiled gratefully as she grabbed a handful.

I glanced over at Lance and could tell by their body language that he liked Jen more than she liked him. He was leaning in toward her, but she seemed to be leaning closer toward me to put more distance between them.

The previews began, and I looked around the theater. As my eyes adjusted to the darkness, I noticed a couple in front of us who were already making out. To the left of them was an older woman who was also looking at them and shaking her head in disapproval. Three rows up from her, I saw … Michael.

Michael wasn't alone though. He was there with Raina.

I sat up a little straighter to get a better view. I could tell they were sitting side by side, but I couldn't tell whether or not they were holding hands.

The movie started, and as if he'd been waiting for it, Ben pulled a flask from his jacket pocket. He held it up against my soda, his eyebrows raised in question. I just shook my head. Ben frowned for a second, disappointed that I wouldn't drink with him. He then proceeded to pour the entire contents into his own drink.

A few minutes and three gulps later, Ben moved his arm to the armrest between us. His palm was tilted toward me, inviting my hand into his. I popped a handful of popcorn into my mouth and carefully clasped my hands together in my lap. Ben sighed and gave up, taking another gulp of his spiked soda.

The movie was a little cliché but not the worst I'd seen. There were a few scenes that caught me off guard, causing me to jump in my seat. Each time, I looked over at Michael to gauge his reaction, but he remained unfazed. By the fourth unexpected event in the movie, I wondered if there was anything that could startle him. Raina, on the other hand, jumped at every part and hid her eyes beneath her hands.

"Please ... don't!" the actress in the leading role begged.

She was strapped to a gurney in a mental institution while the attractive psycho killer, who was dressed like a doctor, pulled out several scalpels and knives, trying to decide which one to use. The killer decided on a scalpel and approached the victim, who was panicking and trying to untie herself.

I glanced over at Michael and noticed that instead of watching the movie, he was talking to Raina. She shook her head at him and stood up, wiping tears from her face. As she hurried past our row, I noticed that she was breathing heavily and shaking. She was having a panic attack.

Michael sat there for a moment but then stood up and hurried after her.

I watched them both leave, unsure of what to do. I realized that whatever was going on was none of my business, but a part of me still felt compelled to follow them. I'd had more panic attacks than I could count over the past few years. Maybe there was something I could do to help her calm down. I could help her count slowly and take deep breaths. That usually worked on me.

I looked down at my watch, and the movie only had ten minutes left at most. I contemplated on waiting until the end of the movie but decided against it.

"I'll be right back," I whispered to Jen and stood up.

She gave me a questioning look, so she must not have seen Michael.

Ben moved his long legs out of the way, so I could pass. As I walked past him, he unnecessarily put his hands on my hips as if trying to help me. I debated on slapping his hands away but instead chose to just ignore him. It was better to not give him any more attention than necessary. I didn't want him following me.

As I exited the theater, I glanced around for signs of Michael or Raina. I didn't see them in the hall, so I headed out to the main lobby. Almost immediately, I noticed Michael pacing outside the entrance to the ladies' restroom.

"Natalie," he said as I approached him. He sounded more surprised than happy to see me. "What are you doing here?"

"Just seeing a movie. I'm on a non—never mind." I shook my head, switching gears. "I hope this doesn't seem crazy, but I saw you and your girlfriend leave the theater, and she seemed upset, so I wanted to see if everything was okay."

He stared at me, dumbfounded. I could tell he hadn't been expecting that. He probably thought I was a stalker. A crazy stalker who had meltdowns at work.

"Right. Uh," he stammered, "my sister isn't feeling well."

"Would you like me to check on her?" I tried to seem nonchalant by the distinction that she was his *sister*.

Again, he seemed surprised. "I don't think that's a good idea."

"Are you sure? I don't mind." And I meant it. Even though she had been rude to me in the café, I wanted to help Michael.

"I think you should go," he said firmly.

I opened my mouth, unsure of what to say but knowing I was going to protest.

"I mean it, Natalie. This isn't a good time. It's just going to make it worse if she sees you."

I didn't understand. *How could seeing me make it worse?*

Michael looked past me, and his face hardened. I followed his gaze and noticed Jen, Lance, and Ben waiting for me by the exit. Jen looked amused, but Ben crossed his arms across his chest, clearly annoyed that I was talking to another guy. Ben thought this was a real date despite my attempts to thwart him.

I turned back to face Michael, who was glaring at Ben.

Michael then turned his glare on me. "Please go before she comes out," he repeated.

Speechless, I turned and walked away.

"Who was that?" Ben asked when I returned to our group.

"No one," I replied flatly. "Just a customer from the café."

Jen stared at me with a puzzled expression on her face, but I just gave her a look that said, *Don't ask.*

Ben talked my ear off on the car ride home. I didn't really hear him though as I kept replaying the interaction with Michael in my head. Michael had seemed almost annoyed that I was there. It had been clear that he didn't want my help and somehow thought all I would do was make the situation worse.

Lance dropped me off at my house first, and Ben insisted on walking me to my door. I had been hoping that he would skip this formality, but he was determined to win me over despite my best efforts to keep things neutral between us.

"Thank you for dinner," I told him and offered him a handshake.

Ben took my hand and yanked me forward, pulling me close to him. "I had a great time," he whispered in my ear.

Instinctively, I pulled back. He looked confused, obviously not used to rejection from women. His expression faded into a smile, as if he were in on a secret.

"It's okay," he said. "I like hard to get." He gave me a swift kiss on the cheek before strutting away. As he was about to get in the car, he turned to me. "I'll catch ya next time."

I smiled politely, counting down the seconds until I could go in the house and scrub my cheek clean.

SIX

In less than one hour, I would be at Jen's mercy as she dressed me up for the Halloween masquerade ball. The masquerade would take place at the Casa de la Belleza, a luxury hotel that Jen's dad managed. The hotel was hosting the party as part of a fundraising event, but her dad had given her an extra ticket after she insisted on bringing me with her.

The party was scheduled to end around one a.m., so Jen's dad had booked a room for Jen and me to share, so we wouldn't have to go home so late.

I added a pair of pajamas to my overnight bag and did one last check to make sure I'd packed everything. My bag was small and light since Jen was supplying most of what I needed to get ready.

As I made my way to the hotel, I walked past the tapas restaurant where we had gone the other night with Ben and Lance. My cheeks began to feel hot as I recalled my encounter with Michael at the theater that night. I was still embarrassed about following him and by his subsequent rejection. It had been three days, and I hadn't seen him since.

When I got to the hotel, I was amazed to find that Jen's father hadn't just booked us a room; he'd booked us a two-bedroom suite. There was a living room, a dining room, and even a balcony overlooking the hotel's elegant pool area. I couldn't fathom how much a suite at a five-star hotel cost.

Jen, who already had her makeup finished and her hair in hot rollers, gestured for me to sit at the vanity, so she could begin primping me. I didn't have a lot of experience in primping, so the majority of the hair tools and makeup applicators were foreign to me.

I spotted a tube of lipstick and felt reassured. At least I recognized something on the vanity.

"How are things with you and Lance?" I asked Jen as she began working on my hair.

She frowned. "I'm not sure. He tried to kiss me, but I just don't know. I think we're better off as friends. I think Lance and Ben are coming tonight though, so I'll see how it goes."

I wasn't thrilled about the idea of seeing Ben, but I decided to just continue to put distance between us. Jen was a little confused about Lance, but I wasn't at all confused about Ben. My instincts told me he was trouble, and I wasn't interested in getting involved with him.

Jen styled my hair up into a soft bun and then started working on my makeup. I wore makeup but nothing to this extent. She opened various powders and creams and did something called contouring, where she made my cheekbones stand out. I asked her where she'd learned to apply makeup like this.

"I used to do pageants when I was younger," she replied, blushing.

For some reason, she was embarrassed to admit this to me. I wasn't surprised at all though. I could see Jen showcasing her dazzling smile and personality while winning over pageant judges. She was a natural at that type of thing.

"It comes in handy though," she continued. "When I do field assignments, I'm always camera-ready."

Jen was a journalism student at St. Augustine College and worked at their news station a few hours per week. They sent her all over campus and throughout the city to cover stories. She was so good that she'd recently received an internship at one of the news stations in Jacksonville. She was only working there one Saturday a month but was excited to have the experience on her résumé when she graduated.

When she was finished with my makeup, I wanted to look in the mirror, but she refused to let me look until I put the dress on.

"You need to see the whole transformation," she told me.

I promised not to peek as Jen went to the closet to retrieve the dress she'd brought for me. I obeyed her until she finally told me to open my eyes. When I did, she revealed the most beautiful dress I had ever seen. It literally took my breath away.

The champagne dress was floor-length but not too voluminous. It had sheer cap sleeves, a sweetheart neckline, and just enough beading detail to keep it from looking too plain. It was simple but very elegant.

"Do you like it?" she asked, worried by my lack of response. "It's actually one of my former pageant dresses."

I was astonished. "Like it? It's amazing!"

Jen helped me put on the dress and then immediately told me to close my eyes again. I blindly followed her as she led me toward the cheval-style mirror in our room. She told me to stop walking and open my eyes. I couldn't believe what I saw.

I saw me but a different version of me. I looked glamorous, and even though I was a little concerned about the amount of makeup applied to my face, I had to admit, Jen really knew what she was doing. The makeup colors she'd chosen brought warmth to my face, but I still looked somewhat natural. I looked like I was glowing, much like I had that morning after I woke up after sleeping for two days.

"You're a knockout," she said.

"I can't believe it," I replied, still unsure if I was really looking at myself.

Jen walked behind me and placed a masquerade mask over my eyes. She carefully attached a satin white ribbon to hold it in place. The mask wasn't what I'd expected; it was so much better.

I'd thought the mask would be large and clunky, making it difficult to see, but that wasn't the case at all. Knowing me well, Jen had picked out an elegant but lightweight mask. The gold Venetian-style mask was simple and not overpowering. The mask was merely a decoration, like an elegant piece of jewelry. I still looked like me when I was wearing it.

Jen removed the hot rollers from her hair, which gave it the perfect amount of curl and bounce. She pulled her dress out of the closet, and it matched her bubbly personality perfectly. Instead of being a floor-length, traditional gown, it was a short hot-pink dress with a full tulle skirt. The bodice looked almost like a corset, but it was strapless and covered in sequins.

As Jen got dressed, I put on a pair of borrowed heels and was appreciative that mine were much shorter than the stilettos Jen had chosen for herself. I stood up and walked around the room to get a feel for the shoes. I didn't wear dress shoes often and would be mortified if I tripped in two-inch heels.

Jen emerged in her hot-pink dress and looked stunning, as usual. She put on a black lacy mask and tied it in place with a hot-pink ribbon.

"Let's get our party on!" she said, clapping her hands together with excitement.

The masquerade was held outdoors, so heaters had been placed throughout the large white tents to keep guests warm. It was now dark outside, but the tent was beautifully lit with sparkling chandeliers hanging from the ceiling and candles set at each of the cocktail tables. The use of amber uplighting cast a warm glow on the tent walls, making the party seem extravagant but intimate at the same time. Beneath our feet was carefully placed blue-and-yellow Talavera tile flooring.

Although the party had just begun, there were already about a hundred guests in the tent area. Everyone was dressed in elegant masquerade attire, with the exception of a few men who opted not to wear masks.

I noticed one guy in particular standing on the opposite side of the room. He was wearing a black tuxedo with a white shirt, a black necktie, and a simple black mask, which made him look mysterious and sexy.

We approached the bar and were greeted by a bartender wearing a white mask that covered just the right side of his face. I ordered a soda and was surprised when Jen ordered the same.

"My dad isn't a big fan of me drinking even though I'm old enough now," she explained.

With our sodas in hand, we assembled a small plate of hors d'oeuvres and stood around a cocktail table. Before taking a bite, Jen spotted the dessert table and left to fix us a plate while I held our table.

As she walked away, I quickly noticed how many guys turned around to stare at her as she walked past them. One guy even ran into a cocktail table because he was watching her instead of where he was going. I almost laughed aloud but stopped when I noticed the mysterious guy from across the room walking my way.

He was about halfway across the room when the light of one of the chandeliers caught his bright blue eyes beneath the mask. I tensed as I realized who it was.

"Hi," Michael said when he reached me. "I thought that was you."

Unsure of what to say, I just stood there, silent.

"About the other night," he continued, "I'm sorry for being rude to you. You just caught me off guard."

"You were trying to take care of your sister, and I was in the way," I acknowledged, realizing maybe I shouldn't have taken his rejection so personally.

"Raina was upset, and I was worried that if she saw you there, it would set her off."

"Why would seeing *me* set her off?" I asked. *What could I have possibly done to make his sister hate me so much?*

"It's complicated, but trust me when I tell you that it's better for you if I leave you out of it."

"I don't understand," I told him, even more confused than I had been before.

I waited for some sort of explanation, but he just stood there, refusing to give me one.

I saw Jen talking to her dad at the dessert table. "Excuse me, Michael. I need to go thank the host," I said, not trying to hide the frustration in my voice. "I'm sure we'll bump into each other again later."

He nodded slightly but didn't say anything as I walked away.

I made my way over to Jen and her dad.

"Natalie!" Mr. Walsh greeted me. "I'm glad you could make it."

I'd met Jen's dad a handful of times since moving into town, and every time I saw him, I found myself amused by how much he and Jen were alike. They were both always so upbeat and welcoming.

"Mr. Walsh," I greeted him in return. "Thank you so much for the invitation and for allowing us to stay at the hotel tonight. I feel like I'm in a movie or something."

"I'm glad you're enjoying yourself, and I know my Jennie will stay out of trouble if she's with you." He smiled at Jen, and she jokingly rolled her eyes. "Look, I have to check on the valet situation, but you girls have fun. Eat lots of food. I think we catered enough to feed the entire city."

Mr. Walsh hurried off, and Jen suggested we go back to our table to devour the chocolate goodies she'd found. I plucked a white chocolate truffle from her plate and noticed that Michael was nowhere in sight.

As we finished our hors d'oeuvres and dessert, I filled Jen in on my conversation with Michael. She listened intently and then admitted she was just as confused as I was about the situation.

"So, he didn't tell you what she was upset about. Just that it's better you don't know," Jen said, processing the story out loud.

"I don't get it," I said with a hopeless shrug.

The band started playing one of Jen's favorite songs, and several partygoers ventured onto the dance floor. I braced myself. It was just a matter of time before Jen tried to pull me out there.

"How's it going, ladies?" Lance asked as he and Ben approached our table.

I got a whiff of Ben's strong, musky cologne and almost gagged.

"I was just thinking about dancing," Jen replied. "I love this song!"

Lance offered his arm to escort Jen to the dance floor, but Jen paused, raising an eyebrow at me.

Ben put his arm around my shoulders. "Don't worry," he told her, alcohol strong on his breath. "I will take good care of her."

"I'll be fine. Go have fun," I insisted, ducking from under Ben's arm.

Jen flashed me a wide smile and bounced away.

Ben polished off the rest of his drink and looked at my empty glass on the table. "I'm going to get another. What can I get you?" he asked.

"A soda," I replied with a smile.

Ben shot me a disapproving look.

"We're going to see that wild side of you at some point," Ben said, pointing at me as he stumbled to the bar.

I tried to shake off a chill as it ran up my spine. I couldn't put my finger on it, but something about Ben creeped me out.

I looked around but could no longer see Jen and Lance on the crowded dance floor. I could, however, see Michael. He was talking to a man and woman at a nearby table. The man and woman had their backs to me, but Michael was facing me. He immediately made eye contact with me as if he anticipated I would be looking for him. I looked away.

"All righty," Ben said as he returned and handed me a glass of soda. "One soda for you and another real beverage for me. Cheers!"

We clinked our glasses together, and Ben kept his eyes glued to me as he took a big gulp of his drink.

I looked down at my soda without taking a sip. Something didn't feel right. My soda looked fine, but there was something deceitful in the way Ben was carrying himself. A familiar pang surfaced in my stomach, and I quickly figured out what it was.

"Are you freaking kidding me?" I asked Ben, slamming my glass down on the table. Soda sloshed all over him.

"What the hell's your problem?" Ben jumped back and angrily wiped soda off his sleeve.

The lights flickered as the knot tightened in my stomach. The danger wasn't over. I looked out onto the dance floor, trying to find Jen.

I started to walk away, but Ben grabbed my arm. Out of the corner of my eye, I saw Michael leave his conversation and start walking toward us.

"Get away from me," I forcibly told him.

I brought my hand back, ready to slap him, but he let go, holding his hands up in defeat.

I stormed away from Ben before Michael reached us. I needed to find Jen. The knot grew more intense, and I knew she was in trouble.

"Natalie," I heard Michael call from behind me, but I continued walking. When he caught up to me, he ripped off his mask and tossed it onto a nearby table. "Are you okay? What happened?" Michael threw a hateful glare back in Ben's direction.

"I need to find Jen," I replied without slowing my pace.

I scanned the crowd and felt the onset of panic when I couldn't find her.

"I'll help you find her, but can you tell me what's going on?" Michael asked, still trying to figure out my erratic behavior.

I spotted a speckle of hot pink in the crowd on the dance floor, and I took off. It felt like a never-ending sea of people as I pushed my way toward Jen. The masks that seemed so elegant before now felt sinister as they blocked my path. Partygoers bumped into me and gave me dirty looks, but I didn't care. All I cared about was reaching Jen.

When I finally made it to Jen, Lance was with her. And as I had suspected, she had a fresh drink in her hand.

"Natalie!" Jen cheerfully greeted me, thinking I'd changed my mind about dancing.

I didn't say anything back. I just grabbed her by the hand and pulled her off the dance floor. Lance and Michael followed us, both of them confused.

I took the drink out of Jen's hand and looked down at it. The drink was still pretty full, and the knot in my stomach started to ease up. I was right.

"What's up?" Lance asked, narrowing his eyes at me.

His fake innocence infuriated me.

"Don't even try it," I snapped. "You know exactly what's up."

Jen put a hand on my arm. "Natalie, what's wrong?"

"This creep is trying to drug you," I replied, not taking my eyes off Lance.

He squirmed under my fuming gaze.

"Ben put something in my drink too."

"That's crazy," Lance said with a nervous laugh. He expectantly looked at Jen. "You don't believe her, do you?"

Jen turned to me, and I knew she must be thinking my accusation was farfetched.

"How do you know that?" she asked.

"I just know," I replied.

She studied me for a moment, and I started to worry that maybe she thought I was crazy.

What if she doesn't believe me?

"That's the most ridiculous thing I've ever heard," Lance said. "You can't possibly believe this crap."

Without saying a word, Jen gently took the drink from me. My heart sank.

What am I going to do if she wants to leave with him?

Even if she didn't want to be my friend anymore, I couldn't let her leave with him. He was dangerous.

Jen approached Lance, and a large, smug smile spread across his face.

She raised the glass up toward him. "Drink it," she told him.

"What?" Lance asked, his smile quickly disappearing.

"Drink it," she repeated. "If there's nothing in it, then you shouldn't have any issues with drinking it yourself."

Lance took the glass from her and stared down at it. He looked up at me and then at Jen. His face hardened as he dumped its contents onto the floor. "I don't have to prove anything to you."

"Well, you just did," Jen replied.

"Seriously?" Lance said, pointing at me. "You're going to believe this freak over me?"

Michael stepped forward, now inches from Lance. "That's enough. You need to walk away," Michael warned, his voice low and intense.

"Good luck, man," Lance said to Michael with a chuckle. He pointed at me again. "You're going to need it to deal with this prudish nutcase."

Without hesitation, Michael punched Lance in the face. *Hard.* Although it didn't look like Michael had put much effort into it, Lance fell backward onto the floor.

Everyone around us gasped in shock. Blood gushed from beneath Lance's mask, and he jumped up, ready to fight.

Mr. Walsh must have seen the punch because he rushed over with one of his security guards at his heels. The security guard grabbed ahold of Lance before he lunged at Michael.

"What's the problem over here?" Mr. Walsh demanded, eyeing Michael.

Jen quickly rushed to Michael's side. "It's not Michael's fault. He was just trying to protect Natalie, who was protecting me. Lance put some kind of drug in my drink. Ben did the same to Natalie."

Mr. Walsh's face turned a deep crimson color, and the veins in his neck began to bulge. I could tell that he also wanted to punch Lance, but he was forcing himself to stay composed because he was at work.

"You have zero evidence," Lance insisted.

The security guard searched Lance's pockets but found nothing.

Mr. Walsh turned to the security guard. "Find the other boy and get them both out of here. They are not allowed to step foot on this property again. If they do, call the police and have them arrested for trespassing."

"Yes, sir," the security guard replied before pulling Lance away.

Mr. Walsh's face faded to a lighter shade of pink. "Are you feeling all right, honey?" he asked Jen.

"I think so," Jen replied.

"Did you drink any of your soda?" I asked her.

Jen slowly shook her head. "I don't think so, but I'm not sure."

"Let's get you to your room. I'd like Dr. Sanderson to give you a quick examination. She is here somewhere, and I know she wouldn't mind looking in on you. If she gives you the all-clear, you can rejoin the party," Mr. Walsh told her.

"Yes, Daddy," Jen replied.

A woman wearing a suit with her hair in a tight bun approached Mr. Walsh. She was clearly oblivious to the chaos that had just occurred.

"Sir, the mayor is looking for you. He'd like to have a word about the speech he'll be making later," she told him.

"I'll go with Jen," I volunteered, putting a protective arm around her.

"I think Dr. Sanderson should examine you as well," Mr. Walsh said to me, ignoring the woman.

"Thank you, but I'm okay," I told him. "I didn't drink any of mine."

"Sir," Michael said, "with your permission, I'd like to walk the girls to the room to make sure they get there safely. Just in case security hasn't located Ben yet."

"Thank you, Michael," Mr. Walsh replied as he shook Michael's hand. "I appreciate you looking out for them."

Michael walked us up to our room, and thankfully, we didn't run into Ben. I hoped security had found him by now.

"I'm going to hang out here for a few minutes just to make sure that jerk doesn't show up," Michael said as Jen opened the door to our room.

"You don't have to do that," I told him. "We've already disrupted your evening enough."

"You are welcome to come in and sit down," Jen told Michael, flashing a quick smile at me. "We have an official waiting room and everything. Come see."

Jen opened the door to the room and gestured to the living room. Michael looked at me and waited for me to nod before entering the room.

The phone rang before we could even sit down, and Jen answered it. It was her dad calling to let her know that security had located Ben. Although they hadn't found any evidence on him, they'd escorted him off the property.

As soon as Jen hung up the phone, there was a knock at the door. Michael immediately walked to the door, looking out the peephole. He turned to us and smiled as he opened the door for the doctor.

Dr. Sanderson was a petite woman in her late fifties with silver-blonde hair. She was wearing a navy sequined ballgown and carrying a black medical bag.

Dr. Sanderson gave Jen a thorough examination, checking her pupils, blood pressure, and pulse. She asked Jen a series of questions, including whether or not she felt intoxicated, disoriented, or confused.

"You're not showing any symptoms, so you must not have taken a sip of that drink," Dr. Sanderson told Jen as she put her stethoscope back into her bag. "You're a very lucky girl that your friend got to you first. Rohypnol is unfortunately popular right now, and most victims don't get as lucky as you did."

I let out a sigh of relief.

Dr. Sanderson zipped up her bag and smiled at Jen. "I'm okay with you going back to the party, but from now on, when you go to a party, make sure you get your own drinks and never leave your drinks unattended. This could have ended very badly for you. Got it?"

"Yes, ma'am. Thank you," Jen replied.

Dr. Sanderson left to rejoin the party. I assumed Jen would want to do the same, but instead, she started taking off her jewelry.

"I think I've had enough excitement for one night. I'm going to stay in and just go to bed. It's been a long night," Jen said. "You two should go back though and enjoy the rest of the party."

Before I could respond, Jen hugged me tightly. "Thank you," she whispered to me before letting me go. "I don't want to think about what would've happened if you hadn't been there."

"Try to rest," I said, grateful she was safe.

Jen thanked Michael as well before going into her bedroom and closing the door behind her.

"I don't really want to go back to the party," I admitted to Michael when we were alone. "I'm not really a party person. I was only there because Jen had asked me to be."

Assuming I wanted him to leave, Michael stood up.

"But there are supposed to be fireworks at midnight, and we should have a great view from our balcony if you want to stay and hang out for a while," I quickly added.

"Sure," he replied with a small smile.

"There's just one thing I have to do first," I said, and I pulled off my shoes. I let out a deep, relaxed breath.

"All better?" There was a hint of amusement on Michael's face as he looked down at my bare feet.

"Yes," I replied. "I used to wear heels every now and then to school, but I haven't worn them since I moved to St. Augustine. I walk everywhere here, so heels aren't really an option."

"Speaking of St. Augustine," he said as he held open the balcony door for me, "I realize I came across pretty intense that day I walked you home. It's none of my business why you moved here."

I stepped outside and rested my arms on the railing. He stood beside me. Without my shoes on, I was suddenly aware of how much shorter I was than him. He was at least eight inches taller than me without my shoes.

"It had been a rough day for me, and I might have overreacted a little," I admitted. "I moved here because I needed a fresh start." It wasn't a lie, and it was a cleaner version of the truth. "How about you? Were you born and raised here?"

"No. I've moved around a lot throughout my life," he said without offering further explanation.

"That must've been tough, especially when you were younger," I said, angling myself to face him. "Starting new schools and making new friends and all. I had a hard enough time with that, and I never had to change schools."

"I had Raina," he replied with a shrug. "She's always been my best friend. Do you have any brothers or sisters?"

I cringed a little but tried to remain composed. There wasn't going to be any way around the question unless I wanted to lie, and I didn't. Not to Michael. "I ... had a sister. Her name was Becca." I turned away, facing the railing again.

"I'm sorry," he softly replied. "What happened to her?"

"She disappeared," I admitted, surprising myself with my candor. "Four years ago. We never found her." I couldn't help but shiver.

"What was she like?" Michael took off his jacket and placed it on my shoulders.

"Thank you. Becca was the best sister anyone could ask for. She was my role model." I took a deep breath and tightened my grip on the railing. "She was never afraid to be herself and to stand up for what she believed in. She was protective of people she cared about, especially me. She liked to read and draw. She was also a pretty good cook, something I am not."

I let out a small laugh. "One time, we tried to make our mother breakfast in bed, and I set the toaster on fire. Becca quickly put it out with the fire extinguisher but refused to even let me pour the milk into the cereal after that."

He smiled, and we stood there in silence for a moment. I was in shock that I'd actually opened up to someone about Becca.

I looked up at the sky and focused on the stars. I used to do this a lot right after her disappearance to calm myself. I would look at the stars and remind myself that Becca was under the same blanket of the night sky. Somehow, the thought made me feel like she wasn't so far away.

"Can I ask you another question?" he asked, and I nodded. "How did you know about the drinks?"

The question caught me off guard, and I stiffened.

He continued, "I'll be honest with you. I was keeping an eye on Ben. He has quite the reputation, and I didn't trust him with you. But somehow, I missed it. I didn't see him put anything into your drink. How did you know?"

Avoiding his eyes, I shrugged. "I had a feeling," I replied honestly and hoped he wouldn't pry.

I didn't want to start lying to him now. Despite the fact that I'd opened up to him about Becca, I wasn't ready to tell anyone about my intuitive abilities. He'd already seen me have a meltdown at the café. If I told him that I'd literally had a gut instinct about the drinks, he would really think I was crazy for sure.

"Okay," he said.

I could tell he wasn't buying it, but he didn't push the issue.

A loud popping noise startled us, and we both jumped. Laughing at ourselves, we looked up in awe as starbursts of green, yellow, red, and purple exploded into the sky. It was evident that Mr. Walsh had spared no expense at the fireworks display. It was a magical ending to his elaborate event.

During the grand finale, I looked up at Michael, and I couldn't help but wonder what he was thinking. He looked down at me, and I could see the reflection of the lights dancing in his eyes before the last of the fireworks faded away. It was hypnotizing.

He leaned in toward me, and I held my breath.

He reached his hands behind my head and untied my mask, gently removing it from my face. I'd completely forgotten that I was wearing it.

"There," he said with a thoughtful smile. "Doesn't that feel better?"

I nodded and let out my breath. In an equally terrifying and exciting way, it did.

SEVEN

I startled awake at the sound of clapping thunder. It took me a minute to realize that I was home, in my own bed, lying in a cold sweat. I sat up and ran my hands through my dampened hair.

Over the past several years, I'd grown accustomed to having nightmares. Especially those that took me back to the night Becca had disappeared. In my usual nightmare, instead of getting knocked out, I chased the faceless man who had taken her. But no matter how hard I ran, he was always just out of reach.

This dream had been different.

As I was chasing Becca and the intruder, I followed them into the woods; however, these weren't the woods near my parents' home. These were the same woods from my car-accident dream.

As soon as we entered the woods, Becca and the intruder disappeared. I noticed something lying on the ground, near the tree I'd hit. My mangled car was gone, but the dent I'd made in the tree remained. I walked closer to see what was left behind from the wreckage. There, lying on the ground, in perfect condition, was Becca's journal.

I heard a flutter from up above, and when I looked up, I saw the black raven from my car-accident dream perched on a branch. His dark eyes were fixed on me, as if waiting for me to open the journal.

The alarm clock on my nightstand said it was two a.m., but I turned on my lamp and climbed out of bed anyway. I grabbed Becca's journal off my dresser and sat back down on the bed, letting the journal sit unopened in my lap.

I still wasn't sure I wanted to open it yet. If it wasn't going to bring me closer to getting the answers I needed, would it be worth the pain of reliving memories I could never get back? Could I handle it?

At the masquerade party last week, I had been able to open up to Michael a little bit about Becca, and that was absolutely a step forward. I'd never been able to do that before, not even with Jen. Despite that success, was I strong enough to face whatever Becca's journal contained?

I could imagine that this journal consisted of Becca's visions about her relationship with Seth and the future she'd probably foreseen with him. It might predict her graduating high school, going to college, and getting married. Or maybe those visions never existed because, on some level, Becca had known there wasn't a future. Either way, it would be devastating to know.

I sighed at the realization that the more I resisted reading the journal, the more it would haunt me.

My hands shook as I opened the cover. The first page just had her name, but I felt my eyes sting at just the sight of her handwriting. It had been a while since I saw it.

I took a deep breath and turned the page. Flowers were drawn on the page but not just any flowers. They were the flowers that Seth had given Becca for her birthday. The sketch was done with a black pencil, but I remembered the vibrant red roses and how they had shown up on our doorstep with a love note. I smiled at the memory of my father giving my mother a look that asked, *Should we be worried?* In the bottom corner of the page, Becca had written the date July 1. Her birthday was July 7.

The next page contained a sketch of St. Augustine. It was of the famous Bridge of Lions with the strip of stores and restaurants lining State Road A1A in the background. She must have sketched this in anticipation of our family vacation. The date said September 20. We had taken our family vacation that October.

The following sketch was also of St. Augustine, drawn September 30. It was of St. George Street. I admired how she'd captured the ambiance and peacefulness of the city. As much as I'd loved St. Augustine when we vacationed here, it wasn't until I'd actually moved here that I really learned to appreciate all of its charm. Becca had even drawn a guitarist performing on one of the side streets.

I started to move to the next page when I caught a glimpse of the Cuna Café in the background. I held the journal closer to get a better look, and sure enough, the street performer was actually down Cuna Street, and the café was behind him.

I didn't remember the Cuna Café when we had been on vacation. I was pretty sure Carl had told me he opened the café the year after we visited, but maybe I was wrong.

I turned the page and froze. A sharp chill ran throughout my body. I wanted to slam the journal closed and throw it across the room, but I couldn't move. My body felt like a block of ice. I couldn't believe what I was seeing. It wasn't possible.

There, drawn out on the page in great detail, was the car accident from my dream.

In the center of the page was the same tree. My car was smashed against it, almost split down the middle. The front end was completely gone; it was merged with the tree trunk. It was just as I remembered it.

It didn't make any sense. *Why would Becca envision something I would dream about four years after she disappeared?* Yes, it was a terrifying nightmare, but I'd had a million of those since she went missing. Why would this one be any different from the rest?

I turned the page, but it was blank. I closed the book, unsure of what to think or feel. I just sat there, stunned.

The thunder rumbled outside, and the faint glow of lightning peeked from behind the curtains in my bedroom. The hairs on my arms stood on end, as if sensing the electricity in the air. As a lightning bolt crashed just outside my apartment, I understood why she had drawn the accident in her journal.

I darted out of my room and through the house. I could hear the rain picking up outside as I grabbed a flashlight from the kitchen drawer.

Even though I was still in my tank top and pajama pants, I opened the front door and stepped outside. Barefoot, I trampled through the wet grass to my car, slushing mud against the bottom of my pants.

The rain poured down on me, but I barely noticed as it soaked my hair and pajamas. I was on a mission because I had to see for myself what I knew to be true.

I shone the flashlight on my car and held my breath, bracing myself for the fact that the world as I knew it was about to change.

Sure enough, beneath the small beam of yellow light and beads of rain was a completely smooth, evenly painted surface on my back right bumper. There was no trace of a scratch having been buffed and painted. It was as if I'd never bumped the neighbor's mailbox with the car. With shaking hands, I ran the tips of my fingers over the bumper.

This isn't my car.

I backed as far away from the car as I could until my back was flat against the outside wall of my apartment. Unable to take my eyes off the car, I slid down until I was sitting on the soaked ground with my legs pulled toward my chest.

My head swirled with a million questions. *If this isn't my car, then where did this car come from? Did the accident really happen? Was Michael really there? If he was, why would he have gone through such great lengths to cover it up?*

Let's say the accident had happened. There was no way I could have survived it. As I remembered it, Michael had pulled me out of the wreckage, but unless he was secretly a doctor, I didn't see how he could've saved me. Without a doubt, my injuries would've required me to go to the hospital and have surgery. I probably would've died before we ever made it to the hospital.

Maybe I wasn't crazy after all. Maybe what had happened to me in the café that day was connected to the accident. But how?

I wasn't sure how long I sat there in the rain before I finally got up. In a daze, I stumbled back inside. Like a zombie, I changed into dry pajamas and climbed back in bed, not even bothering to towel-dry my hair. I calmly closed my eyes, knowing I wouldn't be able to sleep.

The next morning, I was awake before the alarm went off. My eyes felt gritty and puffy from tossing and turning all night, but I forced myself to get out of bed and quickly shower. I hurried to get dressed, throwing on the first pair of jeans and sweater I could find in my closet. As I headed out the door, I pulled my hair up into a messy bun.

I was a woman on a mission, in need of answers.

There was a chill in the air, and the ground was still damp from the storm the night before. I walked twice as fast as usual toward St. George Street, dodging puddles along the way. I glanced down at my watch and was relieved to see that it was eight fifty-five a.m. The Treasure Chest should open in five minutes.

I didn't really have a game plan for when I got there. Michael might not even be there when I arrived, but it was the only way I knew to get in touch with him. One way or another, I needed to see Michael today and get the truth.

A few minutes later, The Treasure Chest came into view, with an Open sign on the front door. Without hesitation, I entered the store, startling a woman who was standing behind the counter. The woman relaxed when she laid eyes on me.

"Good morning," the woman greeted me with a warm smile. She appeared to be in her mid-forties with wavy light-brown hair that hung slightly below her shoulders. She had a trail of freckles that started on one cheekbone, crossed over her nose, and landed on the other cheekbone.

Although I didn't see a resemblance to Michael, I wondered if she was Michael's mother.

I glanced around, looking for Michael, but there was no one else in the store.

"Hi," I replied, forcing a smile. "Do you know where I can find Michael?"

The woman grew pale, as if she'd just seen a ghost. "Who are you? What do you want with Michael?" she asked, not hiding the alarm in her voice. She was afraid of me.

"My name is Natalie," I told her, softening my voice. "I'm a friend of Michael's."

I wasn't sure if Michael and I were technically friends, but I was desperate to ease this woman's fears, whatever they were.

"I don't mean to cause any trouble," I assured her. "I just need to talk to him. Please. It's important."

She warily stared at me. "You're the girl who works at the café, aren't you?"

I wasn't sure if she'd been in the café before or if Michael had mentioned me to her, so I just nodded in response.

"Michael!" she called, not taking her eyes off me. "You have a … visitor."

"Thank you," I said.

Michael came out from a room behind the counter and stopped short, obviously surprised to see me there.

He quickly noticed the expression on the woman's face. "This is Natalie. Natalie, this is my mom, Lorena," Michael introduced us.

"Hi. It's nice to meet you Mrs. ..." I realized I didn't know his last name.

"Nolan," she offered. "But you can call me Lorena."

"I need to talk to you. Privately," I told Michael, sounding calmer than I felt. I didn't want to freak Lorena out again.

"Sure," he replied. He put a reassuring hand on Lorena's shoulder. "I promise it's fine. I'll call you later."

She flashed him a small smile but said nothing in response.

Michael came from around the counter and motioned to the front door. He put his hand on the small of my back as he led me outside.

"I'm sorry for dropping by like this, but I needed to see you. I need answers," I blurted out.

Michael froze and glared down at me. "Not here." His voice was low and controlled. "Let's go."

Michael walked several steps ahead of me in silence all the way to the waterfront. Because it was still so early, we had the area to ourselves.

Michael leaned against the railing, facing the water. I stood next to him, keeping careful distance. He seemed angry with me. As I waited for him to say something, I couldn't help but notice how tense his back muscles were as they slightly protruded from beneath the long-sleeved black shirt he was wearing.

He ran his hands through his hair and sighed as if he'd just lost a battle with himself. He turned to me and asked, "How did you figure it out?"

"There was a scratch on my bumper, and now, it's gone," I told him bluntly.

He laughed, but for the life of me, I couldn't imagine what was funny.

"I have to ask you," I continued, pressing forward, "just to confirm for my own sanity, the accident was real, wasn't it?"

"Yes," he replied without hesitation.

His response caught me off guard. I would have thought someone who had gone through so much effort to cover his tracks would put up a little more of a fight in telling the truth.

"You were there. You saved me," I said. "Why?"

"Because you were dying," he stated matter-of-factly. Then, his eyes softened. "And I couldn't let that happen."

"How did you do it? And how did you even know I was there? Were you following me?" I had so many questions, and I could feel myself getting flustered.

"My family moved here nine months ago. Shortly after, I started having these dreams," he replied, staring back out at the water.

I followed his gaze and saw a sailboat in the distance.

"The dreams were about this girl I'd never met. Every night was a different dream but always about the same girl."

The sailboat disappeared into the horizon.

Michael looked down at his hands as he began to mindlessly pick at a loose string on the hem of his sleeve. "The dreams never went away," he continued. "They went on for months. Then, one day, it happened."

"What happened?" I asked. I didn't understand any of this or what it had to do with the accident.

He turned to face me. "Raina and I were taking a walk one morning, and there you were. You were in the café. I could see you through the window. You were ... *real*."

"I don't understand." *How could he have been dreaming about me?*

"At first, I decided to stay away. I didn't know what to think of it. But I couldn't stay away. I had to know more about you, to know for sure that you were the same girl." He leaned in closer toward me. "My family thought it was some kind of trap and had me convinced to leave town, but then I had a new dream. It was about your accident, and you died in my dream."

He paused, assessing the shock on my face. He hesitated but then continued, "I began having that dream every night after I first saw you, and every night, the details would get clearer and clearer, to the point that I was able to figure out where it was. I could almost pinpoint the exact location of the accident."

"So, you followed me."

"Yes. When I overheard you telling Jen that you were driving to Jacksonville, I decided to wait in that area just in case," he explained. "I was close by when I heard your accident. Even then, I was scared I would be too late, and I almost was."

I shook my head as I tried to put all of the pieces of his story together. "How did you save me? Are you, like, an EMT or something?"

"No," he replied, shifting his feet. He took a deep breath. "I can heal people. I healed you." He looked away, as if ashamed by this revelation.

There was a stone bench a few feet away. I walked over to it and sat down.

"Why did you cover it up?" I asked him. "Why didn't you just tell me?"

"It's a long story, but there are people that would come for me if they found out where I was. I couldn't risk it."

He closed the gap between us and squatted down in front of me. I could feel the intensity of the situation radiating from him as his eyes searched mine.

"Natalie, you have to give me your word that you won't tell anyone about this. You can't tell Jen. You can't tell anyone. Ever." He gently grasped the sides of my arms. "I saved your life, and now, I need to be able to trust you. I need to be able to trust you with my life."

"I won't tell anyone," I assured him. "But I need to know everything."

"I've debated on telling you the truth for a while, but I just couldn't," he said. "You can't imagine how hard it is, having a secret like this."

"Trust me; I do understand," I said. If anyone understood what it was like to hide who you really were, it was me.

"And most of all, I didn't want to put you in any more danger than I already have," he added.

"Danger? You saved my life!" I tried to make a conscious effort to keep my voice down.

"Natalie, you don't understand the kind of trouble I could cause for you," he said. "You don't understand how many times I've tried to walk away from you because I don't want to drag you into all of this. There's so much you don't know about me. It ... it's just not safe."

Michael stood up, and I instinctively grabbed his hand, afraid he would leave. He looked down at our hands, and I immediately released him, recalling the day I'd accidentally touched his hand in the café and he'd jerked it away.

He stared at me, and I worried that I'd crossed a line with him.

"Would you come with me?" he asked softly. "It'll be easier to show you than to explain it."

"Yes," I replied, standing up. I had no idea where he was taking me, but I was eager to know the truth.

He led me a few blocks away from the waterfront until we turned down a residential street. We stopped when we reached a single-story brick house with a white front door and white trim. The outside of the house and the yard were well kept but very plain. A navy-blue SUV sat in the driveway.

"This is my house," he said, leading me to the front door. "My parents and Raina live just down the street."

"Is that your car?" I asked, wondering if someone else was already there. I hoped it wasn't Raina's.

"Yeah," he replied. "I usually just walk to work since it's so close by." He unlocked the door and stepped aside, allowing me to walk in first.

The inside of Michael's house wasn't what I'd expect for a young bachelor. It was very clean and had a lot of character. The walls were exposed brick, and the floor was black walnut wood. In the corner was a built-in fireplace with a beautiful black mantel. I'd never understood why someone would build a fireplace in a home in Florida until now. It added a nice, cozy touch to the room.

There was an entryway table with picture frames on it. Michael motioned for me to sit down in the living room, so I stole a quick glance at one of the photos. It was a photo of Michael, Raina, Lorena, and a man with salt-and-pepper hair at the beach. I assumed the man in the picture was his dad.

I moved further into the living room and sat down on a brown leather couch. Michael walked over to the TV and put a disk in the DVD player.

"Are you sure you want to do this?" he asked.

I nodded without hesitation. Whatever it was, I needed to know.

Michael pushed play and immediately stepped back, folding his arms across his chest. He began to chew on his thumbnail. He was nervous. Whatever he was about to show me was deeply personal.

The video began, and all that was in view was a small room with gray walls, a tiny bed with a white blanket and no headboard, and a round metal table with two metal chairs. The room was very sterile-looking and reminded me of a hospital. There was a little bit of a glare, and I realized it was because the camera was filming through another layer of glass. It was being recorded from some type of observation room.

"We're set up. Bring him back in," a man's voice said, but I couldn't see him because he was off camera. The voice was cold, void of emotion.

The door to the room opened, and a little boy walked in, looking down at the ground. Right behind him was a tall, middle-aged man with a thin face and a long, pointed nose. The man was wearing a lab coat and black pants and carrying a clipboard. The little boy appeared to be around seven or eight years old with blond hair. The man put his hand on the boy's shoulder and guided him to sit down in one of the chairs. The man sat in the other.

The door opened again, and another man walked in, pushing a two-tiered metal cart. This man was younger, in his late twenties, but was wearing a blue coat instead of a white one. The little boy looked up, and as soon as I saw his blue eyes, I recognized him. It was Michael.

I glanced over at Michael, but he kept his attention locked on the TV. His face was expressionless.

Michael on the TV tensed up when he saw the younger man walk into the room and close the door behind him.

"I told you, I can't," Michael yelled at the tall man sitting across from him at the table.

Neither men acknowledged his comment.

The man in the blue coat put on a pair of white gloves and picked up a scalpel from the top of the cart. Without hesitation, the man walked over to Michael, forcefully lifted his arm, and sliced the scalpel across his forearm. Michael didn't cry or scream, but I cringed in horror as I watched blood begin to ooze down his little arm. I closed my eyes. This was too much.

"Heal yourself," the voice from the observation room said.

I forced my eyes back open.

Michael placed his hand on top of the injured arm, but nothing happened. Blood just continued to seep through his fingertips.

"Do you want us to cut you again? Heal yourself!" the voice demanded.

"I don't know how," Michael insisted.

"I'm not playing this game with you again," the voice said. "Bring in the girl."

"No!" Michael protested, but the door opened anyway.

Someone shoved a little girl with dark hair into the room, slamming the door closed behind her. It was Raina.

Raina must've known what was going to occur in the room because she began to cry. She tugged at the door handle, trying to escape.

The man in the blue coat began to walk toward her, and Michael stood up.

"Leave her alone!" Michael screamed and tried to go to his sister.

The man in the white coat grabbed him by the uninjured arm to restrain him.

"Heal that cut on your arm, and we'll leave her alone," the voice said calmly.

"I can't!" Michael insisted.

"Well then, we'll begin to chop her into pieces until you feel motivated to do what we've told you to do," the voice replied, this time with detectible agitation.

The man in the blue coat took another step closer to Raina, and she screamed.

"That's enough!" a different voice said from the observation room.

A few seconds later, the door to the gray room opened, and another man in a white coat entered. He was in his thirties with dark hair. Raina ran to him and buried her face in his jacket. He put a reassuring arm around her and gently stroked her hair.

I leaned in a little to get a better look at the man and recognized him from the photo in Michael's living room. He was the man I'd thought was Michael's dad.

"You're out of line, Dr. Radford," the voice said, this time audibly angry. "You are not permitted to interfere."

The screen went black, but I continued to stare into the TV. A single warm tear slid down my cheek, and I quickly wiped it away. That definitely explained why Raina had reacted the way she did at the theater during the movie. It reminded her of her own personal horror movie.

Michael turned off the TV and paced around the living room.

"I know that was unpleasant to watch, but I didn't know a better way to explain it," he said. "This was one of the tamer videos."

I blinked at him, unable to comprehend what could be worse.

"How did you end up there? What was that place?" I asked.

"It's a lab facility owned by a man named Chad Henley. Raina and I were born there," he replied.

I looked over at the family picture on the table.

He followed my gaze. "That's my dad, Alexander. He was the chief scientist who, well, created us. His conscience couldn't deal with how we were being treated, so one day, about six months after this video was made, he took us out of there. He and his wife raised Raina and me as their own, but we've been on the run from Henley ever since."

I opened my mouth but had no idea what to say. Even though I wasn't on the best terms with my parents at the moment, I couldn't imagine being born without a family and a place to call home. Just seeing that awful gray room on the video was enough to give me nightmares. I had no idea how a child could cope with that.

Michael stopped pacing and sat next to me on the couch. "I need to know what you're thinking."

"Well ..." I said, trying to put my thoughts into words. "I think you're very brave."

He tilted his head. Clearly, this wasn't the answer he had expected, but it was true. What had happened to him and Raina was terrible, but for him to risk being discovered to save my life had been incredibly brave.

"What did you think I was going to say?" I asked, now wanting to know what was on his mind.

"I thought you would want to leave. Out of fear for what I am. Whatever that is," he replied, swallowing hard. His eyes narrowed, as if he thought this could still be a possibility.

"No, I don't want to leave," I told him. And it was true. I wanted to better understand him. "I don't understand why this company would create you just to hurt you."

"They created us with what they called 'talents,' so they could try to replicate them," he replied.

"They wanted to find a way to heal people?"

How could a company that's okay with torturing children also want to help people? It didn't make any sense.

"Not exactly," he clarified. "They already had a way to give us the talents at birth, but what they were really after was a way to bottle them and make a profit off them. In my case, he wanted to be able to create a miracle medicine."

I didn't understand, and the expression on my face must have shown it.

"For example," he continued, "Henley believed if he could reproduce my healing abilities into a form that could be administered to a regular person, he would be able to cure everything from cancer to broken bones to the flu. He was hopeful that he could even find a way to reverse the aging process. People would pay a fortune for that kind of medicine. That's why he was so insistent on me healing myself. He needed to study the process in order to find a way to replicate it."

"But in the video, you kept saying you couldn't heal yourself," I said.

"And I can't. I can heal people and animals but not myself."

Michael lifted up the sleeve of his shirt, revealing several lines of scars from where they'd cut him. I gently touched his arm, feeling the jagged reminders from the nightmares of his childhood. He curiously looked at me.

"Why aren't these people in jail?" I asked through clenched teeth.

I removed my hand, and Michael pulled his sleeve down.

"In order to expose them, Raina and I would have to expose ourselves," he replied. "The majority of the world wouldn't be accepting of us. That's why Henley couldn't just charge a fortune to have me heal people directly. The world would never accept that. If we were to expose Henley, we'd be hiding from all people instead of just a group of people. I don't care so much about what happens to me, but I can't do that to Raina. She just wants to try to live a normal life, and after all we've been through, she deserves that."

I understood what he was saying, and he was right. I'd gone through great lengths to hide my own intuitive abilities because I knew how cruel people could be toward those who were different.

"I would also have to expose my dad," he continued. "Even though he was the one who saved us over and over, he would still be held accountable for creating us in the first place."

I glanced again at the family photo on the wall. Even though Michael and Raina weren't their biological children, you'd never know. You could feel the love in their family coming through in the picture. It was in the smiles on their faces, in the light in their eyes. It made me homesick for the family I'd had before Becca disappeared.

Michael's cell phone chimed, and he pulled it out of his pocket to look at it.

"I need to get back to the shop," he said. "We are getting a shipment today, and I need to be there to help my dad unload it."

"Of course," I told him.

"Come on, I'll drive you home." Before I could protest, he added, "I insist."

"Can I ask you a question?" I asked Michael as we got into his SUV.

"Sure."

"What made you believe that your dream of my car accident would actually happen?"

His dreams made me wonder if he had some intuitive abilities as well.

"Do you remember that day in the café when you spilled my water?" he asked, glancing at me.

I could feel my cheeks flush. "Of course. How could I forget? It was so embarrassing."

"Well, I'd dreamed that before," he said. "It felt vaguely familiar when you spilled the water, but when you touched my hand, I was certain it was the same as my dream. I realized that if that dream came true, the accident dream would come true as well."

"You mentioned earlier that your family thought the dreams were a trap. Did they think I was working for Henley?" I asked.

"Yes," he replied. "They thought it was a possibility. They thought maybe Henley was using you to lure me out."

We pulled into my driveway, but I sat for a second instead of getting out of the car. Michael took a deep breath but didn't say anything.

"Thank you for saving my life," I told him. "Thank you for risking all of this to save me, someone you really don't even know."

Michael looked away for a second, as if debating on how to respond. Finally, he turned back to me.

"That's the thing though. I feel like I know you," he replied. The way he looked at me made my heart skip a beat. "I knew in my heart that you didn't work for Henley. There's just something about you, Natalie ... and I couldn't let you die."

EIGHT

"Come on, it'll be fun," Jen said, swiveling in her chair as I walked from one end of the bar counter to the other, restocking napkins.

"I've heard that before," I replied sourly. My skin crawled as I thought about the masquerade, although I had to admit, I'd enjoyed watching the fireworks with Michael.

"Pleeeease," she begged.

I stopped and couldn't help but chuckle at her exaggerated puppy-dog eyes. It was Jen's day off, and she had come all the way to the café after class just to beg me to go to a bonfire party with her tomorrow night. Apparently, she knew me well enough to know that if she texted me, the response would have been a very simple, concise no.

"Let's just go for an hour, and if you hate it, I promise we'll leave," she persisted.

"Fine. *One* hour."

The café door opened, and I anxiously glanced in that direction, hoping it was Michael. I'd been doing that all day. This time, it was really him. He looked around until he found me. He smiled at me as he took his usual seat, and it did not go unnoticed by Jen.

"You should invite him," she whispered as I put his slice of cake on a plate.

I ignored her and walked over to Michael.

"I was beginning to wonder if I'd see you today," I said as I placed the cake in front of him.

"I had a break at work, so I thought I would stop by for a quick snack." He was visibly more relaxed today than he was yesterday.

"So, what are you inviting me to?" he asked, catching me completely off guard.

How in the world did he hear that?

Maybe extreme hearing was one of his superpowers. He had admitted to overhearing my conversation with Jen about going to Jacksonville as well.

"A bonfire party at the beach tomorrow," I replied, one hundred percent confident there was no way he'd want to go.

"What time?"

"Seven." I prepared myself. *He'll make an excuse about having something else he needs to do.*

He nodded thoughtfully. "I have to work until six thirty, but I can meet you there."

Out of the corner of my eye, I noticed a woman at one of my other tables trying to get my attention, and I realized she was ready for her check.

"Okay, sounds good," I told Michael before rushing off to deliver the check to the woman.

Did he really just agree to go?

I dropped the check off and heard the door chime again. Instinctively, I looked at the doorway and was surprised to find Seth standing there.

"Seth?" I questioned as if it wasn't really him and I was just seeing a mirage.

"Hey you!" he said, grinning ear to ear as I approached him. When I reached him, he scooped me up in a big bear hug, lifting me off my feet. "I bet you didn't expect to see me again so soon."

"No, I didn't," I told him. "But I'm glad you're here. Let's get you some lunch. It's on me this time."

I led him over to the bar counter, and he sat on the stool next to Jen. Jen stopped eating and stared at him. I didn't think I'd ever seen her speechless before.

"Seth, this is my friend Jen," I introduced them.

Seth looked at her, and his eyes widened. His big smile returned as he offered her a handshake. "Nice to meet you, Jen," he said.

She was still speechless.

"So, what brings you to St. Augustine?" I asked Seth.

"Well," he said, "I was hoping I could crash for a couple of days until my apartment is ready. Apparently, this move is happening faster than I thought."

"Of course you can," I assured him. "I don't get off work for another hour though."

"That's okay," he replied. "I actually need to do a little shopping, so I'll just meet up with you later this evening."

Jen gave me an expectant look and discreetly nodded her head in Seth's direction.

"Um," I started, hoping I was interpreting her correctly, "Jen is a St. Augustine shopping expert."

She nodded at me in encouragement.

"You really should bring her along. She'll help you find whatever it is you're after."

Seth raised his eyebrows and looked at Jen, who just smiled innocently at him.

"I would be happy to," she told him.

"That would be great," he replied.

I glanced over at Michael's table, but he wasn't there.

"Excuse me for a sec," I said and walked over to the empty table.

His cake was finished, and once again, he'd overpaid for his order with cash on the table.

I dashed out of the café and saw Michael on foot, about to turn onto St. George Street.

"Michael!" I called after him.

He stopped but didn't turn around.

I jogged over to him. "Leaving so soon?"

"I have to get back to the shop," he replied, finally turning to look at me.

"Oh," I said, trying to hide the disappointment in my voice. "I get off work in an hour, and I was actually hoping we could meet up. I still have some more questions about … you know, everything."

"Sure," he said, glancing over my shoulder, back at the café. "I've got a few things to wrap up at the store, but I'll come back and meet you here in an hour."

"Perfect. See you then," I replied before rushing back inside.

That was strange. Why do I get the feeling he's upset with me?

When I got back to the café, I checked on my tables and then made my way back over to Seth and Jen. They were both laughing hysterically. Jen's face was red from laugh-crying.

A little while later, after eating a turkey sandwich, Seth left with Jen to go shopping. The café was busy, so the last thirty minutes of my shift went by quickly. As soon as Jessica arrived to relieve me, I hurried to the back to get my purse and left.

Michael was waiting for me outside, as promised.

"You must be starving," he said when he saw me. Luckily, he seemed to be in a better mood. "There's an amazing pizza place down the street that's always quiet this time of day. I thought it might be a good place for us to talk."

"Sounds perfect," I said. My stomach rumbled to confirm.

Gino's Pizza was only two blocks away, and as expected, it was quiet. It was three forty-five p.m., so it was right in between the lunch and dinner crowds. I'd never eaten there before; however, I often saw a line spilling out onto the street during lunch time, so it must be good.

We ordered our food from the counter and carried it to a table in the very back of the restaurant. There was only one other table occupied in the restaurant, and it was at the front, so it felt like we had the place to ourselves.

I took a bite of my cheese pizza and cringed as Michael took a bite of his slice topped with extra pineapple. I never understood how people could eat that.

"What? You don't like pineapple?" he asked.

"I do," I said after swallowing my food. "Just not on pizza."

"It's delicious! Have you ever tried it?"

I scrunched up my nose in response.

"You haven't lived until you've tried it!" He held out his slice for me to take a bite.

I caved and took a small bite, only getting one tiny piece of pineapple with it. I was surprised to find I actually liked it.

"Mmm," I agreed, nodding.

"All right, now that we have that out of the way," he said, pleased with himself, "what questions do you have for me?"

"Okay," I said, wiping my mouth and taking a sip of water. I glanced around one more time to make sure the coast was clear.

"How did you replace my car? I mean, if I hadn't realized the scratch was gone, I don't think I ever would have figured it out."

"Alexander has a friend that's been helping us run for years, and it just so happens that he owns a car dealership. It took some work, but he managed to find a car that matched yours perfectly and had it delivered here the next morning," he explained. "It was a long shot; don't get me wrong. But I knew you didn't drive it very often, and from what we could tell, it didn't look like you had personal items in the car, so we decided to try replacing it."

"What did you do with my old car? And how did you even get me out of the car in the first place?" I asked, recalling how mangled my car had been.

"We paid off a guy to tow your car and dump it," he said matter-of-factly. "As for getting you out of the car, I ripped the door off and pulled you out." He casually took a bite of pizza.

My jaw dropped. "What do you mean, you *ripped* the door off?"

"It's another Henley-manufactured skill," he said, looking down at his hands. "I can tap into my adrenaline easily when I need to."

"Like when you hear about moms lifting cars off of their babies? That kind of adrenaline?" I asked.

"Yeah, something like that."

"It's another one of your superpowers," I acknowledged.

He gave me a skeptical look and then let out a small laugh.

"So, what other questions do you have?" he asked, and I felt my cheeks get hot.

"What?" he pushed, clearly noticing my embarrassment.

I debated on whether or not to ask but ultimately decided I needed to know, whatever the answer was.

"Um, I woke up in my bed … in my pajamas …" My voice trailed off.

A hint of a smile tugged at Michael's lips. I could feel my face getting redder, and he must've noticed it as well because he quickly cleared his throat and tried to look serious again.

"No. That was Raina," he replied, looking me square in the eye. "We used your driver's license to find your house. We used your keys to get in, and Raina changed you into your pajamas. I carried you into bed, but I promise I was a perfect gentleman."

I believed he was telling the truth. I let out a small sigh of relief that made him smile again. I didn't understand why he found my embarrassment so entertaining.

I decided to hold off on any more questions as we finished our pizza. A few minutes later, we were leaving the restaurant, and I was hoping Michael wasn't ready to call it an evening yet. I still had so many questions I wanted to ask.

"Have you been to Amistad Park?" he asked.

I shook my head. I'd never even heard of it.

"It's about a fifteen-minute walk from here, but I promise it's worth it."

"Let's go."

A few minutes into our walk, I checked my phone. "Just making sure Seth didn't text me yet," I explained.

No text from Seth must mean he was enjoying his shopping time with Jen.

Michael ran his hand through his hair. "I hope he doesn't mind that you're out with me."

His comment caught me off guard.

Does he think Seth is my boyfriend? Is that why he left the café in such a hurry earlier?

"It's not like that with Seth," I told him.

"I haven't seen him around before," he replied, and I couldn't tell whether or not he believed me.

"He's somebody I grew up with. I've known him my whole life, so he's like my brother. Our fathers are business partners," I said. "He and Becca were dating when she disappeared. I mean, they'd been in love since we were little kids, but they actually started dating about a year before we lost her." I felt a lump form in my throat, and I swallowed, choking it back before I could get emotional.

"We're almost there," he said, his voice a little softer.

I let out a breath, grateful that he'd changed the subject.

"Where is this park?" I asked as we veered off to an unoccupied side street.

I'd never been down this way. There were no houses or buildings, just trees lining the street. At the very end of the street was a rusty wrought iron gate.

"It's at the end of the street."

As we got closer to the gate, I noticed an Amistad Park sign lying on the ground. The white wooden sign was chipping, and the blue lettering was almost completely faded out. The park had obviously been closed for some time.

The gate had a chain and lock on it, so I wondered what we were doing there. Instead of walking up to the entrance, Michael led me into the woods. About one hundred feet into the woods, there was an opening in the gate where several railings were missing. It was just big enough for us to slip through to the other side.

"There's not a No Trespassing sign. I've checked," Michael said with a mischievous grin.

We followed the trail away from the entrance, going deeper into the woods. Even though there was still daylight, the trees blocked out a lot of the sun, so it felt much later in the vacant park. We passed a playground with a broken slide, and I opened my mouth to ask him why we were there when it came into view. Straight ahead was a beautiful white carousel. I couldn't believe it was in such good condition. Someone must have come and restored it after the park closed.

"Wow," I said, staring at the carousel in awe.

"Come on," Michael said, leading the way.

"It's too bad it doesn't run," I told him. "It's amazing."

"Hop on," he said.

I stood there for a moment, confused. There was no way the power was still connected.

"Go," he insisted.

I stepped onto the carousel and climbed on a white horse with a green-and-pink saddle. Michael walked out of sight, and I was about to go look for him when I heard a humming sound, like a motor. The lights to the carousel turned on, revealing all of the brightly colored horses held in place by shiny brass poles. As the music started, Michael ran to the carousel.

"Hurry!" I yelled out to him as he jumped on.

He climbed onto the brown horse next to mine.

The carousel picked up speed, and I watched in amazement as the world spun around us. We passed endless trees until they all started to blend together.

All of the events of the past week started to fade away into the background even if only for the duration of the ride. As my horse rose and fell, I pushed away the fears and uncertainties that had bottled up inside me. I threw my head back and laughed.

I glanced over at Michael. He was watching me, a half-smile tugging on his lips.

When the ride stopped, Michael hopped off his horse and came over to help me get off my horse, which was fully ascended. I brought one leg over the horse and expected Michael to offer me his hand, but instead, he reached up and lifted me off by my waist. He put me down in front of him, and I tried to find the words to express to him how I was feeling.

Alive. Awake.

Before I could say anything, my phone chimed. I dug it out of my purse. It was Seth texting me to let me know he was on his way to my house.

"I'm sorry, but I need to go," I regretfully told Michael. As much as I didn't want our evening to end, I'd already told Seth he could stay.

We left the park, and even though we were closer to Michael's house, he insisted on walking me home.

"That was fun," I said. "I can't believe the carousel still works." Then, it dawned on me that maybe Michael had had something to do with that. "Wait, do you have some kind of ability that made it run?"

"Yes. It's called a generator," he replied with a laugh. "Alexander gave Raina a carousel music box for her sixth birthday. She was obsessed with it, but of course, we had no way to ride one at Henley. She had to leave it behind when we left there." Michael gently guided me to the side of the road as a car passed us. "When I found out about this one, I cleaned it up and hooked up a generator to it, so it would run. She goes out there when she needs to clear her head. I thought you could use that right now."

"It was exactly what I needed."

We turned down my street and saw Seth standing outside, leaning against his car.

"Do you want to stay and hang out?" I asked Michael, stopping while we were still out of earshot.

"I'd better get back to the store to help them close up," Michael replied. "And I think you two could use some time to catch up." He turned to walk away.

"Do you like pancakes?" I blurted out, verbalizing the first sweet breakfast food I could think of.

He stopped and turned around, no doubt confused by my question.

"There's this restaurant on A1A that supposedly has the best pancakes in St. Augustine," I continued. "Would you like to go with me tomorrow morning?"

"I love pancakes," he replied. "I'll pick you up at nine." He smiled before turning again and walking away.

Seth eyed me as I walked down the driveway to the front door. "And who was that?" he asked, a teasing tone to his voice.

I smiled as I let us into the apartment but didn't answer his question.

"Now, I'm really curious," he said, following me into the house.

I closed the door behind us and gave Seth the grand tour, which took all of two minutes.

"The sofa converts to a bed," I told him.

"Has your mother been here yet?" he asked, looking around.

I shook my head, which made him chuckle.

"Don't get me wrong; I think your place is awesome. But your mother ... well, she would hyperventilate."

"That's what I've always thought," I agreed. "Are you hungry?"

"Starving. I worked up an appetite again with all of that shopping."

Seth went out to his car to get his suitcase while I made him a bowl of macaroni and cheese. It had been his favorite when we were kids, so I hoped he hadn't outgrown it. I was still full from pizza, but I sat with him while he ate.

"So, how was your day with Jen?" I asked as Seth popped a forkful of macaroni into his mouth.

"Hmm," he said, grinning as he swallowed his food. "She's lovely."

"Yes, she is."

"In fact, we're going out tomorrow night," he said, his face turning serious. "She said you were going to a bonfire and invited me to go. I hope you don't mind." He scooped up the last of his macaroni.

"Of course I don't."

"She said you invited what's his face," Seth said despite his full mouth.

"His name is Michael." I took Seth's dirty bowl to the sink.

I washed the dishes while Seth dried. Just like old times, he made a point to splash water on me when I wasn't paying attention. It used to drive my mother crazy. We'd finish the dishes with a huge puddle on the floor and soaked clothes.

I grabbed a cup out of the sink and splashed it at him, drenching his shirt.

He stood there in shock for a moment. Then, he quickly seized the spray nozzle on the sink and sprayed it at me.

I shrieked and threw a sponge at him as I ran out of the kitchen. He tried to chase me but slid on the wet floor. He managed to stay upright and hauled the kitchen towel at me. It fell short, missing me by about two feet.

I was hysterically laughing in the living room when he caught up with me.

He stopped chasing me and watched silently while I composed myself.

"What?" I asked, suddenly self-conscious.

He shook his head. "I haven't heard you laugh like that in a long time," he said. "You seem different. Even from the other night when we had dinner, you seem changed somehow. Does it have anything to do with that Michael guy?"

I sat down on the couch, pulling a throw pillow into my lap. "Are we really going to do this?" I asked. "Are you going to talk to me about boys?"

"Look at you, cracking jokes and everything," he teased. He plopped down on the couch next to me. "I've always wanted to have a brotherly chat with one of your boyfriends and never got the opportunity to. I can be quite intimidating if you give me the chance."

"He's not my boyfriend. We're just friends."

"If you like him, don't hold back, Natalie," Seth said as if he could read my mind.

I shrugged. There was no denying that I connected with Michael in a way that I'd never connected with anyone else before, but I didn't know how to proceed from here. I'd spent so much time pushing everyone away that I wasn't sure I knew how to let him in.

Seth shifted his body to face me. "Nat, listen to me," he said, his face serious. "Give yourself permission to be happy. Pain is a part of life. So is loss. There is no way to get around that. But I will tell you this; as much pain as I felt from losing Becca, it didn't outweigh the time I'd had with her. I don't regret loving her for one second."

"It isn't that simple."

Allowing yourself to get attached to people before experiencing that kind of loss was one thing. Being able to do that, knowing what kind of pain could follow, was completely different.

"It is that simple," he insisted.

We sat in awkward silence, agreeing to disagree.

Seth, never being one for tension, decided to break it. "I don't want to have to beat sense into you, but I will," he said with a smile, hitting me in the shoulder with a throw pillow.

Later that night, after Seth retired to the couch, I lay awake in bed. I could hear him snoring lightly from the other room, and it gave me a strange sense of comfort. All throughout our lives, until Seth and Becca had actually started dating, we would stay over at each other's houses. It reminded me of the sheltered life we'd had before Becca's disappearance.

Thinking of Becca inevitably took me back to that night and everything after. As I lay there, I recalled the night after Becca disappeared.

Seth and I were sitting in my bedroom. My parents were downstairs, talking to the police. Seth's parents were also downstairs, comforting my parents.

Seth frantically paced around my room. "She has to be somewhere," he said. "I mean, people don't just disappear into thin air."

It had been a long, exhausting day. I'd spent the better part of the day in the emergency room, getting treated for a concussion. The police had interviewed me several times at the hospital and again after I returned home. I'd relayed every detail over and over to the police at least a dozen times, and still, there were no leads. They'd attempted to have a sketch artist sit down with me, but I had nothing for them to work with. Poor Seth had spent five straight hours at the police station, being interrogated, until they officially ruled him out as a suspect.

"You know I didn't do this, right?" he asked me, dark circles protruding from beneath his eyes.

"Of course I do," I told him, and I knew it to be true. I knew from the core of my soul that Seth was not involved.

"Natalie, I need your help," he pleaded with me. "I know you have some of the same instincts that Becca does even if you pretend you don't. I need you to stop pretending and try to figure out who did this. See if you can figure out who has her and where she is."

My usually lighthearted, carefree best friend was on his knees, begging me for something I could not give him.

I shook my head, heartbroken to disappoint him. "I can't."

"Try. Please just try," he asked, tears welling in his eyes.

Seth and I had been inseparable since I was born. I'd been with him when he fell out of a tree in our yard when he was nine years old and broke his arm, and still, I'd never seen him cry until that moment.

"Please!"

"Seth, I can't," I told him, my voice strained from crying. It felt like razor blades scratching the inside of my throat. "I've tried. I can't find her. I don't know how to find her."

It was so frustrating. I had this intuitive ability that I didn't want, which came out in the most inconvenient times. The one time I needed it to work, to tell me where my sister was and who had taken her, and I got nothing.

My mind and body wanted to cry, but I physically couldn't cry anymore. The reality of it all was setting in. I couldn't bring myself to tell him, but I secretly wondered if the fact that I couldn't pinpoint who had taken her meant she was no longer alive. I'd always felt this unexplainable connection to Becca, but when I'd regained consciousness after the attack, the connection was gone. All that was left was a deep void in my heart where my sister used to reside. I vowed in that moment to never feel that kind of pain again.

Coming back to the present, I grabbed my cell phone off the nightstand. I opened up the image gallery and started scrolling through scenic pictures of St. Augustine and selfies that Jen had insisted we take. Finally, I reached the pictures that I'd saved to my phone but rarely looked at. They were pictures of Becca.

The first picture was of us at St. Augustine Beach during our family vacation. The next picture was of Becca, Seth, and me in Seth's driveway. Seth had just gotten his driver's license, and his parents had bought him a new car for his birthday. Seth's mom had wanted a picture of us around the car with Seth holding the keys. I'd stood on the passenger side of the car while Becca had stood next to Seth, playfully kissing him on the cheek.

I placed my cell phone back on the nightstand. I lay on my side and brought my knees toward my chest, wrapping myself tightly under the covers.

What is wrong with me that I can't allow myself to move on from the past?

Seth, who'd been through losing the girl he'd been in love with his entire life, had grieved like a normal person and was finally able to move on. It didn't mean that he had never loved her or didn't still love her.

If I wouldn't deny Seth a future filled with peace and happiness, why am I denying it for myself?

I closed my eyes and sent a message to Becca, imagining that, wherever she was, she could hear me.

Becca, if you can hear me, I miss you. I think about you every day, but I have to let go. I have to let go of this false hope that you will return as if nothing happened. I have to let go of this guilt for not doing more to stop that person from taking you and for not being able to find you. I have to let go of those things because I know this isn't the life you would have wanted for me now. I know you would have wanted me to be happy. But I promise you this: I will never forget you. I will never forget what an amazing sister and friend you were to me. I love you more than you will ever know.

NINE

"*Go ahead. Open it.*" Becca's voice echoed from deep within my memory. She handed me a tiny pink box with a white bow wrapped around it.

I walked over to my dresser and quietly opened the top drawer, careful not to awaken Seth, who was still asleep in the living room.

"*What is it?*" I recalled a younger me asking.

The present-day me pulled the same pink box from beneath a pile of T-shirts.

"*You're not going to know until you open it,*" Becca replied.

Just as I had done on my fourteenth birthday, I opened the box and took in the beauty of the gift inside. Lying delicately on a pillow of white fluff was a lotus charm necklace dipped in rose gold.

"*It's beautiful,*" I said then and thought to myself now.

I lifted the necklace out of the box and held it up, admiring how the metal gleamed in the morning light shining through my bedroom window.

"*It symbolizes growth and perseverance,*" Becca told me. "*You see, they bloom from the darkest and murkiest of waters into exquisite beauty.*"

I put the necklace on and looked in the mirror. I could almost feel the warmth from the hug I gave her afterward.

"Morning, sunshine," Seth's groggy voice called from the living room.

"Good morning," I replied.

I heard Seth rummaging around the kitchen while I struggled to decide on what to wear to breakfast with Michael. Finally, I chose a pale pink sweater, jeans, and a pair of brown flats.

There was a knock at the door, and Seth yelled, "Got it!"

As I entered the living room, I saw Seth standing at the front door, shirtless in only his pajama pants, eating cereal out of a giant plastic mixing bowl.

"Hi," I heard Michael say. Receiving no response from Seth, he asked, "Is Natalie here?"

"Yep," Seth replied without moving. He smiled and scooped another heaping spoonful of cereal into his mouth.

"Seth, stop it!" I said, swatting him out of the doorway. "And for goodness' sake, put some clothes on!"

Seth cackled, fully aware of his mischief. He grabbed his T-shirt off the sofa and put it on.

"Sorry about that," I told Michael as I stepped outside. I quickly took notice of how Michael's navy shirt made his blue eyes stand out even more than usual.

"You kids have fun," Seth called after us.

As we walked to the restaurant, Michael told me about the new antiques The Treasure Chest had arriving in the afternoon. He'd be heading there after breakfast to help Alexander get them cleaned up and ready for display in the store.

When we got to the restaurant, it was crowded inside, but I noticed empty tables upstairs on the balcony, overlooking the water. It was a little chilly, but it still surprised me that no one was sitting outside, enjoying the view. I suggested sitting up there, and Michael agreed.

We climbed the spiral staircase upstairs, and a few minutes later, we were seated, and our pancake orders were in. I leaned back in my chair, inhaling the crisp breeze coming off the water. Several fishing boats were in the distance, taking advantage of the cool but sunny day.

Michael leaned in and reached his hand toward me. He carefully touched my necklace, turning it over between his fingers.

"That's pretty," he said, releasing it. "It suits you. Is it new?"

"No, I've had it for a long time. I thought it was time to start wearing it again," I replied, running my hand over it.

"Can I ask you a question?" he asked. I detected a little bit of hesitation in his voice.

"Sure." I took a sip of my orange juice.

"What happened to you that day in the café? The day the lights went out."

"Oh, that." I hadn't expected the question; however, a part of me was also surprised it hadn't come up sooner.

"You seemed like you were in distress, and I don't know why," he explained. "It's been bothering me ever since. Have you been feeling pain since the accident?"

"No. Not at all," I told him. "I was in distress though, um ... not the physical kind. Not exactly anyway."

He looked puzzled, and I realized I wasn't making any sense.

"You're going to think I'm crazy," I admitted aloud, looking around again to confirm we were alone on the balcony. It was still only us.

Michael raised an eyebrow. "I tell you I was born in a lab, have the ability to heal people, and can rip through steel, and you're worried that I'm going to think *you're* crazy?"

I took a deep breath, ready to take that first step toward letting him in. "The morning I woke up, after the accident, I felt different. I felt healthy and energized, but I didn't know why. I just thought it was because I'd slept for two days."

"Two days?" he interjected, not hiding the shock in his voice.

I nodded and continued, "But that isn't even the strangest part. So, I felt different, but because I didn't know why, I didn't see the warning signs, like power surges in my apartment. I walked to work like I normally do and even ignored how loud it was on the street. It wasn't until I got to work that I realized I could ..." I hesitated but then decided to rip it off like a bandage. "I could read minds."

Michael narrowed his eyes. "How is that possible?"

"I thought I was losing my mind, but now, I think it was somehow connected to the accident," I told him.

The waitress appeared with our orders, and we sat patiently as she placed our food on the table in front of us. Michael smiled politely but eyed me, eager to continue the conversation the second she left.

Once the waitress was out of earshot, Michael leaned in closer. "I don't understand. That's never happened before," he said in a low voice. "I've healed my parents before. Granted, neither of them had injuries as serious as yours, but I didn't do anything differently."

"I can't explain it," I told him. "But the next day, it stopped. Everything just went back to normal, and it hasn't happened since."

"You could actually hear what people were thinking?" Michael asked, trying to wrap his head around it.

"Yes," I confirmed. "I could clearly hear their thoughts. I could hear everyone. Jen. Carl. The customers. Strangely though, I couldn't hear yours." He nodded thoughtfully, and I continued, "It was so much, so loud that I couldn't take it anymore. The next thing I knew, I was on the floor, and the power was out."

The hostess emerged from the staircase, seating a party of four at the table next to us. Michael and I straightened up in our seats, as if caught doing something we weren't supposed to be doing. We quietly focused on eating our breakfast with an unspoken understanding that we'd pick up the conversation again later.

When we were finished eating, Michael insisted on picking up the check despite my argument of how I was the one who had invited him to breakfast.

"What kind of gentleman would I be if I let you pay?" he asked.

The waitress smiled at him in agreement, and I gave in.

As we stepped onto the sidewalk that ran along A1A, Michael looked at his watch. He needed to head to the store, and I offered to walk with him. Michael was quiet, and I was worried that I'd freaked him out.

He must think I'm crazy. I mean, how could he not?

"You don't have to come to the bonfire tonight if you don't want to," I told him, giving him an easy out.

"Why wouldn't I want to go?"

I shrugged in response.

Michael looked ahead and then suddenly grabbed me by the arm. Before I could react, he jerked me off the street and into the alleyway. He pushed me back against the side of the brick building.

I was about to ask him what was going on, but I noticed that his whole body was tense, ready to fight. My back was to the wall, and his body was only about an inch from mine. His arms were protectively pressed into the wall on each side of me. He was listening carefully, and I tried to as well, but I didn't hear anything unusual.

Michael slowly peered his head out to look onto the street. I knew the coast was clear when his body finally relaxed. He didn't move as he gazed down at me.

"Sorry about that. Are you okay?" he asked, looking me over.

I nodded, unable to speak. It wasn't because I was startled but because I was suddenly very aware of the warmth of his body, so close to mine.

His eyes lingered on my lips, and my heart began to race.

He slowly took a step away, and I regained my composure as I followed him back to the street.

We resumed our walk to the shop, but I could tell his mind was preoccupied.

"What just happened?" I asked.

"I thought I saw a Henley car," he replied. "But I was mistaken."

"Oh." I shuddered at the thought. "Have you seen them before?"

"Many times. But not here yet. We can never be too careful."

"Would you have to leave? If you saw them?" I asked, pretty certain I already knew the answer.

"Yeah," he replied. "We'd have to go and leave everything behind. We always have a game plan, just in case. Here, I'll show you." He detoured down a side street lined with historic homes.

We walked past an old, two-story blue house with paint peeling off it and an overgrown lawn. It was clearly abandoned but would be a beautiful home if someone fixed it up. There was a For Sale sign by the driveway.

"This is our meeting spot," Michael explained without looking at the house. "If any of us sees any sign of Henley, we send out a group text that simply says *Found*, and we immediately leave wherever we are and come here. No returning home, no returning to the store, no stopping along the way. We come straight here."

"Where would you go after you met up?" I hated the thought of him leaving.

He shook his head. "I honestly don't know. Alexander has it all prearranged, but we don't know until we get there. It's for our safety, in case any of us are captured."

We turned down another street, and as The Treasure Chest came into view, I was forced to face the reality that if Henley ever discovered them in St. Augustine, he'd have to leave, and I would likely never see him again. That could happen at any moment. Like Becca, he could disappear from my life.

I walked with Michael to the front door of the store, and he was uncertain about letting me walk home alone. I insisted that I would be fine. After all, it wasn't Henley that he had seen. He let me leave after we exchanged phone numbers, and I promised to text him when I got home.

My walk home was uneventful, but I kept a watchful eye for anything suspicious. As soon as I got home, I sent Michael a text to let him know I was safe. He texted back, letting me know he still planned on meeting me at the bonfire later this evening.

Seth was no longer at my apartment, but I found a note on the coffee table.

Nat,

Apartment leasing office called, so I am going to Jacksonville to sign my paperwork. I'll be back by six for the bonfire.

—Seth

Several hours later, I had the cleanest apartment in St. Augustine. I'd scrubbed every square inch of it in an attempt to do something productive on my day off and to pass the time until the bonfire. I needed to distract myself from thinking about Michael, the danger he was in, and the possibility of him leaving. Around four p.m., I ran out of things to clean and decided to take a shower to freshen up.

As I shaved my legs, I recalled Michael's comment about how he'd been tracked down by Henley in the past. Michael and his family seemed to be so careful that I wondered how Henley had managed to track them down.

Would there ever be a point in time when Henley gave up and just let them live in peace? Is there even a small chance that Michael wouldn't have to leave someday?

I got out of the shower and started drying my hair when I heard the front door open. It was immediately followed by laughter. I recognized it as Jen's laughter, and if she was laughing that hard, I knew Seth was with her.

I put on my robe and went out to greet them. Seth was on the couch, and Jen was practically on top of him, trying to force-feed him something. He twisted his face in every direction, mouth closed, avoiding her.

"Stop being so stubborn and just try it!" Jen told him.

"Help me!" Seth said when he saw me. He grabbed Jen's wrists to keep her hands away from his face. "She's gone mad. She's trying to feed me kale chips!"

Jen stopped fighting him and sat down on the couch. "Natalie," she said, "please tell your friend that they are healthy and good for him."

I crinkled my nose. "Sorry, I'm with Seth. They're gross."

Seth pointed to me. "See," he said proudly.

"I hate to interrupt," I told them. "But, Jen, can you help me get ready? I have no idea what I'm going to wear tonight."

Jen lit up and bounced over to me. She loved any opportunity to play dress-up, and with the exception of the masquerade, I rarely let her do it with me. Seth turned on the TV, completely content to be left out of girl time.

A few minutes later, Jen had pulled out a pair of dark blue jeans, a plaid flannel button-down shirt, a scarf, a puffer vest, and a pair of ankle boots. I wasn't convinced all of the items went together until I put them on. Somehow, they worked, and I looked trendy, like Jen.

"This is a perfect bonfire outfit," Jen told me as she admired her work.

Jen insisted on doing my makeup for me, and it was a back-and-forth deliberation on how much makeup I would allow her to use. After she assured me it would look natural, I relaxed and let her work her magic.

"I'm glad you finally got the guts to ask Michael out," Jen said as she topped me off with a spritz of perfume.

"I didn't ask him out exactly," I corrected her. "It's not a date."

Jen rolled her eyes. "You and this non-date business."

"What about you?" I asked, trying to take the focus off myself. "Is this a date with Seth tonight?"

"Yes," she replied and then took a step back, her eyes wide. "Oh gosh, Natalie. I didn't even think to make sure you were okay with it."

I held up a hand to stop her. "I'm fine with it," I reassured her. "I promise."

She tightly hugged me. "I like him so much," she whispered.

"He's an amazing guy," I agreed, hugging her back. I let go when I heard footsteps.

Seth appeared in the doorway. "You're both already beautiful, so you can't blame me for wondering what could possibly be taking so long," he said.

Jen blushed, clearly under the spell of Seth's charm. I just shook my head and smiled at them.

"Let's go," I said.

It was supposed to be cold outside after dark, so I grabbed a beanie to keep warm. Jen strategically placed it on my head, so my hair looked perfect with it. I never would have thought to do that.

We got into Seth's car, and within ten minutes, we arrived at the beach. The sun had set, and I was glad Jen had made me wear the vest, as it was chilly.

A small crowd of Jen's friends from school had already gathered around the bonfire. A girl with long brown hair, wearing a ton of makeup, ran up to Jen and gave her a hug. Jen introduced her as Sadie, one of her fellow journalist interns.

Headlights turning into the parking lot caught my eye, and I realized it was Michael's SUV. He pulled into the parking spot next to Seth and got out. He looked fresh, like he'd taken a shower and changed after work to get ready for the bonfire. He was wearing a dark gray hooded pullover with a white T-shirt underneath, a black jacket, jeans, and black boots.

"I brought some chairs," he announced, lifting his trunk open to unload them.

Seth and I walked around to help.

Seth reached into the trunk and pulled out a beach chair. He reached in for another one but hissed and yanked his hand back. He squinted in the dark, trying to inspect it. "Shhhhoot. I think I cut my hand."

Instinctively, I grabbed Seth's hand and dragged him closer to a lamppost, so he could see how bad it was.

Michael took the chairs from Seth, and once we got into the light, I immediately saw blood on the chair that had cut him.

I lifted his hand up to inspect it but saw nothing. "Where did you cut it?"

"On the side," he said, gesturing to the side of his hand, near his pinkie.

I inspected it again. It was perfect, no sign of injury. I released his hand.

I locked eyes with Michael, and he immediately took the bloody chair out of the light. Michael had seen the blood too.

Seth flipped his hand around and around, baffled that there was no wound. "Maybe I just pinched it," he rationalized.

"Probably. I'll grab the rest of the chairs," Michael told Seth, his voice nonchalant. "I think your date is already on the beach."

Seth looked down on the beach where Jen was surrounded by a group of friends. "She's pretty popular, huh?"

"Yep," I confirmed, but I knew that wouldn't be a problem for him.

Seth had a certain charisma that drew people to him. His funny, easygoing personality made him someone most people could effortlessly get along with.

Seth left us and made his way down to the beach. He was no longer concerned about the injury to his hand.

Michael turned around and walked back toward his car. I followed close behind him.

Instead of pulling more chairs out, Michael placed the non-bloodied one back in the trunk and then took the bloodied chair over to the faucet used to wash off sandy feet. He was able to rinse most of the blood off.

When he was finished, he tossed it back in the SUV with the other one and slammed the trunk shut.

"There has to be a logical explanation," I said, although I didn't know what it was. I knew Michael never touched Seth, so he couldn't have healed him.

Michael didn't respond. Instead, he grabbed me by the hand, pulling me farther away from the party and toward a gazebo on the other side of the parking lot. I struggled to keep up with him.

Once in the gazebo, he let me go and pulled a pocketknife from his jeans. He opened it and held the blade against the palm of his hand.

"What are you doing?" I asked him, shocked at what he was about to do.

Without saying a word, he pressed the blade into his hand. A clean, superficial wound caused a stripe of red blood to appear, and it began to ooze down his palm. He didn't even flinch, but I gasped at the sight.

He reached his bleeding hand out, wanting me to hold it. I had no idea what he was doing.

"I don't understand," I told him.

"Heal me," he said.

I just stood there, horrified.

"It's the only way to know for sure."

The blood began to trickle from his hand, and it dripped on the ground. It reminded me of the video, and I couldn't stand to see him hurt. I grabbed his hand, unsure of what to do next.

It turned out, I didn't have to do anything specific. Within seconds, the bleeding stopped, and we watched as the wound closed up. His skin tingled beneath my touch. There was a faint, warm current buzzing between our layers of skin. It was strange that I hadn't felt it when I healed Seth though. In fact, I hadn't felt anything at all. I didn't even realize I had done it.

I ran my finger across his palm, amazed that his skin was in perfect condition. Michael closed his eyes, and I wondered if he was in pain.

"Did I hurt you?" I asked, quickly letting go.

He opened his eyes. "No." He looked down at his hand and then back at me.

"What does this mean?" I asked. "I don't understand any of this."

Michael took a step closer, and I could tell he was conflicted on how to answer my question.

"I think you were right earlier today when you said you changed after I healed you," he replied. "I don't know how it's possible, but you've somehow inherited my ability to heal."

TEN

M ichael and I sat quietly on the sand, at a safe distance from the party, trying to process what had just occurred.

I began to worry if there was more to come—if I was going to continue to develop new symptoms from when Michael had healed me. Michael rubbed the back of his neck, and I could tell he was troubled by similar thoughts.

"Have you ever been healed by someone before tonight?" I asked, trying to break the silence.

"No," he replied but offered no further explanation.

"Raina doesn't have the same abilities you do?"

"It's complicated," he said with a sigh.

I sat silently, waiting for him to continue.

"I don't know if Raina can heal or not. I don't know if she is unable to heal or if she's just gotten really good at hiding it all these years."

I recalled how terrified she had been in the video, how traumatic those events in her life had been, and I realized that Raina and I weren't that different after all.

"She has her own abilities though," he explained. "She can move things without touching them. Like she can be on the other side of the room and close the door. It still freaks Lorena out a little bit. Every time, she asks Raina if it was her or if we have a ghost in the house." A small smile started on his lips, but it quickly faded.

"Can you do that too?"

"Yeah, but not as well as she can. The door will move a little, but I can't close it," he said. "Raina was forced to practice using those talents every day of her life until we escaped. She knew if she kept excelling at developing those skills, they would be less inclined to hurt her like they hurt me."

The thought pained me, and I tried to push it away. Even though Raina didn't like me, I still felt empathy toward her. I wouldn't wish that kind of fear on anyone.

"So, healing, strength, super-hearing, and mild telekinesis," I recapped, trying to lighten the mood. "Any other superpowers?"

"Stop treating me like a hero, Natalie," Michael replied, frustration in his voice. "Look at what I've done to you."

"What are you talking about?" *Is that what he thinks? That this is his fault?* "Michael, you saved my life. I wouldn't even be here if it wasn't for you."

He looked away, unconvinced. "I can't shake that feeling from earlier, when I thought Henley had found me. In that moment, I wasn't just afraid for myself; I was afraid for you too. The reality that I've dragged you into something dangerous really hit me today."

"You haven't dragged me into anything," I assured him. "It's who you are … and I want to be a part of your life."

"I'm worried that I'm not good for you," he said, still avoiding eye contact.

My phone chimed, and I reluctantly checked it. "It's Jen, wondering where we went. We should probably go make an appearance," I told him, although I wasn't in the mood to go to a party. But if we didn't go, they would wonder what was going on and probably come looking for us.

Down on the beach, at least a dozen more people had gathered around the bonfire.

"There you are!" Jen called when she saw us.

As soon as we reached her, Jen eagerly introduced us to everyone, including a guy named Justin, who immediately pointed us to a cooler and a keg.

Michael walked over to the cooler and pulled out two bottles of water. He handed one to me. Seth pumped a beer out of the keg for Jen and grabbed himself a water.

"You can drink," I told Seth. "I can always drive us home."

Michael gave me a look.

"I'm good. There's no way I'm letting you near my car," Seth said.

"You've never even ridden with me," I protested, although I knew it was probably for the best.

"Yeah, but the stories your dad tells are legendary," Seth replied.

An hour into the bonfire, I was listening to Jen's friend Cora talk about how she'd recently changed from an advertising major to an art history major. She was bubbly and talkative like Jen but definitely had an edgier look with short black hair and black-rimmed glasses, and each fingernail was painted a different color.

Sadie pulled out ingredients to make s'mores, and Cora left with a few others to find roasting sticks. I glanced at Michael, expecting his face to light up at the sight of the sugary goodness, but he was distracted, his eyes fixed on the fire. His mind was somewhere else, and by the frown on his face, I knew he was still brooding over our previous conversation.

"Do you feel like going for a walk?" I asked him.

I knew what I needed to tell him to help him understand that he hadn't done anything wrong. None of this was his fault.

Michael remained silent but stood up and helped me to my feet.

Michael and I walked down toward the water, strolling along the shoreline. It was so peaceful. The only sound was of the waves as they gently pushed against the sand. The moon was full, providing just the right amount of light to be able to see where we were going.

"I know you think that by healing me, you somehow broke me in the process," I said, ready to lay it all on the table and ease his concerns. "But that's not true. I was already ... defective."

This was my opportunity to tell him the truth. My deepest, darkest secret. A part of me questioned what I was doing, and the other part was telling me to be vulnerable, that I was safe with him. I decided it was now or never.

He stopped walking, giving me his full attention. "What are you talking about?"

I swallowed hard, determined to get it out before I could change my mind. "The night of the masquerade, you asked me how I knew Ben and Lance had drugged our drinks, and I told you, I had a feeling," I said. "And that's true, but it's not the whole truth." I paused, searching for the right words.

Michael intently watched me, trying to figure out where I was going with this.

I took a deep breath and continued, "I've always had this strong sense of knowing—call it intuition. When I was in first grade, my father went on a weeklong business trip to New York. It was the longest he'd ever been gone, and when he returned, he gave me a snow globe of the Statue of Liberty. I brought it to school with me for show-and-tell. Afterward, I placed it in my backpack and returned to my desk. Later in the day, as I went to gather my things to leave, I got this knot in my stomach, and I knew one of the boys in my class had taken it. I hadn't seen him do it, but I was certain he had it." I paused again.

He nodded, urging me to continue.

"So, I told our teacher, and the boy denied it. I was insistent, so she searched his backpack, and there, buried in the bottom, under his lunchbox and jacket, was my snow globe. The funny thing is, I thought I had done a good thing, figuring out who had taken it and getting it back, but I quickly learned that the world didn't think that way. My teacher had me transferred from her class the next day. She saw me as the problem, not him."

I looked out at the ocean, hoping the salty breeze would somehow calm my nerves. "I made up my mind after that day that I was going to hide my intuition from everyone. Only, at the time, I didn't realize what it would cost me."

I felt tears trying to push their way to the surface, and I fought them back. "The night Becca disappeared, I knew someone was in the house to hurt her. I didn't know who or why, but I knew she was in danger, and I allowed my selfishness to get in the way of saving her life."

"Natalie, that wasn't your fault," Michael said, but I held my hand up to stop him.

I needed him to understand who I really was. He deserved to know the truth, as ugly as it was.

"My intuition warned me that something was wrong," I continued, my voice starting to quiver, "but I allowed myself to be paralyzed by the fear of who I was. I should have called the police, but I was afraid. What if they didn't believe me? I talked myself into investigating instead of calling for help. I wasted those precious seconds that could have made a difference."

Michael stepped closer to me. My eyes were fixed on the ground.

He reached out and gently cupped my face with his hands. "Natalie, look at me."

I didn't move. I felt so ashamed. *What kind of person does that?*

"Look at me," he repeated softly.

Reluctantly, I obeyed.

"You can't blame yourself. You did nothing wrong," he said.

A tear managed to escape and rolled down my cheek. He soothed it away with his thumb.

"The only person responsible for taking your sister is the one who took her."

The rational part of me knew coming clean to someone was a big step in the healing process. The emotional part of me was still terrified that, deep down, I was a bad person, a selfish person, a broken person. As I looked into Michael's eyes and felt the warmth of his hands on my cheeks, there was no hint that he saw any of those things in me.

I heard laughter and shouting nearby and realized it was Jen and Seth coming toward us. They lightheartedly splashed each other in the water along the way.

Michael let me go and took a few steps away. I discreetly wiped the tears from my eyes and composed myself.

Jen eyed us, realizing they'd interrupted something.

"Jen's ready to go. She's a party pooper," Seth teased her. He was oblivious.

Jen reached out to playfully smack Seth, but he grabbed her arm and picked her up, throwing her over his shoulder. She screamed and laughed as she pounded on his back. Seth put her down, and they walked arm in arm all the way back to the parking lot.

Michael and I followed them in silence.

"So, Seth wants to come over tonight and see one of my old pageant videos," Jen said as we approached the cars. "He doesn't believe I won the Junior Miss Orange Festival Pageant with fire baton twirling as my talent."

"I can drive Natalie home," Michael offered.

Jen's face lit up. I couldn't tell if she was more excited that she'd get to be alone with Seth or that I'd be alone with Michael.

"That would be great!" Jen said as she ran over to give me a hug good-bye.

Seth gave Michael a warning look. "I can trust you to get her home safe?" Seth asked.

Michael opened the car door for me. "You have my word," he replied as I slid into the passenger seat. "Precious cargo."

Michael was quiet on the drive home, and I started to second-guess my decision to open up to him. Maybe tonight wasn't the right night to reveal so much. Between telling him this morning that I could hear people's thoughts and then healing him at the beach, maybe this was just overwhelming for him.

"I'm sorry I unloaded on you back there," I said as we pulled into my driveway. "I feel like I freaked you out."

"Nothing you told me today changes how I feel about you," he replied, turning off the car. "But I am freaked out. I'm freaked out by what I've done to you."

I sighed, realizing we were back to this. "Whatever is happening to me isn't your fault." I paused but could tell he still wasn't convinced. "You brought me back to life, Michael, and I'm not talking about how you healed me from the accident. For the first time in four years, I feel *alive*."

He leaned in closer to me, and like he was a magnet drawing me in, I moved toward him in return. He stared at me for a moment, and his face softened.

I wanted to say something to him, but I didn't know what. Before I could mutter a word, his face hardened again.

"There's always going to be the possibility of me having to leave," he said, frowning. "You need to know that if Henley's team shows up, I will have to go. I won't be able to see you or call you first because it won't be safe—for us or for you. I don't want to hurt you."

"I know."

As much as the thought of losing him scared me, I knew he was right. If Henley were to find them, he wouldn't be able to risk his or his family's safety to say good-bye to me. I wouldn't want him to.

"I'd better go," he said before I had a chance to respond. "But I think you should take some time away from me to think about what's best for you."

He reached across me and opened my door.

THE UNVEILING

I sat there, unmoving, unsure of what to say. *Is this his way of telling me he wants me out of his life? Is this all too much for him to handle?*

I looked at him, hoping he'd give me clarity but he didn't. He just looked straight ahead, waiting for me to leave.

Rejected and confused, I got out of the car.

"Good night, Michael," I said before shutting the car door.

I walked up to my apartment, and even though I knew Michael was still there, waiting to make sure I got inside safely, I didn't turn around to acknowledge him before going inside.

ELEVEN

"I'm sorry I can't come with you to help you get settled in," I told Seth as he loaded his suitcase into the car.

"It's all good. I know you've got to work," he replied, flashing me a mischievous grin. "Besides, my super-hot *girlfriend* is going to help."

"*Girlfriend?*" I teased without alluding to the fact that Jen had already texted me about their official relationship status. Twice in fact. The first time was to tell me that Seth had kissed her last night and they were officially dating. The second was to tell me not to tell Seth that she'd told me.

I gave Seth a hug, and sadness washed over me. Now that I was finally starting to feel like myself again, I realized how much I needed him in my life.

"Cheer up," he said. "I'm not gonna be far away, and something tells me I will be here a lot to visit—"

"Your super-hot girlfriend," I finished his sentence and rolled my eyes.

Seth laughed as he climbed into his car. "*And* my best friend. She's pretty cool too … for a nerd."

I waved good-bye to Seth, and once his car was out of sight, I headed the opposite direction to work. I was working a double until closing, so unless Michael came into the café, I wouldn't see him. As I recalled how our conversation had ended last night, I doubted he would.

Although I had done my best to convince him that having him in my life had changed me for the better, I knew Michael was feeling responsible for the changes I had been experiencing since he healed me. And while, yes, I did think it was all somehow connected, I'd never felt "normal" anyway. I'd always known I was different.

I managed to go through the motions during my shift as I tried to reconcile our last conversation in my head. Robotically, I tended to my customers, making sure they had everything they needed, but my mind was preoccupied.

Carl called me over, snapping me back to reality. He handed me a to-go order. "Delivery for The Treasure Chest," he said. "I figured you might want to deliver it."

I perked up, thinking maybe Michael had had a change of heart about wanting to spend time apart. My enthusiasm didn't go unnoticed.

"Go ahead and take a thirty-minute break," Carl said as I left the café.

I stepped outside and quickly looked at the ticket attached to the bag. *Tuna melt on whole wheat.* I frowned. It didn't sound like something Michael would order.

I walked to The Treasure Chest and hesitated in the doorway when I saw Raina behind the counter, reading a magazine.

She looked up at me and pursed her lips. "Michael isn't here, and I didn't order anything," she stated before turning her attention back to her magazine.

"I did," a voice said from behind her, coming from the back room.

A second later, Alexander appeared in the doorway. Even though he looked a little older, I recognized him from the photo at Michael's house.

"Why don't you come on back, Natalie?" he said.

I was surprised he knew my name since we'd never formally met.

I walked around the counter, passing Raina, and followed him into the back room that they used for stock.

"I'm Alexander," he introduced himself, shaking my hand. "It's nice to finally meet you. I apologize for Raina. She doesn't deal well with change."

"Change?"

"Please sit if you can stay a minute," he said, gesturing to a small table with two chairs. "I was hoping we could get acquainted."

I was unsure of what to expect, but I sat down anyway.

Alexander handed me cash and dropped the sandwich bag on his desk. He had no intention of eating.

"Michael informed me that he's told you about our ... situation."

I stiffened. "I'm not going to tell anyone, if that's what you're worried about."

He shook his head and smiled kindly. "I wasn't insinuating that you would. Michael has assured me that we can trust you. And as I'm sure you are aware, Michael doesn't trust very easily, so if he says we can trust you with our secret, I believe him."

I sat back in my chair, feeling a little more at ease.

"I'm more interested in understanding how you are dealing with all of this," he said. His question caught me off guard, and he must've noticed. "Michael told me that you are having some side effects from his healing powers. He came to me last night, very concerned about you. You see, this has never happened to anyone he's healed before."

"What did he tell you exactly?" I asked, feeling a little embarrassed. It never crossed my mind that he would tell his family even though it did make sense that he would.

"He said that you slept for an unusual amount of time, and when you awoke, you were able to interpret people's thoughts and impact electrical currents. Then, last night, you demonstrated some healing powers of your own."

I let out a small sigh of relief, knowing that Michael hadn't told him about my pre-healing intuitive abilities. Telling Michael had been a big step for me and not one I was ready to take with a complete stranger.

"Is there anything else about your experience that you'd like to share?" he asked. "I hope you accept my sincerity when I tell you that I only want to help you."

My instinct told me that Alexander was telling the truth, but the part of me that was conditioned to protect my secret held me back from confiding in him. I gave him a tight smile and shook my head.

Alexander frowned. "Natalie, I'm going to level with you about something that I don't think Michael has shared."

The tension in my body returned.

"I need to understand what is causing you to develop these abilities because it poses a danger to my family."

"What do you mean?" I asked, shocked.

"You see, anytime Michael or Raina uses their powers, they give off a burst of energy, which is traceable," Alexander explained. "The amount of energy depends on the magnitude of the usage. Small usage here and there is easily masked in an old city like St. Augustine, especially with all of the frequent lightning storms, but large bursts—like when Michael healed you or like the power outage in the café—draw a lot of unwanted attention."

"Henley," I whispered more to myself than to Alexander.

"Yes," he confirmed, his brows furrowed. "Michael and Raina are quite attuned to their abilities and know how to control them. Michael healing you in Jacksonville likely set off Henley's radar. I'm concerned the incident in the café might have drawn even more attention."

A wave of panic crept over me as I wondered if Michael had left town, and that was the real reason he wasn't there. Then, I remembered Raina was still here and doubted that Alexander would send Michael away without sending Raina with him.

"We have to be very diligent. Henley could come here," Alexander continued. "We've been considering leaving; however, it's a delicate balance. Leaving someplace unexpectedly can also draw too much attention, especially in smaller cities like this one."

"Michael thought he saw one of the Henley cars yesterday, and it really freaked him out," I confessed.

"And with good reason. This is dangerous for all of us, including you. Henley will stop at nothing and spare no one if he thinks he can get to Michael and Raina. You need to understand what that threat means to you. If they were to come here and find out about your relationship with Michael, they would use you to get to him."

The words stung, but he was right. I stood up, unable to sit any longer. I paced around, uncertain of where my feet wanted to take me.

"I would never tell them anything," I insisted.

I would never betray Michael or his family. I would never do anything that would send him back to that horrible place.

Alexander stood up and gently placed his hands on my arms, stopping my pace. "I believe you, but you might not have a choice."

And I understood. I'd seen enough of the video to know, if Henley believed I could lead him to Michael, he would surely try to torture it out of me.

"Chad Henley is an evil man, and if he takes you, I have no doubt my son will try to save you," he warned before releasing me. This was something I hadn't considered. "Please be careful. For you, for Michael, for my family."

I nodded, unsure of what to say to him. I felt flooded with regret. Regret that Michael had risked his life to save mine. Regret that, because I couldn't control myself that day in the café, they were all in danger of Henley coming to St. Augustine and finding them.

"I'm sorry," was all I could manage to say.

"It's not my intention to make you feel guilty," he replied. "I understand why Michael made the decision to save you, and I can't fault him for that."

The door to the stockroom opened. Michael entered but stopped short when he saw me. Clearly, Alexander hadn't told him he was planning on talking to me about this.

It was all clear to me now. Michael's decision to save my life had put a target on his back, and the fact that I didn't understand my newfound abilities made me dangerous to him.

The conversation in the car with Michael last night was his way of trying to tell me that I was putting him and his family at risk. He wanted me to make the choice to walk away, so he didn't have to be the one to do it. He didn't want to hurt my feelings.

"I'd better go," I said, heading to the doorway, anxious to get out of there.

Michael reached out to stop me from leaving. "Wait, I'll walk you."

"No, that's okay. I have to hurry back," I replied, avoiding his eyes.

He leaned in a little closer, his hand still on my arm. "What's wrong?" he asked quietly. His eyes locked with mine, forcing them to make contact.

I faked a smile. "Oh, nothing." I tried to sound casual. "The café is just swamped today, so I need to get back."

Michael hesitated before removing his hand, trying to decide if I was telling the truth. I didn't think he was convinced, but I bolted before he could pursue it any further. I hurried past the counter and out the front door. Raina didn't even look up to acknowledge me.

I felt nauseous as I walked back to the café. The thought of Michael going back to Henley was unbearable. I recalled the video of the little boy who had faced his worst nightmares and thought of Michael today, who still carried the scars on his arms as a constant reminder.

When I returned to the café, I dived right back into my shift, trying to keep my mind occupied. I was extra attentive to my tables, and when the café started slowing down right before closing, I began reorganizing the waitress station, carefully cleaning every square inch.

After the café closed, Carl and Jessica left for a date night, and I headed home.

It was Saturday night, so the downtown area of St. Augustine was alive with locals and tourists enjoying late dinners and music in the outdoor bar areas.

The sound of a woman singing and playing guitar grew louder as I approached one of the most popular hangouts. Dozens of college students gathered around the bar, barely paying her any attention.

I recognized Ben sitting at the far corner of the bar, next to a pretty girl with long blonde hair. They both did a shot, and Ben laughed as the girl gagged. Ben tucked the girl's hair behind her ear and whispered something that made her giggle. She wrapped her arm around his neck, pulling him into a drunken kiss. I looked away and quickened my pace, eager to pass the restaurant. I could feel anger rising up in me as I recalled what had happened at the masquerade. If he were to see me and confront me, would I be able to control my abilities? I couldn't risk drawing any more attention.

I managed to make it to my street without being noticed by Ben. I started to relax until I noticed a black sedan with dark tinted windows parked across the street from my apartment. I'd never seen it before, but I tried not to panic. Black cars weren't uncommon, and it probably belonged to someone visiting one of my neighbors.

I kept an eye on it as I walked to my front door, trying not to be obvious with my suspicion. I went inside my apartment and immediately locked the dead bolt.

Take a deep breath. You are being paranoid.

With all of the lights off in the house, I peeked out the window. The car was gone, confirming my paranoia.

I let out a sigh, and I wasn't sure if it was one of relief, frustration, or a combination of both.

I stood in the living room for a few minutes, debating on what to do next. A part of me wanted to call Michael and try to talk this out, but the reality was, I was dangerous. If I cared about Michael, I would stay away from him.

I wandered into the kitchen and made myself a bowl of chicken noodle soup. When it was ready, I grabbed my laptop and sat at the kitchen table.

I typed *Chad Henley* into the search bar and braced myself for whatever I would find. Knowledge was power, and I felt powerless. If Chad Henley was the enemy, then I needed to make sure I had as much information as possible.

Within seconds, a photo of Chad Henley appeared. He wasn't what I'd expected. In my mind, I'd envisioned a much scarier image based on the voice from the observation room in the video Michael had shown me. I'd pictured a large, evil-looking man full of rage. The man in the picture didn't match that image at all.

The picture of Chad Henley showed a man in his early fifties with brown hair that was turning gray, especially in his sideburns. You could almost see the brilliance behind his hazel eyes. He had a square jaw, and his lips were not set into a smile or a frown but were completely neutral. In the picture, he wore a suit and was posing with several other men in suits. Although I'd imagined him to be very tall and dominating, most of the men in the photo were taller than him.

The caption of the photo indicated it had been taken at a charity banquet, benefiting children with leukemia. Apparently, Henley's company had donated one million dollars to them. I scrolled through a few more of the images, and they were all work-related. There were pictures of him with the mayor, the governor, and even the attorney general. I'd underestimated the reach of his power.

I noticed a link to the C. Henley Labs Incorporated website and clicked on it. They were headquartered in Chicago, Illinois, but had multiple satellite locations throughout the United States. I noticed they had a satellite office in Charlotte, North Carolina. My dad's company had opened a satellite office there when I was about ten years old, and since it was only about a four-and-a-half-hour drive from Richmond, we would usually rent a big house with Seth's family and spend spring break there.

According to the company's mission statement, C. Henley Labs Incorporated was a "medical science research organization, striving to advance quality of life for individuals faced with debilitating illness or disability." If only people knew the truth about who Chad Henley was and what the company was really up to.

My phone vibrated on the table. It was a text message from Michael.

Michael: Everything okay?

No, everything is not okay.
I wanted to tell Michael I was sorry and that if I could go back in time and stop him from saving me after the accident, I would. I wanted to tell him that I was terrified of the thought of him going back to that horrible place where he had been born. I also wanted to tell him that I was selfish and I wanted him to remain in my life, that I didn't know how to picture my life without him in it.

I typed and erased several different responses as I tried to figure out what to say. Finally, I typed:

Me: I agree that we need some space.

I hesitated but hit Send.

My heart sank as I imagined going into work and seeing his empty table.

As if he were waiting on my text, he immediately wrote back.

Michael: If that's what you need, I understand.

I just stared at my phone. It was done.

Maybe this was the closure Michael needed to just go ahead and move away from here. He'd said himself that they were prepared to move, but he'd changed his mind when he had the dream of my accident. Alexander had indicated there was a balance between leaving too soon and staying too long. With me out of the picture, they could let things calm down for a couple of weeks and then just leave town quietly.

I imagined Alexander telling his regular customers that he'd decided to close the shop to retire early and move to Palm Beach or somewhere tropical, meanwhile really preparing his family to move out west somewhere.

I reminded myself that it had never been a matter of *if* but *when* they would leave. My friendship with Michael was never meant to last.

TWELVE

"You look terrible," Jen told me as I dragged myself into the café on a Sunday morning to work the lunch and dinner shifts. "And I mean that in the nicest possible way."

"I haven't been sleeping well," I confessed.

Ever since my conversation with Alexander two weeks ago, I had been dreaming of Henley capturing Michael. Every night, I would wake up in a cold sweat with my heart frantically beating against my chest.

I put my purse in the locker and headed back into the dining area. Carl noticed that I'd arrived and frowned. I didn't normally work on Sundays, but I'd decided to pick up the extra shift to try to keep myself busy. Carl walked over, and I could tell he was hesitant to approach me. I expectantly looked at him.

"Is everything okay with you?" he asked. "Your boyfriend hasn't been coming around. Did you break up or something?"

"He wasn't my boyfriend," I said flatly, catching a glimpse of myself in the mirror. Deep, dark circles surrounded my eyes, and I looked much paler than usual. No wonder he and Jen were both concerned. I looked awful. Not wanting either of them to worry, I tried to smile. "I'm fine. I promise."

The café was slammed during lunch and dinner, and even though I was tired, I welcomed the distraction.

While I didn't actively think of Michael during my shift, I often found myself looking at the front door when I heard it open and chime. Each time, there would be a moment of disappointment when I realized it wasn't him. Jen caught me several times but didn't say anything to me about it.

Over the past couple of weeks, Jen and I'd had many conversations about Michael. Of course, I couldn't tell her the whole story. I'd simply told her that I needed distance from him, which wasn't a complete lie. Jen didn't understand and tried to convince me to reconsider.

"I really think he cares about you, Natalie," she'd said. "Are you sure you can't work this out?"

After the dinner rush, Carl left, trusting Jen and me to close up for him. Jen shot me a knowing smile because the only reason Carl ever left the café before closing was if he had plans with Jessica.

The café was empty, so Jen and I started preparing for closing. I was halfway through rolling my stack of silverware when I heard the door open. I casually looked at the entrance, knowing it wouldn't be Michael. And it wasn't. A middle-aged man wearing a suit walked in and took a seat at the bar counter.

Jen gave me the *who comes in ten minutes prior to closing* look but still managed to give him a warm greeting. I turned my attention back to rolling the silverware until I noticed the man and Jen look over at me. Jen said something to the man and gestured for him to give her a minute. She hurried over to me, and I stood up straight, unsure of what was going on.

"Who's that?" I asked her.

"He says he's with the electric company," Jen replied. "I told him Carl wasn't here, but he said he wanted to talk to you. Why would he want to talk to you and not Carl?"

The bigger question was, why would someone from the electric company be here after nine p.m. on a Sunday night? It was more than a little suspicious, and as much as I didn't want to talk to the man, I needed to get to the bottom of it. For Michael's sake.

I forced a smile and shook my head, trying to defuse Jen's concerns. "I totally forgot that Carl mentioned he'd be coming by. I'll talk to him." I instantly felt guilty for lying.

I tried to appear confident while the man stared at me as I approached him. "Can I help you?" I carefully folded my hands in front of me to stop them from shaking.

"You must be Natalie Clark," he said, and I nodded. "I'm with the electric company, and I'm hoping you can help me sort some things out. Were you working on October 27?"

I instantly recognized that as the date I'd returned to work after the accident, the same day I'd managed to short the electricity in the café. I pretended to think about it and then responded, "I'm not sure. I can barely remember what I did yesterday." I let out a small laugh that sounded too fake.

"Let me see if I can refresh your memory. There was a power outage in the café that day." The man skeptically eyed me.

"Oh, yes," I replied, acting as though I'd just remembered. "I do remember that." I wasn't sure where he was taking the conversation, but I decided it was best to play along in order to figure out how much he really knew. "It must have been quite an outage to send you in here to follow up several weeks later."

"Yes, in fact, it was," he said, tapping his fingers against the top of the counter. "But the funny thing is, Natalie, the power outage was isolated to just this café."

"Maybe there is a wiring problem. You know how old these buildings are." My voice betrayed me as it began to quiver. I cleared my throat.

"I don't think that's what it was," he replied. "We'd like to interview a few of the people who were in the café that day, just as a precaution. Any regulars that you can point me to?"

My stomach dropped, and a familiar knot settled in. As I'd feared, he wasn't with the electric company. They wouldn't send someone out this late to talk about a power outage, and they certainly wouldn't want to interview people about it. My gut told me Henley had sent him, and he was trying to figure out how to find Michael.

I recalled the black car outside my apartment. I hadn't been paranoid after all; Henley was watching me. They must have found me because of the power surge I'd created at my apartment the morning I woke up from the accident, before I went to work. I doubted they suspected that I'd caused the outages, but they likely thought that either Michael or Raina were with me at the time each outage occurred.

"Sorry, can't help you there," I told him. "There's no way to know for sure who was in the café that day."

He narrowed his eyes at me, and I decided to take the upper hand before this got any further out of control. I decided to call his bluff. He wouldn't want to blow his cover because he knew that would cause Michael's family to run.

"What did you say your name was?" I asked. "If you can leave me your business card, I'd be happy to relay it to the owner. Maybe he can recall something I can't."

The man stood up, towering over me. I locked eyes with him, refusing to let him know I was intimidated.

Anger began to build deep inside me, and I focused on trying to control it. I couldn't let him know he was getting the best of me.

Out of the corner of my eye, I saw Jen stop and stare at us.

The man accepted my defiance and took a step back. "Not necessary," he muttered. "I'll be sure to stop back in soon."

The man turned and walked away. I stood there, unmoving until the door slammed behind him. Once he was gone, I let out a huge sigh of relief and sat down. My arms and legs began to tremble from the adrenaline. Jen ran to the front door and locked it before coming to my side.

"What was that all about?" she asked.

I hated lying to her, but I knew I must to protect her. "I don't know. Maybe he's running some kind of scam. He's definitely not with the electric company though." At least the last part was true. "If he comes back in, don't talk to him."

The café phone rang, and Jen headed to the counter to answer it. I struggled with what to do next. I needed to tell Michael, but I couldn't go to his house.

What if that man is watching me?

I considered calling him, but what if they had my phone line tapped? I wouldn't put it past them to have the ability to do that.

In the background, I heard Jen telling the caller the café's hours for the next day.

I realized what I needed to do. I hurried into the back room with my cell phone in my hand.

I opened a new text to Michael that said *Found* and paused. It was his family's code word, and he would know what it meant.

Am I sure about this?

Once I hit Send, there was no taking it back. Michael and his family would leave forever.

I held my breath as I hit Send. As much as I wished it weren't true, that I was just being paranoid, I knew I wasn't. The knot in my stomach told me that Henley was here, and unless I warned Michael, they would surely find him.

I stared at the sent text, contemplating what to do next. Maybe I'd ask to crash at Jen's house tonight, just in case that car was outside my house again.

My phone chimed softly, but it startled me, and I jumped.

It was a reply from Michael.

Michael: Meet me there.

Can I do that? Can I go there?

We never talked about this. He'd always told me that if they spotted Henley, they would leave without saying good-bye, that it would be the safest thing to do.

But what if I don't go? Would he wait too long and get caught? If I went, I would have to be absolutely sure I wasn't followed.

I grabbed my purse and jacket and poked my head into the dining room. I did my best to appear calm.

"Do you mind finishing closing up?" I asked Jen.

Jen looked at the phone in my hand, and a big smile spread across her face. "Of course! I knew you'd come to your senses."

A vision of me coming into the café tomorrow after Michael was gone crept into my head, and I realized I'd have to come up with yet another lie to cover up the real story. My heart began to ache at the thought that I would never see him again after tonight. But if I hurried, I would at least get a chance to see him one last time.

I ducked out the back entrance of the café. I assumed it was safer than going out the front in case that man was out there, waiting for me.

I looked around and made sure the coast was clear before quietly shutting the door behind me.

It was dark outside, and the streets were empty. Since it was Sunday night, all of the surrounding businesses had closed early. It was an eerie contrast to the busyness I was accustomed to on Friday and Saturday nights after closing.

The safe house was only a few blocks away, and the fastest way for me to get there would be to go directly to St. George Street, but I decided to go around the block, the other way toward A1A just to make sure I wasn't being followed.

It was chilly outside, making my breath appear in white puffs as I exhaled. The street was silent, except for the sound of my shoes hitting the pavement in steady, determined strides. One faint streetlight provided inadequate illumination of the surroundings, and I found myself examining every suspicious shadow.

I was close to A1A and was about to turn the corner when I heard a rustling noise. I froze.

I stopped as the knot formed in my stomach. I turned around but saw nothing.

Out of nowhere, someone wrapped their arms around me from behind. One hand covered my mouth while the other firmly grasped around my torso. Without hesitation, I started trying to fight him off, thrashing in his arms, trying to free my mouth to scream. My cell phone dropped out of my hand and crashed on the ground.

A tall man hurried toward us, and even though he was now wearing a black hoodie instead of a suit, I recognized him as the man from the café. As he grew closer, I noticed a syringe in his hand, and panic swept through my whole body. I thrashed against my attacker with all my strength but was still unable to free myself. I screamed against his hand, and the streetlight above us exploded, sending sparks of light shooting toward the ground.

My attacker and the man with the syringe were caught off guard, and I seized the opportunity to free myself from his grasp. My window of opportunity was very short, and within seconds, they were running behind me.

Dashing onto A1A, I frantically looked for someone to flag down, someone to save me. With all of the businesses closed for the night, there was no one out, walking around. Completely alone against my attackers, I ran in the opposite direction of the safe house, unsure of where I would run to but I was determined not to lead them to Michael.

I was almost to the bridge that crossed over the Matanzas River when I saw a car approaching. I waved my arms as I ran toward it, trying to flag it down. The car screeched to a halt, and two men in black hoodies got out and started running toward me.

Knowing the other two men must be closing in on me as well, I veered off the road and onto the bridge. Maybe if I could get on the other side of the bridge, I could flag down someone to help me.

My legs ached, and my lungs burned as I tried to outrun my pursuers on the bridge. I was almost halfway across the bridge when a black sedan flew around the corner. Its tires skidded as it turned onto the bridge from the other side. I was trapped. I couldn't turn around because there was no way I could fight off four men, and I couldn't go straight because the car was cutting me off.

My conversation with Alexander flashed in my mind, and I knew I couldn't be taken captive. Even though I knew in my heart there was nothing they could do to get me to tell them where Michael was, I couldn't risk Michael coming after me out of guilt.

With no time to formulate a plan, I did the only thing I could think of to escape. I clutched the ledge of the bridge and climbed up onto it.

Seeing my intention, the men who were chasing me stopped running and cautiously watched me. They exchanged a nervous glance, trying to decide how to proceed. I was of no value to them if I was dead.

The man from the café was no longer holding the syringe. He put his hands up in defeat. "Natalie," he said, "think about what you're doing."

He took a small step closer, and I looked down. It was a long way down to the water, and I just hoped that if I died, it would be quick and painless.

"We just want to talk to you," he said, but I knew better. "We aren't here to hurt you. We just need to know where Michael and Raina are."

Hearing Michael's name was enough to give me the courage I needed. I closed my eyes, and it only took one tiny step to send me plummeting toward the water.

As I fell, I didn't scream, but I could briefly hear the commotion above me before I slammed into the water. I imagined this was what being hit by a car felt like. Within seconds, I felt excruciating pain in my ribs.

I stayed under the water and swam without knowing which direction I was swimming in. Without a doubt, the men were watching to see if I surfaced, and if they located me, they would try to capture me. I needed them to believe I was dead.

Although in Florida, the water was still a dangerously low temperature, and I knew that I must get out of it as soon as possible. Beneath the surface, I swam with all of my strength. Unable to hold my breath any longer, I allowed myself to surface. I let out a loud gasp for air and prayed that my attackers hadn't heard it.

To my surprise, the current had carried me a good distance from the bridge. It was too strong for me to fight, so I swam parallel toward the shore.

When we were kids, our parents had taken us on a vacation to Virginia Beach. It was the first time I'd ever been in the ocean, and I remembered my dad teaching us to swim parallel just in case we got caught in a rip current. The same logic should apply here.

I continued to swim despite the numbness that was beginning to creep into my hands and feet from the cold water. Reaching shore felt like a never-ending task, but I finally made it. The current had carried me about half a mile away from the bridge.

The shore was lined with rocks that scraped against my flesh as I dragged myself out of the water. Exhausted, I lay there on the rocks, catching my breath.

As soon as I could breathe, I forced myself up. I had to make it to the safe house. Every minute Michael stayed there put him in more jeopardy of being discovered.

As I ran, the pain in my ribs began to subside. My legs, however, were tired and ached from the cold. I saw an empty city trolley parked for the night and ran to it. I crouched behind it, listening intently to the silence. There was no way to know for sure that the coast was clear, and I would have to cross over A1A again in order to get to the house. I decided to chance it. I darted from behind the trolley, dashing through the A1A intersection. To the left, I noticed headlights in the distance, closer to the bridge. They were still looking for me.

Soaking wet, I shivered as I ran. Taking only side streets once past A1A, I managed to remain undetected.

As I rounded the final corner, the safe house came into view. I slowed to a jog to take one last inventory of my surroundings, making absolutely sure no one was following me. When I confirmed I was alone, I sprinted as fast as I could. It took every ounce of energy I had left to make it.

The second my feet hit the driveway, Michael emerged from the shadows on the porch. He was waiting for me. He rushed down the stoop, and I crashed forward into his arms. I tightly hugged his neck, exhausted but grateful to see him.

My legs wobbled beneath me before giving out. Michael picked me up and carried me into the house.

The house was illuminated with several candles and lanterns placed on wooden crates. Michael gently set me on the floor and began digging through an old trunk. I noticed four suitcases next to the trunk and realized they must have pre-packed luggage for unexpected nights like this. He pulled out a plaid blanket and joined me on the floor, wrapping it around me and pulling me to his chest.

He vigorously rubbed his hands up and down my arms, trying to warm me up.

When my breath became a little more even, Michael pulled back to look at me. "Are you okay?" he asked, running his hand through my damp hair.

"I-I think so," I stammered.

"What happened?" He moved his hands back to my arms to continue warming me up.

The concern in his eyes pained me because I knew what I was about to tell him would make it worse. Henley's men were here, and there was no turning back.

I told him the whole story, careful not to leave out any details in case they were valuable. He raised his eyebrows as I told him about taking out the streetlight to get away from my attackers, but he remained silent until I told him about how I'd jumped off the bridge.

"You did what?" he asked, his whole body tensing up.

"I had to," I explained. "There was no other way out."

"You could have been killed."

I sighed. "I think that was a possibility either way."

He clenched his jaw but didn't say anything else. He knew I was right.

I continued to tell him how I'd swum to shore and made it to the safe house.

"I don't think I was followed," I told him, hoping this little bit of information would at least bring him some comfort. There was still a chance they could escape, undetected.

"Where is your family?" I asked. *What if Henley's men spot them while they're looking for me?* "Shouldn't they be here by now?"

"They are fine," he said. "They were on their way home when I sent the message, but they should be here any minute."

He stood up and helped me to my feet. It took me a minute to steady myself, but he kept his arms tightly around me, making sure I could stand on my own. He removed the blanket from my shoulders, letting it hit the floor. He removed my crossbody purse, which I was surprised to find was still attached to me. He then placed his hands at the bottom of my wet shirt.

"May I?"

I nodded, understanding that he wanted to check to see if I needed to be healed. He lifted my shirt to just below my bra. He ran his warm hand against my ribs.

"Does this hurt?" he asked after noticing I was holding my breath.

Blushing, I shook my head and forced myself to breathe again.

He released my shirt and inspected my hands, elbows, and legs. When finished, he took a step back and just stared at me, perplexed.

"What? Is it bad?" I asked, suddenly concerned that I was hurt and just didn't feel it. I'd heard that could happen to people when their adrenaline was high.

I looked down at my hands but didn't see anything wrong with them.

"Did you already heal me?" I asked. I didn't feel anything like I had when he healed me after the accident.

"No," he replied. "I don't know how, but you seem to be fine. I thought you said your ribs hurt after you hit the water?"

"They did," I insisted. "They don't hurt now though. Maybe it was just the shock of hitting the water so hard."

He stared at me, and just as I was about to ask him what he was thinking, the door opened.

We both jumped but were instantly flooded with relief when Michael's parents and Raina walked in. Lorena crossed the room and grabbed Michael, tightly hugging him before turning to me. I took a deep breath, preparing myself for the worst. She had to blame me for all of this. I did.

"Thank you for warning us," she said and hugged me.

I was completely taken by surprise but hugged her back.

"Raina, dig out some dry clothes for Natalie," she said.

Raina, who obviously did blame me, let out a frustrated sigh as she walked over to one of the suitcases and pulled out a pair of ripped skinny jeans and a black sweater. She didn't even look at me as she held the clothes out. I took the clothes and thanked her, although I received no acknowledgment.

I grabbed one of the lanterns and went into the next room, closing the door behind me. I placed the lantern on the floor and quickly changed.

Although they were trying to speak low, I could hear the conversation through the thin walls. Michael filled his family in on the details of what had happened to me.

"Everything is in place for us to leave tonight," Alexander told the family. "I called Stan on the way, and he's got two cars waiting for us at a hotel by the interstate. We'll swap ours out, and we should be in the clear."

"Good," Michael said. "We'll need two this time since Natalie will be with us."

I froze. *Did I hear that right?*

"She's not coming with us," Raina snapped. "You know that's not an option."

"I'm sorry, son, but Raina's right," Alexander said.

"What are we going to do?" Michael snapped back. "Leave her here, so Henley can finish the job? So they can capture her, torture her, and maybe kill her, trying to find us? I won't agree to that. I won't go unless she does."

I'd been so focused on escaping Henley's men and making my way to Michael that I hadn't given much thought about what would come next for me. I guessed I'd just assumed Michael and his family would leave town, and I'd go back to life as usual afterward, but Michael was right. Henley wasn't going to allow me to do that if he thought there was a chance I knew where Michael was.

"I agree; we can't do that to her," Lorena chimed in. "But it's not safe for her to come with us either. It's not safe for us, and it's not safe for her. This could easily happen again in the next town."

They were silent, and I decided it was a good time to come out of the room. Raina glared at me with hatred, and I couldn't blame her. They were having to leave their home because of me, and now, they couldn't even leave quickly because they felt obligated to figure out what to do with me.

"I'll be okay," I said, making up my own plan as I spoke. "I can, um, go stay with someone until this all blows over. I mean, once they realize you're gone, they will leave, right?"

"You can't stay with Jen or Seth. It's too close and too easy for them to figure out," Michael told me. "You have to go somewhere far away from here. You'll have to stay there for a few months at least. And whatever you do, you cannot trigger any power surges, or they will come for you again, thinking it's us."

"Where can you go?" Alexander asked me.

I considered going to my parents but realized that would also be too easy for someone to figure out. I wouldn't want to put them in danger. "I can stay with my aunt in Kentucky." I hadn't seen her in years, but I was sure she'd be willing to let me stay for a while.

Alexander pondered this and looked at Michael.

As if reading his mind, Michael told him, "I will drive her there myself and then come meet you."

"I will drive myself," I said. Michael gave me a look that told me it wasn't debatable, but I quickly explained, "I need to go to Virginia to see my parents first."

"Oh, for crying out loud," Raina said, rolling her eyes. "There is a sense of urgency here! It's not the time for a freaking family reunion."

I ignored her and focused on Michael. I knew he'd understand.

"I can't just disappear on them," I said. "They need to know that I'll be somewhere safe even if I can't tell them where. I'll only stay one night, max, and then I'll go to Kentucky."

Michael nodded. "I'll take you." I opened my mouth to protest, but he cut me off, "It's not a question, Natalie. Let's get in the car."

Within fifteen minutes, we pulled into a hotel parking lot to switch out vehicles. A steel-gray SUV and a black truck were parked in a dark, secluded part of the parking lot. We maneuvered undetected as we moved the luggage over to the new vehicles. I climbed into the passenger seat of the black truck as Michael tossed his suitcase into the backseat.

"I've never left without you before," Raina told Michael, her eyes glued to the ground.

Michael shut the door to the truck and walked over to her. He pulled her into a hug, but Raina's arms dangled at her sides in defiance.

"It will be okay. I'll see you in a few days," Michael reassured her.

Raina looked up, and her teary eyes landed on me. I looked away, feeling guilty for splitting up their family. I imagined this was probably the first time in Raina's life that she'd ever been apart from Michael.

Lorena hugged Michael next, whispering her good-byes to him.

"I will. I promise. I love you too," he replied to her.

Alexander pulled Michael to the side to give him the instructions of where to meet them after he dropped me off in Kentucky. I couldn't hear what they were saying and realized that was the point.

"Please be safe, Natalie," Lorena said as she approached the passenger side of the truck. "Be extremely vigilant for the next few months."

Michael and Alexander returned to us, and it was time to go. Raina got into the backseat of the SUV without another word.

Michael climbed into the driver's seat of the truck and stared at his family's SUV for a second before pulling out of the parking lot. I knew this must be hard for him.

"You can't tell me where you are going to meet them, can you?" I asked as we pulled onto the interstate.

"No," he replied, tightly grasping the wheel.

I looked out the window and silently watched St. Augustine, once my place of refuge, disappear into the past.

THIRTEEN

The truck came to a stop, and Michael opened his door.

"Where are you going?" I asked, lifting a heavy eyelid. I hadn't meant to fall asleep.

"We need to stop for the night," he replied. "I'll be right back." He left, locking the truck behind him.

I forced my other eye open even though they both felt like sandpaper.

As the surroundings came into focus, I realized that it was three fifteen a.m., and we were parked outside of a motel. Having been asleep for at least two hours, I had no idea what city or even what state we were in.

Michael returned a few minutes later, and we drove around to the backside of the motel. He yawned, and his bloodshot eyes showed how exhausted he was.

Our room was 121, but Michael parked several rooms away, so if someone recognized the truck, they wouldn't automatically know what room we were in.

The two-story motel was old but in a remote area, which was why he had chosen it.

Michael carefully dead-bolted the door behind us and pulled the curtains tightly shut as soon as we were inside our room.

"I'll take the couch," he told me, dropping his suitcase on the floor.

I looked over at the dingy couch, which looked as hard as a rock.

"I've slept on worse," he reassured me.

He opened his suitcase, pulled out a T-shirt, and offered it to me.

"This is the closest thing I have to pajamas," he said. "Maybe we can go shopping and get you a few things tomorrow morning."

"No need. I have clothes at my parents' house," I told him, gratefully accepting the T-shirt so I didn't have to sleep in Raina's skinny jeans. "I'm going to take a shower."

I went into the bathroom, closing the door behind me. My reflection in the mirror matched the craziness that had ensued over the past six hours. The curl in my hair was wild from being drenched in the Matanzas River, and what little makeup I'd had on earlier had long been washed away. I dug a hairbrush out of my damp purse and carefully untangled all of the knots in my hair.

The shower curtain had traces of mildew on it, but the shower itself seemed relatively clean. As I ran the soapy washcloth over my body, I couldn't believe that I didn't have any bruises or soreness from my fall off the bridge. Somehow, I was perfectly intact.

When I was finished showering, I dried off and picked up Michael's T-shirt. It was a light-blue souvenir from the Grand Canyon, and I wondered if it was part of their next story. His bag had been pre-packed, and I'd never seen him wear it before. This could somehow be a part of the new identity he was about to assume after he dropped me off in Kentucky.

I slipped on the T-shirt and instantly took notice of how it smelled like him. Because he was so much taller than me, his shirt came to just above my knees.

With one hand on the doorknob, I hesitated before going back into the room. Even though I knew Michael was going to sleep on the couch, sharing a room with a guy I was attracted to was unchartered territory for me. It felt like a big step in a relationship, especially in one as undefined as ours.

Michael was lying on the couch, watching TV, wearing a T-shirt and athletic shorts. He turned his attention to me as I stepped out of the bathroom. I awkwardly stood there.

"You okay?" he asked.

"Yeah, I'm fine." I tried to walk casually over to the bed.

I was about to climb in when I realized that he had taken one of the pillows but did not have a blanket. I peeled the comforter off the bed.

"I'm good," he insisted, realizing what I was doing.

I ignored him and handed him the blanket. "The sheet will be enough for me," I firmly told him. "Just take it."

He reluctantly accepted the comforter. He spread it over himself and turned off the TV. I retreated to the bed, sliding under the thin white sheet. I turned off the light on the nightstand and lay on my side, facing him. He was lying on his back, and as my eyes adjusted to the dark, I noticed he was staring at the ceiling.

"Are you excited to see your parents tomorrow?" he asked.

"I'm more nervous than excited," I told him honestly. "I'm not sure how they are going to react."

"Why do you say that?"

"I didn't really leave on the best terms, especially with my mother. They didn't want me to move away."

There was a soft thud outside, and I jumped, making the old springs in the bed creak. Michael pounced off the couch, as if he had been waiting for something bad to happen. He crouched by the window and gently parted the curtain to the side. My heart began to race, and my body tensed up. I sat up and scanned the room, looking for another way out in case it was Henley. I was ready to jump out of bed. I was ready to fight.

Michael closed the curtain. "It's nothing. Just someone going into the room next to ours."

I started to shake, and even in the dark, Michael noticed.

"It's okay," he said, sitting next to me on the bed. He rubbed a reassuring hand on my arm. "You're safe."

"How are you not completely freaked out?" I asked him, in awe of how calm he was.

He shrugged. "I guess I'm just used to it. I've done this almost my entire life."

I said nothing as I contemplated what it must've been like for him. As a child, I'd slept so peacefully, so confident that nothing bad could ever happen. Sure, that had changed when Becca was taken, but Michael had never had that at all. He had gone from living at the Henley facility to running from Henley, always knowing that evil man was out there, wanting to hurt him.

"I want you to know that I will do whatever it takes to make this right," he said.

"What do you mean?"

He hadn't done anything but protect me. He'd even separated himself from his family to ensure I made it to Virginia and then Kentucky.

What could he possibly have to make right?

"To make sure you are safe and can go back to a normal life," he replied. "Try and get some sleep. I'll hear them if they find us. I'm a light sleeper." He gave my arm one last reassuring rub and then moved back to the couch.

We lay there in silence for a few minutes, and I wondered if he'd fallen asleep. I decided to close my eyes and questioned if I'd really be able to sleep.

The next morning, I awoke to the sound of the bathroom door opening. Michael stepped out, shirtless but wearing a pair of jeans. He rubbed a towel over his wet hair but did not notice that I was awake.

I'd never seen him without a shirt on, and I couldn't help but watch him as he walked over to his suitcase and pulled out a long-sleeved gray shirt. Scars similar to the ones on his arms were also on his back and chest. They were painful reminders etched into his perfect skin. Despite the scars, I couldn't take my eyes off the lean muscle that rested beneath them.

He put his shirt on and turned toward the bed. I quickly closed my eyes, hoping he hadn't caught me staring. His hand gently shook my shoulder, and I opened my eyes, pretending to wake up.

"Good morning," he said.

If he knew I had already been awake, he didn't let on.

"Morning," I replied, sitting up. "What time is it?"

"Nine. I tried to let you sleep as long as possible, but we really need to get back on the road."

I sat up and realized that the comforter was on me. Michael must've placed it on me after I fell asleep.

He reached back into his suitcase and pulled out a brand-new toothbrush still in the box and tossed it onto the bed. "You can have it. I have an extra. I left the toothpaste in the bathroom."

I grabbed the toothbrush and got up.

With ten minutes, my teeth were brushed, I was back in Raina's clothes, and we were in the car on our way to Virginia. We still had another four hours until we got to my parents' house, and I was anxious to put more distance between us and St. Augustine, where Henley was likely still on a manhunt.

"Can I ask you a question?" I asked, realizing I still had so many unanswered questions about Michael and I was running out of time with him.

"Of course," Michael replied.

"How did you escape Henley?"

"At night, they would lock us in our rooms, and Henley would have a security guard and a scientist on duty to watch over things. One night, the security guard who was supposed to be on duty with Alexander called in with food poisoning. While he was waiting for the backup to come in, Alexander seized the opportunity and took us out of there."

"I can't blame him based on that video you showed me," I said.

He shifted uncomfortably in his seat.

I followed it up with a question that I wasn't sure I wanted the answer to. "Was that when he decided to do it? Was that the final straw for him?"

Michael glanced at me, and I could tell he was debating on whether or not to answer my question.

"It was, but there was also something else," he replied, clearly hesitant. "Chad Henley felt that Raina and I were close to reaching our maximum potential, and he wasn't happy with what he considered to be our limitations."

He looked over at me again, and I nodded in encouragement for him to continue. "Alexander found out that Henley had started making plans. He planned to terminate us if our children proved to have stronger abilities than us."

Unable to wrap my head around Henley's plan to *terminate* him, I decided to address the other disturbing piece of the story. "Your children? She's your sister!" I protested, stating the obvious.

"She's not my biological sister. We had different donors," he clarified. "When Alexander created us, Henley specified he wanted a male and a female from different donors but told Alexander it was because he wanted to see if one came out with stronger capabilities than the other. But that was never his true intention."

"So, you and Raina are meant to be together," I said, hoping I didn't sound as deflated as I felt. "You were literally created to be together." It now made sense why Raina hated me so much.

"No," he said quickly. "She's my sister. In every way that matters, she is my sister. We've never had those kinds of feelings toward each other. *Ever*. It would be like someone telling you that you were meant to be with Seth."

He looked over at me to make sure I believed him, and I did. But just because he felt that way about Raina didn't mean she felt the same way about him.

"Raina and I almost ran away once, before Alexander got us out of there," he told me, changing the subject. "They used to keep us locked in our rooms at all times, but one night, a really bad storm came through and knocked out all of the power in the building. For some reason, I decided to check the door to my room and found that it wasn't locked. I went down the hall, and Raina's door was unlocked too. No one knew but us. We could've walked right out of there."

"Did you get caught?" I asked. "Is that why you couldn't escape?"

"No. Raina was scared to leave, and I couldn't leave her by herself," he replied. I frowned, and he continued, "You have to understand; that's all we knew. Raina was terrified that the outside world could be worse. It was even hard for us to imagine an outside world. We had no concept of what that would be like. It's not like we had TV or books or anything that would give us insight into an outside world."

Michael got off at the next exit and pulled into a gas station. As he got out to pump gas, I took a deep breath, trying to relax. I'd tried my best to censor my reactions because I wanted him to be honest with me, but it broke my heart to think about all that he'd been through. It made me angry that someone like Chad Henley was walking free while Michael and his family had to live their lives on the run.

This whole time, I'd feared Michael going back into captivity to be tortured for the sake of research, but now, I realized he faced an even grimmer possibility. If Henley captured Michael and succeeded in creating someone with stronger abilities, Henley would kill him. I shook my head, trying to remove the thought.

Michael got back in the car. "What's on your mind?"

I couldn't tell him what I was really thinking. I didn't want to think it, much less say it out loud. "What, um, should I do about the people back home?" I asked, avoiding his question with another question. "It's almost time for my shift. Jen and Carl are going to wonder where I am."

He contemplated this as he put his seat belt on and started up the car. "The safest thing for you is to have no contact, but your parents are friends with Seth's parents, right?" he asked, and I nodded. "It will probably get back to them anyway that you are there. Can you trust Seth and Jen not to tell anyone where you are?"

I nodded again, but he didn't look fully convinced.

He reached over and opened the glove box. Inside were six cell phones. He pulled one out and handed it to me.

I called Jen first. Seth was with her, so she put me on speakerphone. At least I could get this over with in one call.

"How did it go?" she asked. "Did you make up with Michael?"

"Um, it's complicated," I said. "I need you to do me a favor."

"What's wrong?" Seth asked, knowing me all too well. He knew something was up.

"I am going to my parents' for a little while, but if anyone asks you where I am, I need you to tell them you don't know. It doesn't matter who asks. You can't tell them where I am," I said.

"Are you in some kind of trouble?" Seth asked, and I cringed at the alarm in his voice. The last thing I wanted to do was make him worry. "Natalie, what's going on?"

"I'm okay. I need some time away to clear my head. It would just be better to do that without any distractions."

There was silence on the other end of the phone, and I wondered if the call had disconnected. Or maybe they'd muted themselves.

"You would tell me if you needed help, right?" Seth finally asked.

"I would," I assured him. "Right now, I just need your word that you won't tell anyone where I am."

Seth and Jen reluctantly agreed to my request. Before hanging up, they made me promise to call and check in periodically, so they would know I was safe. I wasn't sure when that would be feasible, but I promised.

"That was harder than I'd thought," I told Michael as I hung up and dialed the number to the café.

Carl answered the phone, and that call went more smoothly. Since Carl had no idea where my parents lived, I didn't have to worry about him accidentally sending Henley in their direction. I told Carl that I needed time off to tend to a family emergency and asked him to keep it confidential. Carl agreed, and although I didn't have the same level of trust with Carl that I had with Seth and Jen, I sensed that he was sincere and would respect my privacy.

"Do you really think I'll be able to go back once this all blows over?" I asked Michael after I hung up the phone.

"I would prefer you didn't, just to be safe," he replied. "But I do think Henley will eventually move on. They will start asking around about me and Raina, and pretty soon, they will find out where we worked, where we lived, and conclude that we are long gone. They will leave St. Augustine and start the hunt all over again."

I hoped he was right. I wanted to be able to go back. It wouldn't be the same without Michael, but at least I could be with my friends. It was ironic how I'd moved to St. Augustine, so I could be alone, and here I was, longing to go back to avoid loneliness.

We reached the Richmond city limits, and I started to feel anxious about seeing my parents. I wished I could've given them some notice that I was on my way, but it would have only concerned them more if I'd called them from a number they didn't recognize. It was three days until Thanksgiving, so they would probably think I'd come home for the holiday. It would be difficult to explain to them why I couldn't stay.

I also wasn't sure how they were going to react to me showing up with Michael. I'd never had a real boyfriend, and with the exception of Seth, I'd never had any close male friends. It was going to be a lot for them to take in. I tried to envision how that introduction would go.

Should I introduce him as Michael or by another name? Is that even his real name? Does he change it everywhere he goes?

"Are you going to change your name?" I asked, although I doubted he'd tell me what his new name was going to be.

"Just my last name. Raina and I keep our first names. I know it's risky, but it's the first thing we were able to choose for ourselves, and our parents insist that we keep it," he replied.

"What was your name before you left Henley?"

"At Henley, we didn't have names." He was so matter-of-fact with his response, but I sat there, dumbfounded.

Even though Chad Henley had had a hand in bringing their lives into the world, he clearly didn't view them as people. He couldn't—

or wouldn't—look past his selfish ambitions long enough to see their human lives.

Michael exited the interstate to go to my parents' house, and I directed him to their neighborhood. It looked exactly the same.

Each lot sat on about two acres, and every home had been custom-built. It was quiet and peaceful; you'd never suspect anything bad ever happened here. Outsiders would never know that every home had installed a private gated entry at the end of their driveway after the intruder came into our home. Seth's house had been the only one with a gated entry prior to Becca's kidnapping.

We passed Seth's parents' house on the right. Behind the black wrought iron fence was their gray four-story Queen Anne–style Victorian home. I used to have a dollhouse that looked just like it, except it was pink. At the base of the driveway were two stone pillars, each topped with black ravens standing guard. The image of the raven on my dashboard after the accident flashed in my mind, but I quickly forced it out of my head.

"It's two houses down on the left," I told Michael. "The one with the brick privacy wall."

You couldn't see our house from the road now that the privacy wall was there. My mother had insisted on having it installed to ensure that whoever had taken Becca wouldn't come back one night and take me. As crazy as it might seem, that never worried me. If they wanted me, they would have taken me while I was unconscious.

Michael pulled into the driveway and stopped at the closed gate. He rolled down his window, and I gave him the passcode to open it. Fortunately, my parents hadn't changed the number, and it still worked. Michael drove down the brick-paved driveway until we reached the house.

"Ready?" he asked.

I nodded. I wasn't sure if I was, but we'd come too far to turn around. I needed to see them and make sure they knew I was okay before I disappeared for a while. It was the right thing to do.

We got out of the car, and I just stood there, staring up at my childhood home. It was a three-story brick home with black shutters and white columns on the front porch. I recalled how I'd turned around to look at it one last time before I left for Florida, and I'd honestly thought it'd be the last time I ever saw it. I had been in so much pain at the time that I couldn't imagine ever coming back.

With one foot in front of the other, I forced myself to climb the four steps up to the front door. I paused when I reached the door, debating on what to do. I still had a key to the house, but it didn't feel right to use it. I didn't technically live there anymore, and since we were showing up, unannounced, I didn't want to scare anyone. I decided to ring the doorbell and just use the key if no one answered.

There was no answer after the first ring, so I tried again. A few seconds later, I saw the silhouette of a figure approaching through the glass door. I braced myself as I realized it was my mother.

The door opened, and my mother stood there, silent and confused. I could tell she'd never imagined that I'd just show up unexpectedly. Her emerald eyes looked me up and down, and I knew she was thinking that I didn't look like myself—because I didn't.

"Natalie," she managed to say just above a whisper.

"Hi, Mother."

Before I could contemplate what to say or do next, she took two steps toward me and pulled me into a tight embrace. I hugged her back and fought the tears welling in my eyes. It felt good to hug her, and I hadn't realized how much I'd missed it. Out of the corner of my eye, I saw Michael smiling at us.

Mother pulled away. "I can't believe you're really here," she said as she smoothed my hair.

"It's good to see you," I said.

"And who is this?" she asked, looking at Michael.

"This is my friend Michael."

Michael reached out and shook her hand.

"We're heading to New York to visit his grandparents, so I thought we'd stop by and say hi," I told her.

Mother skeptically eyed me for a second, and even though I was pretty sure she knew I was lying, she decided to just focus on the fact that I was home and didn't question it.

"Of course," she said. "Come on in. Are you hungry?"

"Starving," I said. I couldn't even remember the last time I had eaten something.

Michael and I followed her into the house, through the entryway, living room, and into the kitchen. She must have just finished lunch because there were still sandwich ingredients sitting out on the counter. I grabbed two plates out of the cabinet and made turkey and Swiss cheese sandwiches for me and Michael.

I took a bite of the sandwich, and my mother watched me as if she thought I would disappear into thin air. She gave me a half-smile, her mind obviously preoccupied. She looked good though. Much better than when I'd left. The bags under her eyes were gone, and instead of wearing her pajamas all day, she was dressed nicely in a pair of black pants and a silky violet button-down shirt.

"I'm going to get your father," she said as Michael and I finished our lunch.

"He's home?" I asked, surprised.

Mother bit her lip. "We're supposed to be leaving for Greece tonight. We fly out at five this evening. We'll be there for three weeks. We didn't think you were coming home for Thanksgiving, so we decided to make it a second honeymoon."

"Oh, wow," I replied. "That's amazing."

When I'd left, we could barely get my mother out of the house, and now, she was going all the way to Greece.

"We can postpone it though, if you want," Mother offered.

I could tell she was conflicted about me being there.

"No, please don't," I insisted. "We can only stay the night anyway—and we can stay in a hotel if you're leaving tonight."

"Nonsense," she replied. "This is still your home, Natalie. It always will be."

Mother left the kitchen to get Dad, and I put our plates in the dishwasher.

"So far, so good?" Michael asked once Mother was out of earshot.

"Better than good," I confirmed.

A minute later, Dad walked into the kitchen.

"It's about time you came home," he said as I stood up and gave him a hug. He kissed me on the top of my head.

"Dad, this is Michael," I said.

"Nice to meet you, sir," Michael said as he shook my dad's hand.

"You didn't come here to tell me you two had eloped, did you?" Dad asked him.

"No, sir."

"Then, it's nice to meet you too," Dad said with a smile.

A little while later, we went outside and got Michael's suitcase out of the car. Mother asked where mine was, and once again, I lied and

149

told her that I'd accidentally left it at home. It was far-fetched, but it was the best I could come up with.

"Can I talk to you a second?" Mother asked me.

Dad offered to show Michael to the guest room to give us some privacy.

Mother pulled me into the living room and motioned for me to sit with her on the couch. I knew she thought my story didn't add up and wanted clarity on what was really going on. Unfortunately, there was no way I could tell her the truth. I just hoped I could find a way to put her mind at ease. That was the whole point of coming home to see her in the first place.

"I need to ask you something, and please tell me the truth," she said, and I braced myself. "Are you and Michael living together?"

"What? No!" I said, shocked. "Why would you think that?"

She sighed with relief. "Well, you show up out of the blue, in love with this guy, heading up north to meet his family, and you only have one suitcase. You can't blame me for thinking that maybe you were living together."

"It's not like that at all. Michael is just a friend." Even though it was true, it felt like a lie.

She narrowed her eyes at me, debating on whether or not to believe me. "Okay, if you say so." She didn't sound convinced.

"We're *not* living together," I insisted.

"I do believe that," she said with a sincere smile.

I looked around the living room, taking in the familiarity of it. Everything was so pristine, so perfect. There wasn't one stain on either of the white couches, not one scuff on the hardwood floor or one speck of dust on the coffee table. I noticed the family pictures sitting on the fireplace mantel and immediately looked away.

I glanced down at my watch and realized that my parents would be leaving for the airport soon. It would be my last opportunity to have a heart-to-heart with my mother for quite some time.

"I'm sorry for the way I left," I told her.

She turned to me, no doubt surprised by my openness.

"And I'm sorry that I haven't called."

"I'm sorry too," she replied, taking my hand into hers. "After you left, I had a lot of time to think and reflect on how we'd left things. I'd thought I was doing the right thing as a mother, by trying to protect you, but all I had done was drive you away."

"I know you were just trying to protect me."

Mother shook her head and squeezed my hand tighter. "I never told you this, but after we lost Becca, I had this dream that you died in a car accident."

My stomach dropped, and I shifted uncomfortably in my seat.

"It felt so real that I was terrified to let you out of my sight," she continued. "Every day, you'd leave for school, and I'd watch the clock, just waiting for you to come home. I thought if I kept you close, I could keep you safe. I realize now that it was an irrational fear, and it wasn't fair to you."

"Do you still have that dream?"

Her dream has to be a strange coincidence, right?

"I don't," she replied. "They stopped about a month ago."

Dad and Michael came into the living room, carrying several suitcases and travel bags.

"Maureen, we need to load up the car and head to the airport if we're going to make our flight," Dad said.

Mother turned to me, and I nodded encouragingly at her.

"Go and have a great time," I told her. "I'll be back to visit as soon as I can. I promise."

FOURTEEN

I stood at the bottom of the staircase, afraid to take the first step to go upstairs. I looked over at Michael, positive that he must think I was crazy, but there was no trace of judgment from him.

"You can do this," he told me. "You're ready."

I nodded, trying to convince myself. Slowly, I took a step and then a second. Each step got a little easier.

Michael was right behind me as I stopped halfway up the staircase, eye-level with a collage of family pictures.

Over the past several years, I'd walked by them, deliberately avoiding looking at them. This time, I decided to stop and acknowledge them. I was face-to-face with Becca's last school picture. She smiled warmly, and her eyes were so bright, so full of life.

"I can see the resemblance," he said, and he was right.

Becca's hair was darker and her smile wider than mine, but you could easily tell that we were sisters. We both had our mother's green eyes.

Next to her class picture was mine from the same year. I looked happy, completely unaware of how much my life would be changing only a few months later. I'd had several class pictures since then, but my parents never replaced this one. I thought it was because they wanted to remember me this way.

I took a deep breath and continued up the stairs.

To the far right of the hallway was Becca's room, and to the far left was mine. As much as I wanted to go to my room and change into my own clothes, I turned right instead. If I was going to face this, there was no point in delaying it.

We walked to the closed door that led into Becca's old bedroom.

"This is where it happened," I told him.

The memory of waking up after the intruder had knocked me unconscious and realizing that Becca was gone replayed in my mind. I sat down on the floor with my back against the wall, on the spot where I'd woken up after the attack.

Michael joined me on the floor but didn't say anything. He just sat with me while my fingers traced the seams in the wood floor.

"You would think that what happened right here would've been the scariest part for me," I said after a few minutes. "Knowing that someone had been in my house and could have taken me or killed me, but that really wasn't it. It was the fact that I was helpless. I was useless."

I looked up to see Michael watching me, listening attentively. Something in his eyes urged me to continue.

"After Becca was taken, I would just spend hours alone in my room, meditating, trying to trigger something in my intuition that would tell me where she was. When that didn't work, I would just randomly roam through the woods or the mall or nearby neighborhoods, hoping that she would magically appear. I couldn't find her though, and I felt helpless. I'm still terrified of that feeling."

"Helpless is the last thing that comes to mind when I think about you," he said. "You're so much stronger than you realize."

I laid my head on his shoulder. *How can I explain to him that I feel helpless right now, that I know I'm going to lose him soon and there's nothing I can do to change it?*

The doorbell rang, and I lifted my head. Michael and I looked at each other, eyes wide. It was now after nine p.m., and I had no idea who could be stopping by at this hour.

"Henley wouldn't ring the doorbell," I reasoned as we stood up. "But maybe you should stay here just in case."

"Just in case, I'm coming with you," he insisted.

The doorbell rang again, and we walked downstairs to the foyer. We gave each other one last look, preparing for the worst as I opened the door. Standing on the front stoop was Seth's dad, which made sense because he knew the code to the gate. In fact, Seth's family had keys to our house, and he could have just walked in if he'd wanted to.

"Natalie," he warmly greeted me. "Your dad told me you were here, but I had to see for myself."

"Hi, Mr. Weber," I replied, relieved that it was him. "Would you like to come in?"

Mr. Weber looked past me and saw Michael standing by the staircase. "No, that's okay." He handed me a manila folder. "I just needed to drop this off for your dad. He'll need it when he gets back from his trip."

"I'll leave it on his desk," I told him.

"Your dad says you're just passing through?" Mr. Weber asked.

"Yes," I replied. "We're just staying the night and heading out in the morning."

"I spoke to Seth this morning, and strangely, he didn't tell me you were coming into town," Mr. Weber said.

I shifted awkwardly on my feet. "It was kind of a spontaneous road trip."

Mr. Weber smiled. "Of course. I remember being young once. Where are you headed?"

"To New York to visit my friend's grandparents," I replied, motioning to Michael.

"Well, I'll leave you kids to it. Safe travels," Mr. Weber said.

"Bye," I told him, and he walked down the front steps, back to his car.

I closed the door.

"Seth's dad," I explained to Michael.

"You were right about Seth," he said. "He can definitely keep a secret if he didn't even tell his own father."

I placed the paperwork on my dad's desk, and Michael and I headed back upstairs. This time, I turned left at the top of the stairs.

"This is my room," I told him as I opened the door.

I half-expected that my parents had transformed my bedroom into a home gym or another guest room when I moved out, but I was pleasantly surprised to find they hadn't changed a thing.

The walls of my bedroom were still painted a light gray, a nice contrast to my all-white furniture, white curtains, and white bedspread. On top of the bed were bright yellow pillows and a dark gray cable-knit blanket. A large painting of colorful wildflowers hung above my bed. There were no photos of family or friends in my room, but a display of trophies and awards that sat on a shelf above my desk was evidence that I'd once lived there.

"Honor student, science award, soccer trophy," he said, reading from the various items on the shelf. "Smart *and* a jock," he concluded with a smile.

"Yeah, that was a long time ago," I said, slightly embarrassed.

I'd never had a guy in my bedroom—with the exception of Seth, but he didn't count.

"No pictures of ex-boyfriends?" Michael asked.

"No," I replied. "No boyfriends."

And it was true with the exception of Zac Bates, my first and only boyfriend in the eighth grade. We had been young, and it wasn't serious. We'd broken up two months before Becca's disappearance.

Right before she'd disappeared, I had been interested in another boy in my class, Craig Talbot, but I'd stopped talking to him when I returned to school. I'd stopped talking to him just like I'd stopped talking to everyone else in my life.

"I find that hard to believe," he said as he sat down in the desk chair.

"How about you?" I asked, although I wasn't sure I wanted to know. "I bet you've left a trail of broken hearts throughout the United States."

He laughed. "Dating isn't exactly an option for me. I wouldn't want to date someone that I couldn't be honest with, and, *Hi, my name is Michael, and I was born a lab rat,* isn't really a great pick-up line."

I hadn't thought of it like that. I'd always noticed the way girls looked at Michael and assumed he had a long line of ex-girlfriends still swooning over him.

Michael stood up, and I felt nervous.

"We should probably get some sleep," he said, breaking my train of thought. "We should plan to get on the road early tomorrow."

"Okay," I replied. Before I could overthink it, I walked over to him, put my arms around his neck, and hugged him. "Thank you for everything. I couldn't have done this without you."

Michael put his arms around my waist, tightly hugging me back. He buried his face in my hair. He gave me another squeeze and then released me before taking a deliberate step back.

"I'll see you in the morning," he said before leaving to go sleep in the guest bedroom. It was in the next room, but for some reason, it felt too far away.

After Michael went to bed, I went downstairs and double-checked all of the locks on the doors. I wanted to set the alarm, but I wasn't sure if my parents had changed the code.

I went back upstairs to get ready for bed. I took a quick shower and put on an oversize T-shirt and a pair of yoga pants. Feeling relaxed for the first time in two days, I yawned and climbed into bed.

I didn't even realize that I'd drifted off to sleep until I recognized that I was in a dream. It was my usual nightmare, and I was in the woods by my house, chasing after the faceless man who'd taken Becca. I was in a long nightgown, the type I had worn when I was a little girl, and barefoot.

"Stop! Come back!" I yelled.

I was running as fast as I could, but the man was always just out of reach. He darted behind a large tree. I stopped running and slowly walked around to the other side of the tree, trying to sneak up on him, but when I got to the other side, he was already gone.

This was taking a different turn from my usual dream.

As I stared into the darkness, trying to understand where he had gone, I felt a tap on my shoulder. I turned around to see Becca standing in front of me. I took a step closer, ready to throw my arms around her but she stopped me.

"You need to go," she said.

"I don't want to go," I protested.

It was rare that I dreamed I was talking to Becca. Even though it wasn't real, I didn't want it to end.

"Natalie, they are coming," she replied firmly. "You need to go. Now!"

Instantly, I woke up, my heart pounding. My stomach started twisting into a knot.

This can't be happening again.

I jumped out of bed and dashed out of my room. The door to the guest bedroom was closed. For a split second, I recalled how I had been confronted by the intruder when I got to Becca's room. I only hesitated for a second before throwing open the door to the guest bedroom. Michael heard me enter his room and immediately woke up.

"What's wrong?" he asked, sitting up.

"We need to go," I told him. "Henley knows you're here, and he's coming."

He climbed out of bed, wearing nothing, except a pair of boxers. He quickly pulled on a shirt and a pair of jeans.

"Go put on your shoes but don't turn on any lights," he said.

I ran back to my room. I didn't bother to change. I just threw on a pair of shoes, put on a jacket, and slung my crossbody purse over my shoulder. Michael was waiting for me in the hall when I got there.

He took me by the hand and silently led the way down the stairs. We stopped at the bottom of the staircase, listening for anything out of the ordinary but only heard silence.

"Do you have a back door?" he whispered.

I nodded and pointed back toward the kitchen.

We quietly made our way through the kitchen to the laundry room, where there was a door leading out to the backyard. We stepped outside, and I closed the door behind us.

Michael and I hurried along the side of the house and crouched behind a bush. I could see Michael's truck in the driveway, but I knew he wanted to make sure no one was out there, waiting for us. I didn't see anyone, but the knot in my stomach hadn't gone away, so I believed we were still in danger.

Without saying a word, Michael pulled the car key from his pocket and pointed to the truck. I nodded. He reached out his hand and held up one finger and then two. On three, we were both up and sprinting toward the truck. When we were almost to the truck, Michael hit the button on the key to unlock and start the truck. We both jumped in, and the second my door shut, Michael slammed on the gas to get us turned around and out of the driveway.

As we reached the end of the driveway, I noticed the gate was already open, which was strange. Maybe it was still open from when Mr. Weber had visited earlier. Or maybe Henley was already here. Either way, I didn't want to stay and find out. The tires of the truck squealed as Michael turned onto the road leading out of the neighborhood.

Michael looked in his rearview mirror. "There's someone behind us."

I looked out the passenger-side mirror.

"It doesn't mean it's them," he added as I spotted a pair of headlights in the distance behind us.

It was too dark, and the car was still too far away to tell if it was them.

Michael made the turn onto the main road leading back to the interstate, and the car behind us turned as well. It still didn't mean it was Henley though. Almost everyone leaving the neighborhood had to turn in this direction to get into town.

To test them further, Michael made the next right, heading down a less populated street that didn't lead to the interstate. The car, still a good distance behind us, made the turn as well.

Michael and I exchanged a nervous look.

Michael then turned left, down a much more secluded street that didn't have any houses. We passed an auto body shop that was closed, and everything past that was just woods.

The car turned down the street behind us, and Michael hit the accelerator, now confident they really were following us. The speed limit on the street was forty-five, but we were closing in on seventy miles per hour. I glanced behind us again, and the car was speeding up, clearly trying to keep us in eyeshot.

Michael slammed on the brakes and made a sharp right turn. For a moment, I was afraid the truck was going to tip over. I held on to the grab bar above the window until we were through the turn. Michael immediately hit the accelerator again until he hit eighty miles per hour on the empty street.

Michael made another sharp right turn, and I heard the brakes screech on the car behind us as it tried to slow down enough to make the turn. It overshot the turn, and the driver had to stop and slam the car in reverse to turn onto the road. Before they were in view again, Michael intentionally veered off the road into the woods. We barely missed the trees as they whipped by us. I closed my eyes, terrified of hitting a tree the way I had the night Michael had to save me.

A second later, Michael stopped the truck and shut it off. I opened my eyes and saw Michael turned around in his seat, waiting to see what would happen next. He had one hand on the ignition, waiting to turn it back on if needed, although I wasn't sure where we would go. We would only be able to go so far into the woods in such a large vehicle.

I turned around in my seat as well, eager to see what was going on. I couldn't make out the road, but I did see headlights heading parallel to where we were, which meant the car was on the street we'd just left. I held my breath, waiting to see if they would spot us.

The car picked up speed and zipped past the opening we had taken into the woods. They thought we were still on the road.

I let out a sigh of relief and looked at Michael. "That was close."

"Too close," he replied.

"How did they figure out where we were? We were so careful. Do you think it's possible they were following us the whole time?" I asked.

"I don't think so."

We sat there until we were confident the coast was clear. Michael carefully drove us out of the woods and then turned back onto the road. Instead of turning the direction we had originally been going, he turned in the opposite direction.

"Reach into the glove box and pull out a phone," he said.

I opened the glove box. "Does it matter which one?"

"Use any, except the one you used earlier today," he replied, and I selected a phone. "Send a text message to a contact named Cliff. That will go to Alexander's friend, Stan. Text: *Swap R-K-V-A*."

I did as he'd requested. "What does that mean?" I asked.

Michael turned onto the interstate.

"We have to get another car, or we'll never make it to Kentucky," he replied. "Once Stan receives that, he'll have a car ready for us in Roanoke in less than an hour."

It was the middle of the night, and I was about to voice my concern about Stan sleeping through the message when the phone chimed with an incoming text message. The message didn't make any sense to me, but I read it aloud, "*H-R-G-Y-T-K*."

Michael nodded. "Good. He'll have it waiting for us off the exit in a hotel parking lot on the right side when we get off the interstate in Roanoke. We'll be looking for a gray truck."

"Wow, I can't believe he got it set up that fast," I said. "Does he know the whole story about your family?"

"He does," he replied. "Stan was Alexander's best friend, growing up. He was the only person my family trusted to help us disappear, but it hasn't been easy for him. His relationship with us could easily be discovered by Henley, and they would come after him the same way they came after you."

"But sometimes, you have to do the right thing for the people you care about regardless of the consequences," I said.

Michael tightened his hands on the steering wheel. "But you shouldn't take unnecessary risks."

I didn't respond.

"I mean it, Natalie," he continued, sounding almost angry with me. "I have to know you are going to be careful once I leave. No more jumping off bridges. No using your abilities. If you draw unwanted attention to yourself, Henley will come after you."

I wanted to reassure him, but I couldn't. There were so many scenarios where I could see myself breaking that promise.

"I can't control what I don't understand," I told him instead. "I don't know how to turn my abilities on or off. It's not like they came with an instruction manual."

He shifted in his seat, and I knew he saw my point even though he didn't like it.

"I didn't say anything before because I would prefer that you not use your abilities at all, but there is a way for you to practice with less risk of being detected. Maybe practicing a little wouldn't be a terrible idea, so you can feel more in control of them."

"Okay," I replied. "How do I do that?"

"You can practice during thunderstorms, but there has to be lightning. Henley's detection devices get thrown off by the electricity in the lightning," he explained. "But this doesn't mean you can go crazy. Practice in short bursts, and don't do it every time it storms. Never practice where anyone else can see you, and don't practice healing because that involves another person. If someone sees you and word gets out, it's just a matter of time before Henley finds out. Got it?"

"Okay. What about mind reading?" I asked. "Would that require a thunderstorm?"

Michael gave me a nervous look. "Do you want to try that again?"

"Not really," I replied honestly. "I think it's more of wanting to know how to control it in case it somehow turns itself back on again. I want to be able to turn it off."

He contemplated this for a second and then replied, "I don't know how that works exactly, but Alexander seemed to think it was undetectable by Henley because it's not projecting anything outward. I didn't talk to Alexander about your intuition, but I don't think that would be detectable either."

If neither Michael nor Raina had the ability to read minds, I wondered how Alexander could be confident it was undetectable. I decided to just wait and test it out during a thunderstorm for the first time, just to be safe.

"Did Alexander say anything else when you told him about my new abilities?" I asked, intrigued by the possibility of learning to control them.

Michael pulled his lips into a thin line, and I could tell he was holding out on me.

"What?"

"Like I said, I didn't tell him about your intuition, but I think you're right about how you inherited your new abilities," he said.

"You do think it's connected to my intuition somehow?"

"We're able to use our abilities because we can tap into a part of our brains that most people can't access. When I healed you, I activated that part of your brain," he replied.

"But you said you've healed your mom before, and she's never developed any abilities."

He nodded in agreement. "You're right. When I healed you, I transferred some of my energy to you. That's really all my ability boils down to. Transmitting energy in a different way than most people can. The difference between you and my mom is that the energy remained. You absorbed it, and it stayed with you. Alexander says that doesn't normally happen."

"If you didn't tell Alexander about my intuition, does he have any theories on why the energy remained with me?" I asked, hoping it would shed some light on why I had any abilities, including my intuition. *Why me?*

He sighed and pushed his head back further into the headrest. "He does." He paused, but I remained silent, waiting for him to continue. "He thinks you might be a course correction."

"A course correction for what?"

"For me and Raina," he replied, his eyes fixed firmly on the road. "For our existence. We were never meant to be born, much less with the abilities we have. We were never meant to have an unnatural advantage."

"He thinks it's some type of evolution," I said quietly, processing the theory.

As I pondered Alexander's theory, the less it sat well with me. Although the science of it made sense, the part where Michael believed he should never have been born bothered me. This was bigger than just science. It had to be.

Regardless of how he had come into the world or how extraordinary he was, Michael was a living, breathing human being. He was more than just his abilities. He was caring and resilient and brave. Those weren't traits that could be created in a lab.

There was no way we had been brought together by accident or merely the result of something as simplistic as cause and effect. I had to believe that we'd met for a reason and that this hadn't all been a product of chance. Maybe Michael and I had been brought together for a reason far greater than we were able to comprehend at the moment. Maybe we had been brought together for a reason far greater than science could explain.

FIFTEEN

"I wish you had gotten some sleep," I told Michael as I pulled into Aunt Gael's driveway.

We'd been in the car for a total of seven hours after switching out vehicles in Roanoke. I managed to sleep a little right after that, but when I woke up around eight o'clock this morning, Michael was exhausted, so I insisted on taking over driving. With my track record, it took a lot of convincing, but eventually, he agreed. As much as I'd tried to reassure him that I wouldn't wreck the car, he'd refused to sleep.

"I'm good," he stubbornly insisted as he got out of the car.

There was a blue sedan in the driveway, which I assumed belonged to Aunt Gael. We walked up to her house, a beautiful two-story white cottage with a wraparound porch. I knocked on the door without knowing exactly what I was going to say when I saw her.

Aunt Gael opened the door, and although I knew she was surprised to see me, she smiled wide with excitement. Before she could say anything, I apologized for unexpectedly showing up.

"Oh, please," she replied with a laugh. "Family doesn't need an invitation. Come on in." She stepped aside and motioned for us to enter the house.

We walked into the living room, which had so much color and personality, just like Aunt Gael. Even though Aunt Gael was my mother's younger sister, she was the polar opposite. Mother was controlled and organized. Aunt Gael was more of a laid-back free spirit. She just took life as it came.

Although their personalities were very different, Mother and Aunt Gael did look a lot alike. Aunt Gael was about ten years younger than Mother, but she looked a lot like Mother had at her age.

They had the same prominent cheekbones and button-shaped noses. They also had the same shade of strawberry-blonde hair, and even though Aunt Gael's was flat-ironed straight, I knew it was naturally curly like Mother's.

I introduced Aunt Gael to Michael, and she motioned for us to sit on the couch, which was black-and-white striped and decorated with bright pink-and-white fuzzy pillows.

"What brings you by?" she asked, sitting across from us in a black velvet armchair.

"Actually," I said, sitting up a little straighter, "I was hoping you wouldn't mind if I stayed here for a little while. Maybe a month?"

"Or two," Michael chimed in. Aunt Gael curiously looked at him, and he quickly clarified, "Just her though. I'll be leaving tomorrow."

My heart sank when I heard him say it.

"Okay ..." Aunt Gael replied, but I could tell she was processing the request, not really answering the question. "Does your mom know?"

"No," I replied. "And I kind of need it to be our secret."

It was a long shot to ask this of her, but it was much safer if my parents didn't know where I was. If Henley was watching them when they returned from Greece and thought they knew where I was, it would put them in danger.

Aunt Gael skeptically eyed me, and I was worried she was going to say no.

"I get it," she said, to my surprise. "She drives me crazy too. Believe me, I also wanted some space from her back in the day. Sure, you can stay."

I let out a small sigh of relief, and out of the corner of my eye, I could see the tension release from Michael's posture.

"I'll show you to the guest rooms," Aunt Gael said, standing up.

We followed Aunt Gael down a narrow hallway. "The bathroom is on the left, my bedroom is at the end of the hall, and your bedrooms are on the right." She stopped outside the first door on the right. "Natalie, you can stay in here in the guest bedroom, and, Michael, since you're only here the one night, you can stay on the pullout futon in the office." She pointed to the second door on the right, which I assumed was where her office was.

As if she already knew I didn't have anything, Aunt Gael asked me if I'd brought any luggage. I repeated my same story about forgetting my suitcase.

Aunt Gael gave me a funny look but didn't press the issue.

"Well, there is a shopping center about two miles away that has pretty much anything you'd need," she said, turning to head back into the living room.

Aunt Gael offered to heat us up some leftover sweet and sour chicken for lunch, and we were only a few bites in when she announced there was chocolate silk pie in the fridge for dessert later.

"I think your aunt is my food soul mate," Michael whispered to me, making me giggle.

"I need to check in on the store, and then I have book club tonight," Aunt Gael announced as Michael and I washed our dishes from lunch. I'd forgotten that she owned a bookstore. "And by book club, I mean, I get together with my girlfriends, talk about a book for five minutes, and then spend the rest of the evening drinking wine."

Aunt Gael gave me a spare key to the house before she left and provided directions to the shopping center. She also recommended a restaurant called The Backyard for dinner. "It's a nice, romantic atmosphere, and they have live music outside," she said with a grin.

I glanced over at Michael, and he seemed unfazed, so I just nodded in agreement with her suggestion.

Shortly after Aunt Gael left, Michael and I headed to the shopping center. I could tell that shopping wasn't his favorite thing to do, but I was glad that he hadn't asked to stay home while I went. It was our last day together, and I wanted to spend every minute I could with him.

Our first stop was the drugstore to pick up some basic toiletries like toothpaste and shampoo. Next, we went to a clothing store, and I did my best to quickly pick out a few basic items to get me through a couple of days. I could always come back later in the week to buy more. As I walked to the register, carrying my new jeans, shirts, boots, pajamas, and socks, I discreetly scooped up a couple of bras and several pairs of panties and shoved them into my pile.

Even though our situation was far from ordinary, it felt nice to do something normal with Michael, like shopping. Aside from our evening eating pizza and riding the carousel, everything we'd done up to this point was tainted with some kind of an abnormal distraction.

The masquerade had been a disaster with Lance and Ben trying to drug me and Jen. Then, our pancake breakfast had been overshadowed by the Henley sighting, which wasn't likely a false alarm after all. And of course, there had been the bonfire where we realized for the first time that I'd inherited Michael's healing abilities.

I paid for my new clothes, and we headed back to Aunt Gael's, so I could take a shower and change out of my T-shirt and yoga pants from the night before.

When I was finished with my shower, I dressed in one of my new outfits—a pair of jeans and an oversize black sweater that wanted to fall off my right shoulder. As I began to towel-dry my hair, I wandered into the living room, expecting to see Michael hanging out, watching TV, but he wasn't there. I went into the kitchen, thinking maybe he decided to sample the chocolate pie that Aunt Gael had mentioned, but he wasn't there either.

My heart began to race as I considered the possibility that maybe he'd left without saying good-bye. I sprinted to the front door and threw it open.

I let out a sigh of relief when I saw his car was still in the driveway.

The door to Aunt Gael's home office was partially open, so I knocked lightly and slowly opened it. Michael was asleep on the futon, and despite being a light sleeper, he didn't wake up to the sound of me coming into the room. I stood there for a minute, watching him take in deep, peaceful breaths.

I quietly backed out of the room and closed the door behind me, not wanting to disturb him. He was exhausted, and there was no telling how long he'd be driving by himself to his next destination tomorrow.

I walked back to the living room, but I wasn't in the mood to watch TV, so I wandered over to the bookcase. Maybe I could find something interesting to read to pass the time until Michael woke up.

I searched the first shelf filled with various romance novels, which were definitely not my thing. The second shelf had mysteries and thrillers. A mystery might be a possibility, but I decided to keep looking. I started looking through the bottom shelf of nonfiction books when a book titled *Keen Intuition* caught my eye. I pulled the book off the shelf and sat down on the couch.

The book was written by a psychiatrist named Dr. Patrice Keen and was based not only on her studies on the subject, but also her personal experiences. I opened up the book and was only a few pages in when I stopped on a quote from Albert Einstein. It said, *I believe in intuition and inspiration. Imagination is more important than knowledge. For knowledge is limited, whereas imagination embraces the entire world, stimulating progress, giving birth to evolution.*

The author went on to express how she viewed her intuition as a gift—a way to not only listen to her instincts, but also her heart. I realized that my heart had been hurting for so long that I didn't know if I would be able to hear it if it were trying to speak to me. And tomorrow, it would be completely broken all over again.

"Sorry I dozed off," Michael said as he entered the living room, rubbing his eyes. "What are you reading?"

"Nothing," I replied, shutting the book and placing it back on the bookshelf where I'd found it.

His stomach rumbled, and mine rumbled in response.

"Do you want to check out that restaurant Aunt Gael recommended?" I asked.

"Sure," he replied. "Let me grab a quick shower first."

The Backyard restaurant looked like a small wooden house, not like a restaurant. They had a limited amount of seating inside in case of inclement weather, but their main seating was outside behind the restaurant.

It was set up like an elaborate backyard. There were about a dozen rectangular wooden tables—some with benches, some with chairs. Each table was staged beautifully with a colorful table runner, candles, and small white vases with daisies. It was cold outside, but there were several outdoor heaters set up. And even though it was past sunset, the backyard was illuminated with lanterns and thousands of twinkle lights strung across the back porch, across the back wooden fence, and through the trees. It was almost magical.

The hostess sat us at a table close to where a man was set up, playing guitar and singing. To the left of our table and in front of where the man was singing, there was an open space where a few people were dancing and enjoying the music.

Our waitress greeted us, brought us some water, and took our orders.

Michael immediately knew what he wanted as soon as he looked at the menu. He ordered sweet chili shrimp and pineapple kabobs. I had a harder time deciding but ended up ordering barbecue grilled chicken and a spinach salad.

Once the waitress walked away, I noticed Michael carefully scoping out the restaurant from his seat. His eyes scanned the perimeter of the yard and then assessed every other patron seated at nearby tables.

"Are you worried that someone from Henley is here?" I asked, leaning in and trying to keep my voice down.

He turned his attention back to me. "It's habit," he replied calmly. "Everything looks normal though. But you should do that when you are in public places, at least for a couple of months." He hesitated and then added, "There's something else I need you to do for me."

I nodded, taking a sip of water. "Anything."

He leaned in closer, his voice low. "If something happens and they find you here, I want you to do anything necessary to get away safely."

"Okay, so in other words, I have your permission to jump off bridges," I said with a teasing smile.

Michael frowned, his face serious. "I said, *safely*. If you are captured, I want you to do anything Henley demands to get him to release you. Tell him anything he wants to know about me if you think there is a chance he will let you go. Even if it means he will have a better lead in tracking me down."

I shook my head in defiance. "I won't agree to that."

He ignored me and continued, "But you cannot, under any circumstance, show him that you have abilities. If Henley finds out about you, he'll never let you go. Do you understand?"

I was about to reiterate to Michael that I would never betray him when our waitress came by to refill our water.

"This is a great song," she said, looking at Michael. "You should ask this lovely lady to dance with you." She smiled at me before walking away.

Michael and I stared each other down, neither of us caving on what I should do if I were captured by Henley. Frustrated, he sighed and sat back in his chair.

I looked out at the dance floor, more to break Michael's gaze than to watch couples slow dance, but he misinterpreted my interest. He stood up and walked over to my chair, extending a hand.

"No, that's okay," I told him, letting him off the hook from the pressure the waitress had put on him.

He raised his eyebrows and pushed his hand even closer to me, determined to give me what he thought I wanted. Halfheartedly, I took his hand, hoping that he didn't feel it was yet another obligation. He'd already done so much for me by saving my life and then taking me to see my parents and making sure I made it to Kentucky safely. He could have just left me in St. Augustine to find my own way here.

As he led me out to the dance floor, I realized that I'd never actually slow-danced with anyone before. It wasn't like I had gone to prom or homecoming in high school. I'd always come up with an excuse as to why I couldn't go when I was asked. I looked up at him, unsure as to what I should do.

I wasn't even convinced he really wanted to dance with me, which made me feel even more awkward.

Michael took a step closer, still clasping my hand. He wrapped his other arm around my waist. I carefully placed my hand on the side of his arm.

He pulled me a little closer, and my heart fluttered and then began to beat wildly in my chest. We started to move, gently swaying back and forth.

My right hand, still in Michael's, rested on his chest, and I could feel his heart beating. It was calm, which somehow began to calm mine. I leaned closer to him, resting my head on his shoulder. I closed my eyes, focusing only on his heart.

I could feel his breath in my hair, and just like that, the calmness was suddenly washed away and replaced with a sense of dread. This was too much. His heartbeat might be steady and calm, but mine was back to fragile and terrified.

I stopped dancing and took a step back, away from him. I looked up at him and knew he was about to ask me what was wrong, so I desperately glanced around, looking for an out. I spotted our table and noticed our meals had been delivered while we were dancing.

"Our dinner is getting cold," I told him.

He looked over at the table and back at me. Before he could ask for further explanation, I left him no choice but to follow me off the dance floor and back to our table.

My appetite was completely gone as I pushed the food around on my plate and forced myself to occasionally eat a forkful of salad. I hoped that if I looked busy eating, Michael would avoid asking me questions.

He occasionally glanced at me as he took steady, silent bites but didn't say anything.

We finished our dinner, and Michael drove us back to Aunt Gael's house. He attempted to make small talk with me on the way home, which felt much more forced than our usual conversations.

I felt distant, disconnected, but I didn't know how to overcome it. I didn't want our last night together to be like this, but I couldn't pretend that his leaving wasn't going to destroy me.

As we were about to get out of the car, he asked me to pull out one of the cell phones from the glove box.

"Why don't you cut us a couple of slices of that chocolate pie, and I'll join you in a sec?" he said. "I'm going to call Alexander and check in to make sure they got to the new place safely."

I went into the empty house while Michael stayed outside to call Alexander. As I shut the door behind me, I was tempted to stay and try to eavesdrop. Maybe if he didn't know I was listening, he'd slip up and give a hint as to where he was going. But then I recalled our conversation at dinner and how Henley would try to get me to talk if they found me. I knew in my heart that I would never tell him anything but decided it was still better if I didn't know. I couldn't be forced to tell what I didn't know.

I pulled the pie out of the fridge and realized this would be the last time I ever did this for Michael.

As I started cutting the pie, a wave of emotion came over me like a kettle hitting a boiling point. Despite my head screaming to keep it together, it boiled over, and tears began to stream down my face.

"They're safe, and I'm ready for some pie!" Michael announced cheerfully as he walked into the kitchen. He stopped in his tracks when he saw me. "What's wrong?"

I tried to hold it together, but the emotion overtook me, and I began to sob.

He walked over to me, placing his hands on my shoulders. He turned me around to face him. "Hey. Talk to me."

I tried to take a couple of deep breaths as I wiped the tears away, willing my emotions to get back under control.

"Natalie, I'm sorry," he said, taking my lack of response as unwillingness to talk. "I didn't mean to scare you at the restaurant. That was never my intention. I just need to be able to leave here, knowing that you will be okay."

"I'm not going to be okay," I said, my voice shaky but audible. I wiped the remaining tears from my face.

"All you wanted was space from me, to feel safe, and all I've done is continue to put you in danger," he replied, his voice tight.

I shook my head. "That's not it at all. I never wanted space from you."

I looked up at him. His eyes were filled with confusion and compassion.

"But you said—"

"I didn't mean it," I said, cutting him off. "I just said it because I thought you'd be safer without me in your life."

Michael looked away, as if searching for an invisible answer.

"I don't understand," he said, looking back at me.

"I don't know how to control my abilities, and I was scared I would do something that would lead Henley to you."

"What are you saying?" he asked, a hint of desperation in his voice.

"I don't want space from you," I replied. "Not now. Not ever. *I love you*, Michael." The last part just came out of my mouth. I hadn't intended to say it, but I meant it. I'd never been in love before, but I had no doubt this was it.

Michael just stood there, silent. The tension was thick, and it made me nervous.

What is he thinking?

Michael took a step closer as he processed what I'd just revealed.

Did I just royally mess things up between us?

"Say something. *Please*," I begged, unable to take it anymore.

Without a word, Michael completely closed the distance between us. Before I could comprehend what was happening, his lips were on mine.

Although his lips were soft, his kiss was hard and intense. I reached my hands up behind his head, weaving my fingers into his hair as I pulled him closer. With his hands wrapped tightly around my waist, we stumbled back a few steps until I was pressed against the kitchen cabinets. In one swift motion, he effortlessly lifted me up, so I was sitting on the counter.

His lips moved down to my neck, and my head began to spin. I never wanted him to stop. I never wanted him to leave.

My hands found their way under the back of his shirt, and I ran my hands up his scarred back, feeling the warmth of him.

Michael kissed me on the lips again and then gently pulled away. Without opening his eyes, he leaned his forehead against mine.

"I have to leave tomorrow," he whispered, out of breath.

I wanted to cry and scream at him not to go, but I couldn't.

"I know," I replied. It had to be this way regardless of how unfair it was.

He lifted his forehead from mine and opened his eyes to look at me.

"I don't want to leave you. I would stay with you if I could," he said.

"I know."

Michael leaned into me, his arms around my waist and face buried between my shoulder and neck. I wrapped my arms around his neck, tightly clinging to him. I wanted to stay like this forever.

We heard Aunt Gael's keys rattling in the front door and quickly parted. I hopped off the counter.

As Aunt Gael made her way into the kitchen, I was in the process of smoothing out my hair. Michael played it cool, pulling spoons out of the drawer and placing them on the pie plates.

Aunt Gael was onto us though. She eyed us with an amused smirk as she put her purse down on the counter.

"Just in time. Would you like me to cut you a slice?" Michael casually asked Aunt Gael.

"No, thanks," she replied, flashing me a knowing smile. "I'm really tired, so I think I'm going to go to bed. Don't stay up too late."

Aunt Gael gave me a quick kiss on the cheek, grabbed a bottle of water out of the fridge, and headed to her room. Michael and I let out a quiet laugh when she was out of earshot.

174

Michael and I sat at the table and ate our pie. It was a little too rich for me, but he devoured his. I pushed the last few bites that I couldn't finish in front of him, and he didn't hesitate to eat it.

I yawned as I grabbed our dirty plates and loaded them into the dishwasher.

"You should try to get some sleep," he told me, rubbing my back.

"But then it will be tomorrow," I protested.

He took my hand. "Come on. I'll tuck you in."

Michael led me down the hall and into the guest bedroom. My new pajamas were lying folded on the bed with the other new clothes I'd purchased today. He handed the pajamas to me.

"Go change. I'll be here when you get back," he said.

Reluctantly, I took the plaid pajama bottoms and fitted T-shirt and went into the bathroom to change. When I returned to the bedroom, Michael had cleared the other clothes off the bed and had the covers pulled back. I yawned but couldn't imagine how I would be able to fall asleep.

I crawled into the bed, and he sat down next to me, pulling the covers over me. He leaned down and lightly kissed me on the lips.

"Good night," he said, but it felt like good-bye.

He turned to leave, but I reached out and grabbed his hand.

"Will you stay with me?" I asked. "Just until I fall asleep?"

I lifted the covers up and scooted over, so he could climb in. He took off his shoes and climbed into bed with me, fully clothed.

He lay down on his back and stretched out his arm for me to cuddle up to him. I laid my head on his chest, comfortably fitting under his protective arm.

"I love you too," he whispered.

SIXTEEN

Sunlight danced in front of my eyelids, coaxing my eyes to open. I was confused by sleep and unfamiliar surroundings, so it took me a minute to remember where I was. When I did, I immediately sat up in bed, scanning the room. There was no sign of Michael.

He'd promised to stay with me until I fell asleep, and even though I'd been under the assumption he would go back to his room and I'd get to say good-bye to him in the morning, I got a sinking feeling that he was already gone.

I got out of bed and hurried down to the office. The door was closed, but I didn't bother knocking. I just entered.

Michael wasn't there, and the futon was back in the couch position with his pillow and blanket neatly folded on top. The Grand Canyon T-shirt he'd let me borrow was lying across the back of Aunt Gael's desk chair. He'd left it for me.

Michael was gone, and by design, I would have no way to ever get in touch with him again.

I picked up the T-shirt and pressed it to my face. It still smelled like him.

I burst into tears.

"Natalie?" I heard Aunt Gael call from another room.

"Coming," I replied, unable to hide the trembling in my voice. I took a deep breath and left the office, dropping the T-shirt off in my room before following Aunt Gael's voice in the kitchen.

Aunt Gael cracked an egg into the frying pan but stopped when she saw me come into the kitchen. "What's wrong, dear?" she asked.

I cleared my throat. "Michael left this morning."

"You still like your eggs over medium?" she asked, and I nodded. "Go ahead and sit. It will be ready in a sec."

I obeyed and sat at the kitchen table while she scooped the egg onto a plate with toast and bacon. She placed it in front of me along with a glass of orange juice. She grabbed her plate and juice from the kitchen counter and sat across from me.

Aunt Gael carefully watched me as I took a small bite of toast.

"I'm sure he'll come visit you when you return home," she said reassuringly.

I shook my head, not taking my eyes off the toast. "It's complicated."

Aunt Gael and I ate in silence for a few minutes. When we were almost done, she reached across the table and put her hand on my arm.

"Loss is never easy, honey, and you've certainly had more than your share," she said.

"I never wanted to feel this way again, and here I am," I replied bitterly. A part of me wanted to be angry with myself for willingly deciding to fall in love with someone that I knew could never be in my life forever.

"There are never any guarantees in any type of relationship," she said. "Sometimes, people leave because of circumstance, and others leave by choice. I don't think one is easier than the other to deal with."

I considered what she was saying and realized that she must think Michael had left by choice. And while that was true, I knew it wasn't because he'd wanted to leave. He'd left to keep us both safe. As much as I didn't want to admit it, it was the right thing to do. Michael and I were safer apart than we were together.

"You probably don't want to hear this right now," she said, pausing until I made eye contact with her, "but it will get easier. The pain won't go away, but it will get easier to deal with. Just like it did with losing Becca. Every day will get a little easier."

It was hard to fathom, but deep down, I knew she was right. At this point in time, I couldn't imagine my life without Michael. It felt like he was permanently branded on my heart, and I couldn't comprehend how it would ever heal and be whole again. And maybe it would never heal completely. Maybe it would just scar over. Either way, I would have to learn to live without him. There was no other choice.

"Was he your first real love?" she asked with a small smile.

I hadn't seen her in years, not since the search parties for Becca ceased, but she must've sensed that this was unchartered territory for me.

I dipped my head and took a deep breath, trying not to open the floodgates again.

"Your first love is always the hardest," she said softly. "I'm going to offer you some unsolicited advice, and take it from someone who has gone through many, many breakups. Stay busy. Find something else to focus on. It will keep you from focusing too much on him."

I nodded and tried to force a smile. I appreciated her attempt to help me through this.

For a normal girl and a normal breakup, this would be great advice. If I were a normal girl, I would just go home and carry on with my life. I'd call up Jen for a girls' night. We'd binge-watch sappy movies, and I'd cry over other people's love stories instead of my own. I would go back to work and find a new hobby to occupy my spare time.

For me, however, it wasn't that simple. I couldn't go home. I couldn't call Jen—or anyone else I knew for that matter. I couldn't do anything, except wait for it all to blow over. And when it did finally all blow over, I knew I would still worry about whether or not Michael was safe. If Henley did find him, I would never know. I shuddered at the thought.

I helped Aunt Gael clean up from breakfast and then retreated back to the guest bedroom, feeling exhausted. I closed the curtains tight and climbed back into bed, pulling Michael's shirt close to me. I closed my eyes, trying to imprint the image of Michael into my memory. I had no pictures of Michael to remember him by.

When I opened my eyes again, it was much darker in the room, and I knew I'd been asleep for a long time. My mouth felt like cotton.

I groaned as I got out of bed to get a drink of water. I stumbled into the living room, where Aunt Gael was watching the evening news. She didn't say anything when she saw me, but she threw a sympathetic glance my way.

I wandered into the kitchen and poured a glass of water, fully planning to drink it and go back to bed, when I heard the TV in the next room.

"In Omaha, Nebraska, officials are investigating a mysterious series of power outages throughout the city," the news reporter said.

I darted into the living room.

The reporter, a young woman that reminded me of Jen, stood in front of a building that said *Nebraska Power*. "This comes just on the heels of similar unexplained outages in St. Louis and Kansas City earlier today. Nebraska Power released a statement saying they have not yet located the root cause of the strong power surges that triggered the outage but have managed to restore power to all homes and businesses."

I stood there with my mouth gaping open. *Could it be Michael? Is he leading Henley away from here, giving them false leads?*

"Do you mind if I use your laptop?" I asked Aunt Gael, recalling seeing a laptop sitting on the desk in her office.

"Not at all."

I dashed out of the living room, down the hall, and into the office.

I flipped open the laptop and waited anxiously while it powered on. As soon as the home screen appeared, I opened the internet browser and searched for Harrodsburg, Kentucky.

A map appeared in the results, and I clicked on it. There was an option to get driving directions from Harrodsburg. I typed in St. Louis, Missouri, as the destination. The site told me that it would take a little more than five hours to get from Harrodsburg to St. Louis.

I opened another browser window and searched for a news article on the power outages. It came up right away, and I clicked on it. The article said that the power outage had happened in St. Louis at 8:46 a.m. If Michael had left before 4 a.m. to ensure he was gone before I woke up, it was possible he could have made it to St. Louis by 8:46 a.m. to cause the power outage.

I went back to the map, erased my search, and typed in directions from St. Louis to Kansas City, Kansas. According to the site, it would take approximately four hours to get there. I toggled back to the news article. The power outage in Kansas City occurred at 1:10 p.m. That was around the time Michael would have arrived there.

Once again, I went back to the map. I searched for directions from Kansas City to Omaha, Nebraska. The site said it would take almost three hours to get there. I took a deep breath and flipped back to the article. The first power outage in Omaha occurred at 4:33 p.m., and another one occurred at 4:56 p.m., about ten miles away from the first. I couldn't help but wonder why he would trigger two outages in the same city—unless he was concerned that Henley wasn't picking up the signals.

I looked at the clock on the laptop, and it was almost 7:30 p.m. There hadn't been an outage since. I tried not to panic as I thought through the options. Just because the outages had stopped didn't mean Michael had been captured. He would have to stop them at some point, obviously. But he would be smart about it. He would stop when he knew they were on his trail, and then he would find a way to get as far away from there as possible.

I walked back into the living room to find Aunt Gael still on the couch, watching TV. She stopped biting her nails when she saw me.

"Find what you were looking for?" she asked.

She must've thought my behavior was bizarre, and in fairness, it was.

"I did," I confirmed, sitting on the couch next to her. The news switched over to the local weather. "Would you mind turning that up?" I asked, and she obliged.

"Tomorrow will be a high of sixty-two degrees with severe thunderstorms developing in the evening," the meteorologist explained. "The storms are expected to start between six and seven o'clock and continue throughout the night. Visibility on the roadways will be limited, so you might want to stay indoors if at all possible."

I recalled what Michael had told me about practicing my abilities. Even though he'd preferred that I didn't use them at all, he had seen my point about wanting to learn to control them.

In the long run, knowing how to better control them could prevent me from having a slipup that would draw Henley's attention. The lightning would throw off Henley's trackers, but it would still be risky. If Henley was hours away, thinking Michael was heading west, maybe tomorrow night would be a good time to test it out.

Earlier today, Aunt Gael had suggested that I find something to take my mind off of my heartbreak. Perhaps this could be my thing. Even if I couldn't get through this heartbreak like a normal girl my age, I could get through it in my own way. I could pour all of my focus into this discovery.

"Can I ask you a question?" I asked Aunt Gael.

"Of course, honey." She turned her body toward me to give me her full attention.

"Why do you have that book?" I asked, pointing to her bookshelf. "The one called *Keen Intuition*."

She tilted her head to the side. "Hasn't your mother ever told you? That's a family trait of ours. You have it, don't you?"

"I-I didn't know," I said.

A family trait? I had no idea.

I had known that Becca had it, but Mother never let on that anyone else in the family did. I was careful not to let anyone know I had it, but she also never asked me if I did.

"Oh, yes," Aunt Gael confirmed. "I have it, your mother has it, our mother had it, our mother's mother had it. It seems to get stronger with each generation. Becca's was, well, unusually strong. I always assumed you had it too, but you were much more reserved about it, like your mother."

I thought back to my last conversation with Mother and how she'd mentioned her dream about the car accident. I'd thought it was a strange coincidence at the time, but maybe it was a real premonition. Her fears were real, and she knew they could be real. That was why she'd tried so hard to keep me under wraps when I was living at home. That was why she'd freaked out when I told her I was moving away.

"I had no idea Mother had it," I said, still trying to comprehend this revelation.

"She does," Aunt Gael said with an amused smile. "She just doesn't like to admit it, so I'm not completely surprised that she didn't mention it to you. It wasn't something she liked to talk about."

"Becca just seemed to embrace it," I replied. "She didn't seem to ever question why she had it. She just accepted who she was."

That was just one of many examples of how I wished I were more like Becca. She hadn't doubted herself or felt ashamed of who she was. She had been fearless.

"Are there any other traits in the family?" I asked. "Like reading minds or something?" I knew the question might make me sound crazy, but what if there was more that I didn't know, something that could help me better understand why I could do these things?

Aunt Gael laughed. "No, of course not. What on earth would make you think that?"

I shrugged and forced a laugh. "Just making sure," I said, trying to sound like I was joking.

If my ability to read minds didn't come from Michael and it's not part of my family's genetics, how am I able to do it? Can I do it again? Do I want to do it again?

Just the thought of it made me cringe.

Aunt Gael opened her mouth to say something but then quickly closed it. My heart started to race, as I wondered if she would ask me if I was able to read minds. I didn't want to lie to her if she asked, but it wasn't safe for me to tell her the whole truth.

"What?" I asked, unsure if I would regret asking the question.

"I don't want you to think I'm strange," she replied, looking down at her hands.

"Trust me; you don't have to worry about that."

"There has been some family debate about dream telepathy," she said, looking back up at me to gauge my reaction. "I've never personally done it, but my aunt—your great aunt Ena—supposedly had the ability to do it."

Great-Aunt Ena had passed away two years ago, and Mother couldn't handle going to her funeral, so we didn't attend. I only recalled meeting her a few times in my life and hadn't known her very well. I certainly never heard about any of her abilities.

"I don't know what that is," I admitted.

"Aunt Ena described it as being able to communicate with someone else while sleeping," Aunt Gael explained. "She said she could lie down to go to sleep, and if she could recognize that she was actively dreaming, she could take control of that dream and intentionally contact other people."

"Contact people in her dream?"

"Not exactly," she replied. "I think it was contact with people outside of her dream. She made it sound like it could be anyone. When I was in the tenth grade, I got a really bad report card. Aunt Ena appeared in one of my dreams, and she talked to me about the importance of getting better grades and gave me a bunch of studying tips. It was very bizarre. I asked her if she used dream telepathy on me, but she would never give me a straight answer."

"And you've never been curious to try it?" I asked.

Aunt Gael immediately shifted her gaze, and I could tell she was hesitant to answer.

"It's okay. You can tell me," I said.

Aunt Gael rubbed her lips together, still pondering how to respond. Finally, she admitted, "I did try it once when Becca disappeared, but it didn't work." She shifted her gaze again, and I knew there was more. She glanced back over at me and saw that I was eager for her to continue. "Aunt Ena tried as well."

"And?" I asked, holding my breath.

Her eyes became red and glossy, giving me the answer before she even said it. "And she said Becca wasn't somewhere that could be found. She thought Becca was dead."

SEVENTEEN

"Here are all of our how-to books on quilting," I said, walking an elderly woman over to a bookshelf at the back of the store.

"Thank you," she replied, smiling appreciatively.

"Just let me know if you need help finding anything else," I said before walking back to the register.

Aunt Gael was behind the register, opening a box of new books that had come in today's shipment.

"Go ahead and go," I told her. Aunt Gael had her book club tonight, and if she didn't leave soon, she was going to be late. "I've got this."

In the two months since starting to work for Aunt Gael in her bookstore, I hadn't closed up the store on my own, but I'd seen her do it numerous times.

"Okay," she finally agreed, putting a handful of books on the counter. "Just call me if you need anything."

She gave me a quick kiss on the cheek before grabbing her purse and leaving.

Once Aunt Gael was gone, I turned my attention to a man as he walked up to the register. He didn't have anything in his hands, so I asked, "How can I help you?"

"I'm looking for a book, but I can't remember the name of it," he said. "It's a book about a man who sails around the world."

I concentrated, trying to determine what book he was looking for.

"*Sailor Tom … Sailing Away Tom …*" I heard him think.

I followed his train of thought and recalled seeing the book in our fiction section.

"*Come Sail Away with Tom* by Jennifer C. Clary," I suggested, confident that was the book he was referencing.

"That's it!" he said, delighted to have the mystery solved. He immediately headed to the fiction section to get the book.

I smiled back—not just because I was able to help him, but also because I was able to stop more of his thoughts from flooding my mind. It was something I'd been able to do successfully for over a month, but it still made me nervous every time I did it.

The first time I'd attempted it, I had been terrified that if I started reading minds again, I wouldn't be able to stop. I waited for the perfect moment when there was a thunderstorm outside. Aunt Gael was out running errands, and there was only one customer in the store. It took me a while to relax enough to be able to focus and do it. My heart pounded the entire time I was reading the customer's mind. I was so scared that I would trigger a power outage or be stuck with the ability forever. Once that customer had left and the next customer came in, I'd just relaxed and focused on silence, and everything was normal.

Now, I was at a point where I didn't have to spend as much energy focusing. I could just concentrate a little harder, almost like when you leaned in closer to hear someone speaking softly, and I could hear what people were thinking. Like a light switch in my brain, I could shut off the concentration, turning the thoughts off.

My motivation for reading people's minds was really to fine-tune my abilities just in case Henley somehow tracked me down. If I'd read the mind of Henley's man who came into the café that night, pretending to be with the electric company, I might have known their plan and could've avoided them in the alley when I left.

Recognizing that reading people's minds was a complete violation of their privacy, I practiced it sparingly and only when I was trying to help someone out. I deliberately practiced when Aunt Gael wasn't around so that I wouldn't accidentally pick up her thoughts.

The man returned to the register with his book, and I rung him up. Within a minute of him leaving, the elderly woman also came to the register with three different books on quilting. I rung her up as well and then looked at the clock as she exited the store. It was only one minute until closing, and there were no customers remaining in the store. I flipped the Open sign on the door to Closed and locked the door.

Within an hour, I counted all the money in the register, put the receipts and cash in the safe, locked up the store, and was walking home. It was almost nine p.m. at night, but it was only a fifteen-minute walk back to Aunt Gael's house.

Although the area wasn't populated with tourists like St. Augustine was, I felt safe walking back to her house alone. There was only one time I had gotten scared while walking back at night, and it was when I'd seen a car that looked similar to the one that had been parked outside my apartment in St. Augustine. This particular car had passed me without so much as slowing down, and I never saw it again, which made me realize it was only pure coincidence and not really one of Henley's men.

Thunder rumbled in the distance, and I picked up my pace, hoping to make it back to Aunt Gael's house before it began to rain. I'd forgotten to bring my umbrella despite hearing that it was going to storm tonight. I had actually been looking forward to the storm all day. It had become a usual routine for me to practice my abilities when it stormed, especially on the rare instance when Aunt Gael wasn't going to be home.

A flash of lightning brightened up the sky as I entered the empty house. I immediately headed to my bedroom and sat in my usual spot on the edge of the bed. I didn't know how long the storm would last and wanted to take full advantage of the opportunity.

Noting the closet door was partially open, I focused on it and took a deep breath, relaxing myself. I stared at the door, willing it to move. I stared at it until everything in my peripheral vision started to become distorted.

The door moved an inch and stopped. I let the air out of my lungs, making a conscious effort to breathe normally again.

I'd made some progress with this ability, but I honestly didn't know what I was doing or how to improve. When I'd started, it had taken me several tries before it moved at all. At first, the door would just barely wiggle.

I recalled the conversation with Michael when he described this particular ability and how it was always Raina's strength, not his.

My heart sank, just as it did every time I thought about him. Even though it had been a couple of months since he left, the sting of it was still very present. A day didn't go by that I didn't wonder where he was and if he was safe. They never determined the root cause of the mysterious power outages, which led me to believe that it had indeed been Michael leading Henley away from me. I'd never met anyone so selfless.

It wasn't fair that he had to live his life on the run because of Henley.

My heart rate started to pick up, and I could feel myself getting angry at the thought of Henley trying to track Michael down. I felt a surge from within my body, like the anger trying to come out of me. I worried that I would cause a power outage, so I turned my focus back to the door and thought about releasing that anger on the door.

I must've released it a little too fast because the door slammed shut, making me jump in surprise. I'd never been able to do that before.

Unsure if it was just a fluke, I fixed my gaze on a shoe on the floor. I thought of the night Henley had chased Michael and me away from my parents' home. I allowed the adrenaline to pour out of me and onto the shoe, scooting it across the floor until it hit the baseboard.

I took another deep breath and forced myself to relax. I had to be careful not to overuse my abilities and to not let them get out of control. Any slipup could evoke danger and lead Henley to me.

As I relaxed, I yawned. Using my abilities took a lot of energy, and I was always ready for bed after any successful night of practicing.

I decided to stop practicing for the night and get ready for bed. As I changed out of my clothes, I opted to sleep in Michael's Grand Canyon T-shirt. I tried not to wear it too often because I was worried I would wear it out, but I chose to make an exception tonight. Although Michael's scent was long gone, it still made me feel close to him.

After washing my face and brushing my teeth, I crawled into bed. The storm had subsided, and all that was left was the sound of gentle rain outside. I lay on my back in bed, staring into the darkness for a while, wondering what Michael was doing right at this very moment. I used to lie in bed and wonder the same thing about Becca after she disappeared.

I turned onto my side, trying to turn away from the unpleasant reality that my sister was dead.

After hearing about Great-Aunt Ena's unsuccessful dream connections with Becca, I'd decided to find out for myself. I studied up on it, purchasing multiple books from the bookstore on the subject.

The first time I attempted it, I tried it out on Mother. It worked for a minute, and I didn't actually communicate with her. I just observed, only long enough to see if I could really do it.

When I arrived in Mother's dream, she was dreaming about me and Becca when we were much younger. Becca was about five, and I was two. Mother was taking us on a picnic. It made me wonder if this was a dream based on a memory or if it was something she made up.

In her dream, Becca ran around the perfectly green grass while I squealed and chased her, my tiny legs unstable and desperately trying to keep up. Becca would purposely slow down to let me catch her. Mother looked young and vibrant, sipping on lemonade while sitting on a navy-and-yellow plaid blanket.

In my research, I'd read that it wasn't always wise to make your presence known in dream connections. It could become confusing to the person you were visiting. I didn't want to disturb Mother's dream anyway. She was happy, and I didn't want to ruin it for her. I just retreated quietly back to my own sense of consciousness.

The next day, I remembered feeling a little guilty for visiting her dream though. Just like with the mind reading, it was a huge violation of privacy. But I'd had to test it on someone if I was going to try to make a connection with Becca.

For a week afterward, I attempted to connect with Becca, using dream telepathy, but each time, I came back empty. It was like searching endlessly into nothing but darkness.

When I'd connected with Mother, it'd felt almost instantaneous. As soon as I'd realized I was dreaming and made the decision that I wanted to visit her, it was as if I'd just naturally stepped into her dream.

With Becca, it was different. There was nothing to connect to. It was as if she no longer existed. At first, I'd rationalized that maybe she just wasn't asleep at the time I tried it. I'd then attempted at random times, almost obsessively, but never found her.

I hadn't attempted to connect with Michael. Even though I thought it was safe, I wasn't sure it was a good idea. I was worried that it would make the pain of missing him worse. It would be very difficult to come back to a reality without him in it.

I closed my eyes and focused on the sound of the rain outside, letting it calm me until I started to drift off to sleep.

Instead of my dream starting off as it usually did with me chasing Becca's kidnapper through the woods, my subconscious took me back to the site where I'd wrecked my car.

The car was wrapped around the tree, and the raven was perched above it. It squawked at me as I approached, warning me.

The faceless man appeared from behind the tree, and I stopped. He didn't usually confront me in my dream. My heart began to pound.

I turned to run, and another man, identical to the other, appeared from behind a different tree. I turned to the left and then to the right, only to find myself completely surrounded. My feet began to sink into the ground beneath me, and I was trapped, unable to run.

The faceless men closed in on me as I struggled to free myself. Just when the first one was about to reach me, he walked right past me, completely ignoring me.

One by one, the others followed suit. Still stuck to the ground, I tried to see where they were going in the darkness.

What else could they be after?

A knot formed in my stomach and began to twist as I looked past them.

It was Michael.

He didn't seem to notice me as the men surrounded him.

"Run!" I screamed at Michael, but he didn't hear me.

He just stood there, frozen, as the men closed in.

With all of my strength, I fought to free my feet from the ground to stop them and save Michael, but it was no use.

The raven shrieked again, jarring me to realize that I was indeed dreaming. This wasn't real. It was all made up in my mind, and I was in complete control.

I looked down at my feet, and the mud sank back into the ground and dried up. I was now unafraid of the faceless men, who were merely a figment of my imagination. I looked up again in defiance, confident and ready to fight, but they were already gone. I was too late.

The knot grew more powerful in my stomach, and I urged it to go away. It was just a dream.

It isn't real.

The knot twisted tightly. It was so powerful that I doubled over in my dream, clutching my stomach.

Could someone be punching me in the stomach while I slept?

I wanted to force myself awake, but I had to consider the possibility that maybe the threat was real.

Could my intuition be manifesting itself in my dream to tell me that Michael was really in danger?

It wouldn't be the first time my subconscious had warned me of trouble.

If I allowed myself to come out of the dream, there was no chance I would be able to go back to sleep. If I was going to find out if the threat was real, I had to do it now.

Connecting with Michael in his dream was the only way to know for sure. If I could get into his dream, hopefully, I could confirm he was safe. I would just connect, get the confirmation I needed, and leave.

The fresh wounds of missing him tomorrow would be painful, but it would be nothing compared to wondering and worrying that something had happened to him. I had to know.

Just as I had done with visiting Mother's dream, I willed myself to be connected with him. When I'd connected with Mother's dream, it was like I'd seamlessly transported from my dream to hers. It was almost like one world faded away and a new one emerged.

I focused on Michael, but nothing happened. I couldn't find anything to connect to. It was just like when I'd tried to connect with Becca.

My heart began to pound, and I told myself to remain calm. If I got too panicked, I would wake up. I had to stay asleep to figure out what was going on. I tried again but came up empty.

Come on, Michael. Where are you?

It was possible that Michael wasn't asleep. I had no idea what time it really was here, much less wherever Michael was. He could be anywhere in the world.

I continued to fight the urge to wake up, determined to find another way. Then, it dawned on me. I could try Raina.

Raina hated me and surely wouldn't appreciate me appearing in her dream, but I planned to just take a quick peek to make sure everything was okay. If everything seemed normal, I would quietly leave, and she never had to know I was there.

I envisioned Raina and willed myself to connect with her. Without delay, the woods faded completely to black, and bright white walls came into focus.

I was now standing in a long, very sterile-looking white corridor. It looked like a hospital of some sort. Raina was walking ahead of me in a hurry. My heart began to ache as I realized Raina was dreaming about Henley.

"Michael!" Raina called out. "Michael, where are you?"

191

There was no response.

Raina began to run down the hall, and I chased after her.

We got to the end of the corridor and entered another room. It was the observation room from the video Michael had shown me, but there was no sign of Michael. The door shut after we entered, and we could hear the sound of a dead bolt locking it behind us.

Realizing the room was empty, Raina turned around back toward the door but stopped when she saw me.

"What are you doing here? Do you know where Michael is?" she demanded.

"Raina, what happened to Michael?" I asked.

I didn't know how much time I had before one of us woke up, and if Michael had really been taken, I needed to get as much information as I could from her. We couldn't waste any time.

Raina didn't answer me. She ran to the door and pushed against it, trying to force it to open.

"Raina, please tell me," I begged. "What happened to Michael?"

Raina crumbled to the floor, pulling her legs to her chest. "It's all my fault."

I knelt in front of her, bracing myself for the worst. "What does that mean? Does Henley have him?" I asked.

She began to cry, and I started to worry that maybe she'd wake up before I could find out. I couldn't lose this connection with her until I knew the truth.

"Please, Raina," I tried again. "Tell me. I can't help if you don't tell me."

"They took him," Raina replied. "It's all my fault. It's all my fault," she continued to repeat over and over.

"Stop. Listen to me," I said forcefully, and it worked because she stopped and gave me her full attention. "I need you to tell me where you are. I need to be able to help you get him back."

Raina shook her head. "I can't tell anyone where we are. It's not safe."

"I know that," I assured her. "But you have to tell me. It's safe to tell me."

Raina shook her head again and covered her ears, trying to shut me out. I didn't know the rules for touching someone in their dream but decided this required extreme measure.

I gently put a hand on her arm. Although I couldn't actually feel her arm, I saw my hand lying on it.

"Okay, I understand. You can't tell me," I said, trying to think of how to rationalize with someone who was lost in their own troubled, unconscious mind. "Why don't you just show me? It doesn't count if you show me."

Raina tilted her head to the side, considering my request. Her eyes moved away from me, looking past me. I turned and followed her gaze.

The other half of the room had opened up and was no longer a part of the Henley facility. The second half of the room was now leading to a gray house with large windows and a light oak front door. It appeared to be situated on a residential street.

I turned back to Raina. "Good," I encouraged her. "That's good. Now, I need to know where this house is. Can you show me that?"

I felt a forceful pull; my body was trying to bring me back to a conscious state. We had to hurry.

"Raina, show me."

The observation room disappeared completely, and Raina and I were now in a car driving down the highway. She was driving, and I was in the passenger seat. It was as if the car was going in fast motion, like it was in a time-lapse video.

We slowed down just long enough for me to make out certain signs as we passed them. First was a Welcome to North Carolina *sign as we entered the state. Within seconds, we slowed down again to view a sign that said* Charlotte City Limits, *and then finally, a sign showed us turning onto* Willow Court. *The gray house came back into view as we came to a stop.*

I turned to Raina, who was staring at the house in a daze.

"I'm going to come to you, Raina," I told her.

She looked at me but didn't say anything, so I could only hope she understood and would remember what I said.

"I will be there tomorrow. Don't *leave."*

Unable to hold on any longer, I succumbed to consciousness and jolted awake.

I found myself lying in bed in a cold sweat with my heart pounding. The knot in my stomach persisted, making sure I didn't make the false assumption that it was just a nightmare.

The clock said it was 5:06 a.m. I flipped on the light, jumped out of bed, and quickly dressed. I threw a few articles of clothing into a suitcase, although I had no idea how long I'd be gone.

As I emerged from the bedroom, the house was quiet, and Aunt Gael was still asleep. I walked into the kitchen, grabbed a piece of paper and a pen, and wrote Aunt Gael a note, letting her know I had to leave. I hesitated, wanting to tell her I would be back in a few days, but I decided not to add it. I wasn't certain it was a promise that I'd be able to keep.

As I stepped outside and closed the front door behind me, I pulled out my phone. I dialed Seth's number, hoping he'd answer. I hadn't spoken to him in months.

It rang three times, and he finally answered, groggy from sleep.

"Seth," I said, "I need your help."

"Natalie?" he replied.

The alarm in his voice took me back to the night Becca had disappeared, but I forced myself to focus.

"What's wrong?" he asked, sounding suddenly awake.

"I need your help," I told him. "I need you to meet me in North Carolina."

EIGHTEEN

"Say something," I insisted.

I bit my lip and looked at Seth, who was sitting in the passenger seat of the rental car. Seth didn't respond, so I glanced at Jen in the rearview mirror. She stared back at me with wide eyes.

"It's just a lot to take in," Seth finally replied. "You scared us to death with your random phone call, asking that we hop on a plane to North Carolina. We didn't know what had happened to you. Then, we get here, and you tell us your boyfriend is some genetically advanced human, and somehow, you are too, and now, you need our help to rescue him from some psychotic scientist." Seth looked over at me and reiterated, *"It's a lot."*

"But you believe me?" I asked, flexing my hands around the steering wheel. It sounded so far-fetched, and I knew it was possible that they might think I'd completely lost my mind.

"Of course I do," he replied. "But can you please slow down? I don't know what's more terrifying—what you just told me or your driving."

I looked down at the speedometer and realized I was going twenty miles per hour over the speed limit. I let up on the gas but still kept it ten miles per hour over. Time was of the essence, and I needed to get to Michael's family's house before they decided to leave.

"So, you can, like, read minds," Jen stated.

I looked back at her again.

Her eyes grew even wider as she thought it through. "Are you reading my mind right now?"

"No," I assured her. "You don't have to worry about that."

The GPS in the car told me to turn onto Willow Court, and I obeyed.

"This is it!" I said, pointing to the gray house from Raina's dream.

I still didn't know for sure that his family would be there, but at least I knew Raina hadn't just made this house up out of nowhere in her dream.

I pulled into the empty driveway and shut off the car. I turned to face Seth.

"Now that you know everything, I will understand if you want to leave. I won't blame you if you don't want to be involved," I told him.

Seth eyed the house and then took a deep breath as he looked back at me. "No way," he replied. "No way am I leaving you here to deal with this by yourself."

I turned and looked at Jen.

"No way," she echoed with determination in her voice.

"All right then, let's do this," I said, and we got out of the car.

It felt like we were walking in slow motion up to the door.

What will I do if they aren't here? How will we find them?

We had to find them in order to find Michael.

I rang the doorbell and waited. The house was quiet, and I started to feel nauseous.

I was about to ring the doorbell again when the curtain on the front window moved ever so slightly. Someone was home and checking to see who was at the door.

Slowly, the front door opened, and Raina stood in front of us, pale with bloodshot eyes.

"I was hoping it was just a nightmare," she said with a frown. She looked at Seth and then at Jen. "Who are they?"

"We're here to help get Michael back," I told her. "Can we come in?"

Raina contemplated my request, and just when I was pretty sure she was going to slam the door in our faces, she stepped aside to let us in.

We walked past her into the house, which I was surprised to see was fully furnished. It was like a normal house. It didn't feel like their escape house in St. Augustine with no furniture or electricity.

Raina shut the door behind us. "You didn't answer my question," she snapped.

"This is Seth and Jen," I replied, introducing my friends to her. "You can trust them."

"You say that like I trust *you*," Raina said, folding her arms across her chest. "Which I don't."

The front door opened, and Alexander rushed in. He stopped in his tracks when he saw me and let out a breath. He looked relieved.

"I saw the car out front and didn't know what to think," Alexander explained.

He opened the front door and motioned for someone to come inside. I assumed it was Lorena, and a moment later, Lorena appeared cautiously in the doorway.

"Natalie!" Lorena said. "What are you doing here? It's not safe for you to be here."

"I came to help," I replied. I motioned to Seth and Jen. "We came to help get Michael back."

"Come sit down," Lorena said, motioning for us to get out of the entryway and sit in the living room.

Seth, Jen, and I sat on the couch. Lorena and Alexander sat across from us on the love seat. Even though there was an empty armchair, Raina continued to stand.

"So, I assume you told them everything," Raina said, not trying to hide the accusation in her voice. Without waiting for me to respond, she continued, "Who do you think you are?"

"I'm someone who loves your brother," I blurted out.

Raina took a small step back, clearly not expecting my response. She opened her mouth and then immediately shut it.

"I can help get him back. I have a plan, but I need your help to find him," I said. I turned my attention to Alexander and Lorena. We were wasting too much precious time, arguing about this. "You have to have some idea where they've taken him, right?"

Alexander ran his hand through his hair. "I think they are holding him here, at their Charlotte facility. That's why we came here."

"You weren't here when they captured him?" Jen asked.

Lorena shook her head and glanced carefully at Raina. "We were in Philadelphia," she explained. "There was an ... incident."

I recalled Raina's dream and how she'd said it was all her fault.

"You were with him, weren't you?" I asked Raina gently. I was careful to make sure it didn't sound like I blamed her.

Despite what she might think, I knew it wasn't her fault. And regardless of how much Raina disliked me, I knew what that kind of guilt felt like, and I wouldn't wish that on anyone.

A single tear rolled down Raina's cheek. She immediately wiped it away.

"There was a car," she explained very matter-of-factly, her voice controlled and even. "A drunk driver. I stepped off the curb, and he almost hit me. I used my abilities to divert the car. The driver hit the curb and popped a tire but wasn't hurt."

"They tracked you when you diverted the car," I stated.

"No," Raina corrected me. "A reporter was nearby, but I didn't know. He snapped a few pictures at the scene while Michael was checking on the driver. We didn't know he'd published them in the newspaper and online. We didn't figure it out until two days later when I went to pick Michael up from work and saw Henley's men throwing him into the back of a van. I should've done something, but I froze. I didn't know what to do."

I couldn't help but cringe as she told me the story. If I stopped long enough to think about what Michael must be going through this very minute, I'd lose my mind.

I cleared my throat and tried to focus on the task at hand. We had to get our plan together to get him out of there.

"It's not your fault," I told Raina, but she didn't acknowledge me.

"You said you had a plan?" Alexander asked. "Let's hear it."

Raina hissed and rolled her eyes. Alexander shot her a warning look.

"Yes. I assume pharmaceutical representatives routinely stop by Henley's company to try to sell products, right?" I asked.

Alexander nodded.

"Our dads own a pharmaceutical company," I continued, motioning to Seth. "And Seth actually works for them. If Seth can just get us in the building, I can use my abilities to get Michael out of there."

"I'm coming with you," Raina said. "I can use my abilities too."

Alexander leaned forward, his chin resting in his hand. "Assuming that works, I'm not sure we could make it past all of their security. The second someone spotted me or Raina, it'd be all over."

"You're right. You can't go. Either of you," I said, glancing at Raina. "But they wouldn't be expecting me. *Only* me."

"I can't let you do that," Alexander said. "It's too dangerous. It wouldn't be right. If you got caught, they wouldn't just let you go, especially if they found out about your abilities. Michael wouldn't want that."

"What would be right?" I challenged. "Letting Michael die in there?" My throat felt tight as I choked out the words. "I'm going with or without your help."

Alexander sighed and leaned back into the love seat, contemplating everything I'd said. I knew he was torn between what he felt was right and his love for his son.

"You don't even know us," Lorena said to Seth. "You would be willing to do this for us?"

"I'm willing to do it for Natalie," Seth said.

I smiled at Seth with gratitude. There was no way I could ever repay him for this.

"There's a good chance they will recognize you," Raina told me, and for the first time, she didn't seem to hate my existence.

"That's why I brought Jen," I replied. "Jen's fantastic with hair and makeup. She's going to help create a disguise for me."

Lorena stood up and walked over to me. I stood up to meet her.

She took my hands in hers and squeezed them tight. "Are you sure about this?" she asked.

"Yes," I replied without hesitation.

Lorena squeezed my hands a little tighter. "Then, bring our Michael back."

Two hours later, Jen returned from the mall with my disguise and began my transformation.

While she had been gone, Alexander had gone over every detail he could remember of the Henley facility in Charlotte. He drew out a map that outlined the first door at the security desk that required a passcode to enter. He then drew out all of the hallways and rooms he could remember, including the area he believed they would be keeping Michael. Seth and I had done our best to memorize every detail of the map.

"This is only temporary," Jen said when she caught me staring at my jet-black hair as she finished blow-drying it straight. "It will wash out in a couple of shampoos."

In the next room, Seth changed into a pair of navy dress pants, a button-down shirt, and a tie. He said this was what he would typically wear to work.

When Jen was done with my hair, I changed into the outfit she'd picked out for me—black pants, a white blouse with black flowers on it, and a black blazer. She handed me a pair of flat dress shoes. "In case you need to get out of there quickly," she explained, "these will be easier to run in than heels."

Jen did my makeup, and for the first time, I didn't protest the amount. In fact, I began to worry it wouldn't be enough to conceal my identity. As if reading my mind, Jen handed me a pair of black-rimmed nonprescription eyeglasses. I put them on and felt a little better. Between the hair and the glasses, I barely recognized myself.

"Let's go over the plan one more time," Alexander said as Jen put the final touches on my look by adding a necklace and earrings. She was trying to make me look authentic.

"We check in at the receptionist desk," I recited. "Seth shows the receptionist his work badge, and we ask to see Dr. Bob Meeker. Dr. Meeker should send his office assistant out to get us. Just as we reach his office, I ask to use the ladies' room. The assistant should point me down the hall, and when I'm out of sight, I'll find a hallway on the east side of the building. Once I'm gone, Seth will pretend that he left his meeting materials in the car, and the assistant will walk him back out and will hopefully wait for him at the reception desk while I find Michael and sneak him out."

"I still don't like the idea of leaving you in there," Seth said.

Jen put a reassuring hand on his shoulder.

"I'll be fine," I said, sounding more convincing than I felt.

I looked at the clock and realized that it was almost one p.m. If Dr. Meeker went out for lunch, he'd be back by the time we got there. It was the perfect time to go.

As Alexander gave Seth directions to the Henley facility, Jen pulled me aside.

"Are you sure about this?" she asked. "There isn't another way?"

"There isn't," I insisted.

Jen nodded sadly. "You'd better come back, or I'm going to have to go in after both of you," she said with a nervous laugh.

Alexander walked over to us. "I still feel like I should be going with you. He's my son."

"You can't," I reminded him.

I understood his guilt, but if he were to come with us, we'd surely be discovered.

"Thank you for doing this, Natalie," he said.

"You once told me that if Henley had taken me, you had no doubt Michael would try to save me," I said.

"He would. I know he would."

"Then, you understand why I'm doing this," I said.

The look in his eye told me he did.

Seth jingled the car keys in his hand. "Let's do this thing," he said, trying to sound enthusiastic.

I knew he was trying to hide his nerves to keep Jen from worrying.

Seth and I stepped outside, and as we walked to the car, Alexander, Lorena, Raina, and Jen watched us from the stoop. I gave them a wave as we got into the car. Seth sped off, and I silently prayed that we wouldn't let them down. Michael's life depended on it.

NINETEEN

I tried to keep my hands from shaking by folding them together in my lap. I was glad Seth had insisted on driving us to the Henley facility. There was no way I would've been able to focus on the road to get us there in one piece. My nerves were shot.

"You good?" Seth asked, raising an eyebrow.

"Good," I lied.

The man I loved had been taken by a psychopath, and we were his only hope of getting out of there. Of course I wasn't good.

The video of Michael as a little boy flashed in my mind, and I winced at the thought of Henley intentionally cutting him, trying to force him to do things with his abilities that he wasn't capable of.

I imagined him bleeding from his arms while Henley yelled at him to heal himself. I imagined the scars on his arms getting deeper and more distinct, a constant reminder of the torture he'd endured.

Seth reached over and put his hand on top of mine to stop me from trembling.

"It's not too late to go to the police," he said.

"No," I insisted. "We can't. Not yet. If we went to the police, we'd not only expose Henley, but we'd also expose Michael and Raina. That has to be an absolute last resort."

A sign for C. Henley Labs Incorporated appeared, and Seth turned into the parking lot that led to their two-story office building. It was so normal on the outside; no one would ever expect the horrors that were taking place inside.

I looked around and took notice of all the other office buildings nearby—an accounting firm, a staffing agency, and a party-planning business. C. Henley Labs Incorporated didn't even stand out among them.

Seth pulled into a guest parking space and turned off the car. "Do you want to go over the plan one more time?" he asked.

"No." I just wanted to get it over with. "I can do this. Just remember that you need to pull up to the door on the left side of the building. That's where Michael and I will be coming out of."

"I know you don't want me to call the police," he said. "But if you don't come out, I'm going to call them."

I nodded, hoping it wouldn't come to that.

"Are you scared?" he asked.

"Terrified," I replied. "But not as scared as I am of losing Michael. I can't go through that again."

Seth reached for his door handle.

"You're my best friend," I blurted out before he could get out of the car. "I'm sorry for pushing you away after Becca disappeared. It wasn't because of you. I just didn't know how to deal with the guilt I was feeling. I just want you to know that you've always been my best friend, my brother."

"Don't do that. Don't say good-bye," he replied firmly. "We've got this."

I opened my door.

"Hey," Seth said, stopping me this time. "I love you too, nerd."

I managed a small smile and got out of the car.

Seth hid the car keys on top of the driver's-side tire. If the keys were hidden outside, we knew the car would be available to us when we were ready to escape, just in case things didn't go as planned.

Seth was right behind me as we walked through the front doors of C. Henley Labs Incorporated.

My adrenaline was high, and I was taken off guard by how normal and quiet the reception area was. I didn't know what I had expected, but it wasn't a friendly, smiling receptionist around my age, flowers in colorful vases placed throughout the lobby, and soothing classical music playing in the background.

Seth jumped right into character, quickly taking lead on the plan.

"Hi," Seth greeted the receptionist with a charming smile. "I'm with Clark and Weber. I'm here to see Dr. Bob Meeker."

Seth calmly pulled out his badge and showed it to the receptionist, but she didn't look at it. She was immediately focused on creating a temporary badge for him.

"Are you with Clark and Weber too?" she asked me.

I nodded. I was almost afraid to speak. I wasn't sure I could come across as calm as Seth.

The receptionist didn't even ask me for my name as she handed Seth and me our visitor badges. Seth and I discreetly exchanged a look. Raina had made me a fake Clark and Weber badge because Alexander was adamant that we wouldn't be able to get visitor badges without some type of identification.

"Have a seat, and someone will call you back shortly," the receptionist said.

Seth and I took a seat in the waiting area, but the exchange with the receptionist wasn't sitting well with me.

I stared at the dark gray tiled floor as I tried to block out Seth's thoughts and hone in on what the receptionist was thinking.

The receptionist dialed a number on the phone, and although I couldn't hear what the person on the other end of the phone was saying, I could hear the receptionist's voice and was able to pick up on her thoughts.

"I have two Clark and Weber employees in the lobby for Dr. Meeker," the receptionist said into her headset and then paused.

"Huh. That's strange," she thought to herself.

"I didn't realize he'd checked in earlier," the receptionist replied to the person on the phone. "That must have been when Casey was covering the desk."

I looked up just in time to see her glance over at Seth. The confusion on her face was alarming.

The front door opened, and two men walked in. One of the men was wearing a suit, and the other was in a pair of scrubs. The man in the suit approached the reception desk, and the man in the scrubs walked past us and toward a door on the far-right side of the room. It was the door Alexander had told us to expect Dr. Meeker's assistant to come from.

"Something's not right," I whispered to Seth. "You need to go."

I focused on the man in the scrubs as he approached the door.

"Seven, two, zero, nine, pound," he thought as he punched in the code on the door.

It opened.

"What are you talking about?" Seth whispered back.

205

The phone at the front desk rang, and the receptionist was distracted as she tried to balance taking the call with acknowledging the man in the suit in front of her.

"Go!" I whispered insistently to Seth.

Without hesitating, I stood up and walked to the door with the keypad. I tried to keep my movements quick but minimal, so I didn't draw any attention. The receptionist was still distracted.

I punched in seven, two, zero, nine, pound into the keypad, and the door immediately opened. I slid inside, and to my surprise, Seth was at my heels, closing the door behind us.

"You need to go," I told Seth. "You coming with me wasn't part of the plan."

"Too late now," he replied. "Besides, we're already off plan. What happened back there?"

"Someone from Clark and Weber is already here, so they know we're not supposed to be here."

"How is that possible?" he asked. "I've never heard of this company before."

I pulled Alexander's hand-drawn map out of my pocket and tried to figure out where Dr. Meeker's office was. That was supposed to be my starting point toward finding the right hallway to go down to get to where Alexander thought they were holding Michael.

Seth and I passed a few offices with glass windows, but luckily, each office had their shades drawn and doors closed, so if there were people inside, we couldn't see them, and they couldn't see us.

As we approached a closed door on the left, I noticed the nameplate outside the office said Bob Meeker, MD. I grabbed Seth's arm to stop him from moving forward. If Dr. Meeker had an assistant, she could be nearby and not necessarily in an office.

Wouldn't she most likely sit right outside his office?

We took a few steps closer, and I noticed the wall to the right opened up. Sure enough, there was a desk facing his office. We quietly slid against the wall, closer to the desk, and listened. I didn't hear anything. I motioned for Seth to follow me.

As we walked past the assistant's empty desk, I saw the women's restroom just a little farther ahead on the right, which meant we were on the right track. There were only a few more offices between us and it.

A door handle jiggled from a nearby office. Seth heard it at the same time and grabbed my arm, pulling me behind Dr. Meeker's assistant's desk and to the floor.

The phone on the assistant's desk began to ring, and we heard the sound of heels clanking against the tiled floor. The steps grew closer, and Seth and I could do nothing, except wait for the assistant to come around the desk and discover us crouching behind it.

I closed my eyes, waiting for her to find us. Instead of coming around the desk, she picked up her headset from the other side. She still didn't know we were there.

"Are you sure they said Clark and Weber?" the assistant asked the caller. "I just checked with Dr. Meeker, and he said they weren't expecting anyone else from Clark and Weber for the meeting." She paused, and just as I was about to try to listen to her thoughts, she said aloud, "They left? Yeah, that's odd. I'll be right there."

The assistant tossed her headset on top of the desk, and we heard her heels clanking away, back toward the door leading to the reception area.

Once we heard the door close, Seth and I jumped back up. They were onto us, and we didn't have much time to find Michael and get out of there.

The coast was clear, so we ran down the hall, past the women's restroom, and found the hallway on the east side of the building. We darted around the corner, Seth's shoes squealing as they tried to regain traction.

"That's not supposed to be there," Seth said, referring to a door that was blocking our path.

We came to a stop at the door.

"They must have added it since the last time Alexander was here," I replied, trying to catch my breath.

The door was just like the one in the lobby—thick steel, secured with a keypad. I tried typing in seven, two, zero, nine, pound since it'd worked for us the first time, but the door didn't open. The person we'd followed in didn't have access to this section. This must be where they were holding Michael.

"We don't have time to wait on another person to come through," Seth said. "What do you want to do?"

I pressed my hands against the door as if I'd be able to feel Michael's presence through it. We had to get through. We had to get him out of there.

"I have an idea," I said, recalling Michael telling me about the time he and Raina had almost escaped during the power outage when they were kids.

It was possible that the security breach had been discovered and corrected by now, and it was possible that the breach never existed at this particular facility at all. There was no guarantee that cutting the power off would get us through the door, but still, I had to try.

I closed my eyes and tried to focus. The problem was, I didn't know how to make the power go out. I'd only done it that one time in the café, and it hadn't been intentional. I certainly hadn't tried to make it happen since.

"What are you doing?" Seth asked, the urgency in his voice making me anxious.

"Shh," I hushed him, keeping my eyes closed.

When I'd made the power go out that day in the café, it was because I had gotten upset. It was like all of this tension had built up until it had nowhere else to go but out.

I forced myself to focus on Michael and the danger that he was in. Through my closed eyes, I could tell the lights were flickering. I thought about the scars on his back and chest and began to worry that someone was slicing into his flesh right this very moment. He was suffering, and I wasn't getting to him fast enough. Tears stung at my closed eyes.

Seth shook me back to reality. When I opened my eyes, the power was out. Despite the darkness, I could see Seth staring at me in awe.

"Did you just do that?" he asked.

"Yes," I replied, immediately reaching for the door and opening it right before the backup generator came on.

"Cool."

The generator was providing a minimal amount of light, so we would have a little bit of coverage.

I continued to slowly open the door and peered around it, unsure of what was on the other side. It looked kind of like a hospital. There was a nurses' station, but it appeared to be empty. Directly across from the nurses' station was a room with a closed door. On the door was what appeared to be a patient chart, and I wondered if Michael was in there.

Seth and I squeezed through the steel door, trying not to open it all the way, just in case someone was nearby. We closed it quietly behind us and then crouched behind a cart loaded with medical supplies. It didn't provide much concealment though, so we couldn't stay long. If someone came through the steel door, they would surely see us.

A female nurse emerged from the room with the chart on the door. She attempted to lock the door behind her, but it didn't work. Despite the generator, the doors still didn't lock.

The nurse let out a frustrated sigh as she walked over to the nurses' station and picked up the phone. "The subject is still pretty sedated, but it's almost time for its next shot. And the door to its room won't lock, so you need to send security up," she said.

As I processed her words, I could feel my cheeks flush, my blood starting to boil. She was talking about Michael, and she was referring to him as *it*. I needed to calm down. I needed to be in full control of my abilities, or our cover would be blown.

"It's now or never," Seth whispered, raising an eyebrow.

We both knew there was no plan on what to do next, so we'd have to improvise.

The nurse opened a drawer and started fumbling through it. Behind the nurses' station, on a shelf very close to where she was standing, I noticed a vase with flowers in it. I stared at the vase, willing it to move. I had to be careful though. The idea was to just nudge it, to make it look like an accident. The nurse would just think she hadn't seen it in the poor lighting. I just couldn't send it flying across the room.

The vase wiggled ever so slightly, but the nurse didn't notice. She was still digging in the drawer.

I imagined an invisible cord tied to the side of the vase, gently pulling it off the shelf. Just as the nurse emerged from the desk with a flashlight, the vase dropped to the ground behind the nurses' station. We could hear the shards of glass splattering against the floor.

The nurse jumped in surprise and let out a gasp. She turned on the flashlight and bent down out of sight to try to clean up the mess. I motioned for Seth to follow me, and we silently scurried past the nurses' station and into Michael's room.

Seth softly closed the door behind us, and I immediately surveyed the room, looking for Michael.

There was a hospital bed in the far corner of the room. In the dim lighting, I couldn't tell if it was Michael until I was almost at his bedside.

Michael was unconscious and lying on his back. He was wearing a pair of gray scrubs with thick black straps restraining him to the bed. With trembling hands, I managed to undo the straps.

I shook Michael by the shoulders, but he didn't move. I tried shaking him harder. He had to wake up. There was no way Seth and I would be able to carry him out of there without getting caught.

Michael's head moved slightly, and he groaned.

"Michael, please wake up," I pleaded, running my hand over his head, stroking his hair.

I tried taking his hand in mine and squeezing it, but he didn't respond.

Four different gauze pads were taped to his arm, confirming my fears that Henley had picked up right where he'd left off with Michael. Deep red splotches stained the gauze, showing where his wounds had partially bled through.

Michael's eyes fluttered as he struggled to open them.

"Follow my voice. You have to wake up," I coaxed him.

"Natalie?" he muttered.

"Yes, it's me," I told him, bringing his hand to my lips and kissing it. "You can do this. Wake up."

"Natalie," Michael repeated as he managed to get one eye open and then another. He blinked at me several times, clearly disoriented. "What's happening?" His eyes opened wider as he realized what was going on. "What are you doing here? You have to get out of here …" His tone was urgent, but the pace in which he spoke was sluggish, and I was worried he would drift off to sleep again.

I tried to pull him up into a sitting position, but his body was still limp and heavy.

Seth rushed over to the bed to assist with getting Michael propped up. Seth placed Michael's arm over his shoulders to help him up.

"Come on, man," Seth said to Michael. "We've gotta go."

As they stood, Michael almost fell to the ground, but Seth managed to stable him. I grabbed Michael's other arm and placed it around my shoulders, trying to share some of the weight with Seth.

We made our way to the door, and Seth cracked it open with his free hand. We heard a man's voice talking with the nurse and the sound of broken glass being swept up.

Seth looked at me and shook his head, letting me know the coast wasn't clear. He carefully closed the door. We were trapped.

Michael's eyes started to close, and I could feel his body grow limp again. I tapped his cheek with my hand.

"Stay with me," I urged him.

A loud alarm began to sound, sending an intense shrill throughout the entire building. An outsider would probably just assume it was a fire drill, but we knew the truth.

"They've figured it out," I said.

The knot took hold of my stomach, and I knew trouble was on the way.

Before I could say anything to warn Seth, the door to the room opened up, and a security guard marched in. He was a burly-looking man in his forties with greasy, light-brown hair and a partial beard. He looked more like a convicted felon than a security guard.

The security guard didn't immediately notice us standing to the side of the door. He was focused on the bed we'd just pulled Michael from.

I quickly scanned the room for something we could use to defend ourselves, but Seth reacted more swiftly than I could. Seth let go of Michael, and I wrapped my other arm around him to steady him.

As the security guard realized we were in the room and turned back to face us, Seth was ready for him and punched him in the throat. Seth followed it up by punching the security guard in the face, knocking him out.

Seth grabbed ahold of Michael again, and I stood there in awe. I'd never seen Seth hit anyone. Ever.

"Let's go!" Seth commanded, snapping me back into action.

We did our best to run in sync with Michael between us. The nurse, who was sitting at the nurses' station, jumped to her feet when she saw us emerge from the room. She took a step forward, like she was going to confront us, but as she looked past us, she noticed the security guard unconscious on the floor. She stopped moving and put her hands up, silently pleading with us not to harm her.

I didn't acknowledge her. Instead, I was focused on finding our way to the exit.

According to Alexander, we could escape the building through the back entrance. To get there, I needed to find the other door leading out of this restricted area, go down a hallway, and take a left, and then there should be an exit door. He'd warned me that going through that exit would sound an alarm, but that ship had already sailed.

Seth saw the other door the same time I did, and we made a dash for it, moving as quickly as we could. Michael was slowly regaining strength, but his feet were still listless and his body unsteady.

I was vaguely aware of the commotion behind us as the nurse made a leap for her phone. There was no doubt in my mind that she was calling for more security.

We made it past the first door and entered a long hallway that was partially illuminated by backup generator lights and a pulsating strobe light set off by the alarm. About twenty feet ahead, I could see the hallway where we needed to turn left.

Once we made that turn, we should be close to the exit that led outside. There would still be the challenge of getting to our car, but if we could just make it that far, I was confident we'd find a way to escape. Even if I had to make a scene to get the attention of workers at surrounding offices, I'd do whatever was necessary to get us to safety.

The alarm and accompanying strobe lights turned off, and the power to the building came back on.

"The exit should be right here," I said as we turned left at the hallway.

We're almost there!

My excitement was cut short as we came to a screeching halt.

Standing between us and the exit was Chad Henley.

TWENTY

Chad Henley crossed in front of us, toward his oversize mahogany desk. He leaned against it, arms folded across his chest. He was wearing a white button-up shirt with the sleeves partially rolled up, a black tie, and black pants. Henley's eyes moved from me to Seth to Michael, in the order we were standing.

Michael, although still weak, was now able to stand on his own, unassisted. Two security guards, including the one Seth had previously knocked out, stood behind us to make sure we didn't try to escape or fight back.

Without being prompted, the security guard that Seth had punched walked in front of us. As he stood in front of Seth, staring him down, I noticed the name Chuck sewn into his uniform shirt, like a nametag.

Chuck roughly searched Seth, I assumed looking for weapons that we didn't have. Under Alexander's advice, Seth and I had left our wallets and cell phones with Jen, so the only item the security guard was able to retrieve was Seth's Clark and Weber badge.

"Go ahead, Chuck. Get it off your chest," Henley said, giving a nonchalant wave of the hand.

Chuck drew back his fist and punched Seth in the stomach. I gasped as Seth immediately doubled over in pain. Chuck then punched Seth in the face. I took a step, but Michael shook his head at me, silently cautioning me against intervening. Seth fell backward and huffed in pain. Luckily, he was still conscious.

Chuck took a step to the left and was now in front of me, staring down at me with hatred. My body tensed, wondering if he would punch me as well. Instead, he started to pat me down, searching me, just as he had with Seth.

Chuck patted down my chest and then moved his hands to my back pockets. I glanced over at Michael, trying to distract myself. His jaw was clenched, and his eyes were locked on Chuck. Chuck didn't notice as he dug into my pockets, ripping out my fake ID.

Chuck turned around and nodded at Henley as Seth slowly stood back up.

The door to Henley's office opened from behind us.

"Good of you to join us," Henley greeted whoever had just entered the room, but his tone wasn't friendly.

The footsteps stopped just behind us.

"Seth?" a familiar voice said.

Instinctively, Seth and I turned our heads.

Mr. Weber walked around us and stood to our left, halfway between us and Henley.

My stomach did a flip-flop as I connected the pieces together. Mr. Weber was the person from Clark and Weber who was meeting with Dr. Meeker today. If he was here, it meant he was doing business with Henley.

Is he the reason Henley found us at my parents' house? Had he told Henley we were there?

"Dad, what are you doing here?" Seth asked, shocked.

When Mr. Weber didn't answer him, Seth threw me a desperate glance. He didn't want to believe this was happening. I could only look back at Seth with sympathy.

Henley stood up straight and walked closer. His strides were heavy and intentional, as if he was deliberately trying to be intimidating. I sensed that he liked that people feared him.

"Did you know your son was planning to break into my facility, assault one of my employees, and steal my property?" Henley asked Mr. Weber.

I pursed my lips together and forced myself not to interject. *Michael is not your property.*

"This is all a misunderstanding, a coincidence," Mr. Weber replied. He tried to sound calm and confident, but his shaking voice gave him away. "Seth had no idea of our partnership. I never told him."

Henley cocked his head to one side. "So, I guess that makes it all better, does it?"

"You're working for this guy?" Seth burst out, thrusting a careless hand in Henley's direction.

Henley snapped his attention toward Seth, and without reading his mind, I knew sinister thoughts were running through his head. I could see it in his eyes. I got the sense that Henley liked to feel in control, and Seth's belittlement of him wouldn't go unpunished.

I didn't say anything but reached up and lowered Seth's arm until it was securely resting back at his side. Seth looked down at me, and through his pain and confusion, I hoped he could see the pleading in my eyes. The knot returned and told me that Seth needed to get his emotions under control even though it might already be too late.

Mr. Weber must've also understood what Henley was capable of because he quickly tried again to defuse the tension.

"There must be a way we can sort all of this out," Mr. Weber said. "What Seth did was wrong, and I'm willing to compensate for those wrongdoings. Why don't you let Seth and Natalie go, and you and I can renegotiate my contract?"

Henley let out a small laugh, more for dramatic effect than from genuine amusement. "Money? You think I need a few thousand dollars extra? No, what I need is an investment, insurance that C. Henley Labs Incorporated will make its mark on the world. That's not something you, William, can give me." Henley narrowed his eyes in Michael's direction. "Only *he* can."

"Let them go, and I'm yours," Michael told Henley. "I'll do anything you want."

Henley pondered this for a moment, and then a slow smile spread across his lips. As much as the idea terrified me, I realized this was the moment that I needed to get inside Henley's head. I'd never been inside the head of someone who was evil, but it was the only chance we had of staying ahead of him.

Just as I tried to block out all of the distractions around me, so I could focus on Henley and his thoughts, the knot in my stomach grew deeper, and I knew what was coming. I didn't need to be in Henley's head to know what was going to happen next.

"Well, considering you are already mine," Henley said to Michael, "we'll have to focus on what you can do on behalf of your friends."

My heart began to pound from within my chest. I knew where this was going. *Does Michael?*

"Let's make a deal," Henley said, clapping his hands together, as if the idea had just occurred to him. "Your friends can go when you finally show me that you can heal yourself."

"I can't," Michael replied, his tone calm but firm. "I don't have the ability to do that."

"But I think you do," Henley insisted. "All of the data we have on you demonstrates that you should be able to tap into this specific capability, yet for some reason, you refuse."

Henley nodded to Chuck, who immediately walked over to Michael. He pulled out a pocketknife and unfolded it, revealing a sharp, shiny blade.

I took a step forward, but Seth caught my arm, holding me in place. It was his turn to help me get my emotions back in check. If I were to lunge at Henley, the only thing that would do was get us all killed.

Chuck pressed the blade into Michael's arm and slowly dragged it across. Michael didn't flinch as the blade tore into his skin. Blood started to pool and then slip down his arm. I put my hands over my mouth to keep from screaming.

"Do it," Henley told Michael. "Do it, and your friends can go."

Seth looked at me with such intensity that it forced me to take my eyes off Michael and look at him instead. Seth nodded slightly, and it took me a second to realize what he wanted. He wanted me to read his mind.

"*Can he heal himself?*" Seth asked me silently.

I slightly shook my head in response, trying not to draw any unwanted attention.

"*Is Henley going to kill us?*" Seth asked me in his head.

I looked down at the ground, unable to bring myself to nod or to see Seth's reaction. I hadn't read Henley's mind, but the greater part of me that knew when something bad was about to happen knew it was true. Regardless of whether Michael was able to heal himself or not, I didn't believe Henley planned on letting Seth or me go alive.

During my exchange with Seth, I hadn't noticed Henley walk over to his desk. When I looked up, Henley was walking back toward us, this time holding a black handgun with a silencer on it. He stopped in front of Seth.

"I'll tell you what," Henley said, throwing a side-glance at Michael. "If you can heal yourself before he bleeds out, I will let you heal him next. And if you don't, he'll die, and I'll shoot the girl next."

The knot in my stomach pulsed, and I knew Henley was going to pull the trigger.

I could use my abilities to push the gun away, diverting it away from Seth, but then I would risk the bullet hitting Michael in the process.

"Mr. Henley," Mr. Weber said, his voice clearly laced with desperation.

The edges of Henley's thin lips curled slightly upward. Knowing what was to follow, I instinctively used my abilities to pull the gun toward me, away from Seth and away from Michael.

The gun went off, and at first, I didn't notice anything different. Seth and Michael were both standing, and I still had the knot in my stomach.

It wasn't until I saw Michael take a leap forward, only to be caught by Chuck and the other security guard, that I realized my legs were falling out from under me. The knot in my stomach was replaced by a different kind of ache, one that felt like sharp steel set on fire. It pierced through the knot, knocking it out of my body.

I collapsed, and Seth caught me before I hit the ground. Seth carefully eased me to the floor and put both hands over my stomach. The blood from my stomach leaked between his fingers.

"Dad, help her!" Seth screamed at his father.

I couldn't see Mr. Weber, but his silence indicated he wasn't willing to intervene or challenge Henley.

The world around me started getting quiet, almost muffled. Out of my peripheral vision, I could sense chaos around me.

I could tell Michael was struggling to free himself to heal me. Michael, who had once ripped through steel to pull me out of my wrecked car, was still under whatever sedatives they had given him and couldn't fight off the two guards. Chuck punched him twice in the stomach until Michael was on his knees.

Seth uselessly tried to stop my bleeding. I thought he was trying to encourage me, but I couldn't make out the words he was saying.

The coldness I'd felt before when I was dying in the woods after my accident began to set in. Michael stretched out his hand toward me, desperately wanting to heal me, but he was nowhere close to reaching me.

Henley stood still as a statue, uncaring and unmoved by what he'd done. He was convinced that killing me was justified. I realized that even though I couldn't hear the physical world around me, I could hear Henley's thoughts whether I wanted to or not.

"Why would it have me shoot the girl first?" Henley thought to himself.

He didn't realize I was the one who had diverted the gun away from Seth.

"Interesting. It still insists that it can't heal itself. Maybe once the girl dies and I shoot the boy, it will change its mind."

Hearing Henley think of Michael as an *it* infuriated me. And knowing that he would soon shoot and kill my best friend began to set off a rage deep inside me. I thought about the fresh bandages on Michael's arms and the torture he'd endured at the hands of this madman.

Reality began to set in that once Seth and I were dead, this wouldn't be over for Michael. He would go back into the secure part of the Henley facility, probably to a different location, with no hope of ever being rescued. Sure, Alexander would attempt to save him, but he would be caught and suffer the same fate as Seth and me.

The coldness began to subside and was replaced with a warmth that rapidly turned into heat, like boiling water beneath my skin. The familiar vibrations of healing began to pulsate throughout my body even though I knew Michael was nowhere close to touching me. The stabbing pain in my abdomen dwindled as the heat sensation turned into a flaming fire that now consumed me.

Henley turned away from me and put his attention back on Michael. "You're running out of time," Henley said to him. *"Not that you'd have enough strength to heal her anyway—if you even have enough to heal yourself."*

I heard the last part, but I was pretty sure he hadn't said it aloud.

Henley never intended for Michael to heal me or Seth. He wasn't sure Michael would be able to heal his own wound with the sedatives still in his system. This was just a test to see if he could break Michael down into trying to heal himself. If he could get Michael to do that, Henley would have full control over him.

Seth didn't feel my wound healing up beneath his hands, and I wondered how he couldn't feel the heat radiating off my skin. How could he not be shaking just from touching me? The weakness that had brought me to the ground was gone, and I felt such an intense burst of energy that I worried I might explode.

I jolted up so fast into a standing position that I accidentally knocked Seth over. It was better that he was out of the way anyway. I didn't know if I could control whatever was going on with me.

Chuck let go of Michael and took a cautious step toward me. All I did was think about pushing him away from me, and he flew across the room, smashing into the wall. As Chuck slid down the wall, I noticed the drywall was dented where his head had hit. Chuck lay on the floor, unconscious.

The other security guard made a dash for the phone on Henley's desk, no doubt to call for backup. I envisioned stopping him, and as my eyes followed him across the room, everything started blowing up in the path. First was a window, then several overhead lights, and finally Henley's computer monitor.

The security guard reached the phone, but it flew across the room, out of his grasp. It broke into pieces as it hit the ground. He turned to face me, and before he could think of what to do next, I pushed him into the wall just as I had Chuck, rendering him unconscious.

Henley watched me with wide, greedy eyes. He wasn't scared, but he should be. This rage inside me was all because of him. The intensity inside me began to build up again. A part of me wanted to unleash it all on Henley, to pay him back for everything he had done to Michael and his family and for trying to kill me and Seth. It was a split-second decision on what to do with this energy. I could end all of this right here, right now.

Just as I was certain I was going to launch it all at Henley, I made a last-minute choice to aim it at the wall by the window instead.

As if I'd let off a bomb, a large hole blasted through the wall. The backside of the building was now exposed to the outside.

Mr. Weber ran and crouched behind Henley's desk.

Henley noticed him and thought to himself, *"I'll deal with you later for your mistake."*

Michael stepped around Henley and was at my side. He reached out and gently touched my shoulder. "Come on. We should go," he said.

I debated on what to do with Henley as I stared him down. It wouldn't take much for me to channel another burst of energy, but was that what I really wanted?

As much as I didn't want Henley to exist, I wasn't a murderer. I wasn't *him*.

Seth stood up and ran over to his dad, helping him to his feet. Mr. Weber fearfully watched me as Seth guided him outside to safety.

"Let's go," Michael urged.

I allowed him to take me by the hand and lead me to the hole I'd created in the wall.

Henley didn't make a move. He just watched us carefully. A part of me waited for him to give me a reason to take him out for good, but the other, better part of me was glad that he wasn't forcing me to make that choice.

Michael led me through the hole in the wall, and we stepped outside onto the grass.

"*I'll see you soon, Natalie,*" Henley said.

I stopped and turned to look at him.

Henley cocked his head to the side, and his eyes widened. A small smile slowly spread across his lips.

Henley and I locked eyes, and I realized two things in that moment. One, he hadn't said it aloud. And two, Henley knew I'd heard him. His eyes sparkled with a new curiosity as he watched us walk away.

TWENTY-ONE

"Natalie," a voice said, but I barely noticed.

My eyes were fixed on a small stain on the back of the passenger seat of the car. It was a small blue dot that stood out against the tan interior. *A pen mark perhaps?*

I felt a warm hand on my shoulder.

"Natalie, we're here."

I turned my head to the right, my eyes reluctantly leaving the stain. They landed on Michael, standing outside the car. Seth came around from the driver's side to stand next to him.

"You haven't said anything since we left Henley," Seth said to me.

I didn't respond, but I got out of the car. My brain was in a fog and didn't feel completely connected to my body.

Seth was right. I hadn't said anything since we walked out of Henley's office. Despite my desire to confront Mr. Weber, I had watched in silence as he got into his own car and drove away.

"Can you give us a second?" Michael asked Seth.

"Sure thing," Seth replied and walked to the house.

Michael and I watched as Jen emerged from the house, jumping into Seth's arms as he approached the front door. Seth allowed himself to enjoy the reunion, hugging her tightly for a second. He set her down, and she went to take a step toward me, but Seth ushered her into the house to give Michael and me some privacy.

I was glad that I'd had my suitcase in the car, so I could change my shirt on the way to the house. If Jen had seen the amount of blood that was on it, she would have freaked out.

"Talk to me," Michael said once we were alone. He took my hand in his.

I pulled my hand back and took a step away from him. "It's not safe," I said.

He ignored me and again reached for my hand. "We're safe for now."

I retreated again. He didn't understand.

"No, *I'm* not safe," I insisted. "I don't trust myself right now."

How can I after what I just did at Henley?

I'd had no idea I was capable of destruction of that magnitude. Without a doubt, I could have destroyed that entire building if I put my mind to it. I could have killed Chad Henley, and I'd actually contemplated it.

Ignoring me, Michael stepped closer and carefully wrapped his hands around the sides of my face. He lowered his head, so we were eye-level, forcing me to look at him. "I trust you. Do you hear me? I trust you with my life."

"I don't know how I did what I did," I said, a flood of emotion removing the fog. "It felt almost … uncontrollable."

"You were incredible," he said, pulling me to him, engulfing me in his embrace.

This time, I didn't fight him.

His strength had fully returned. I closed my eyes and listened to his heart strongly beat within his chest. I'd never thought I would get the chance to be this close to him again.

The front door opened, and Lorena stepped out, followed by Raina. Lorena waved, and I reluctantly pulled away from Michael.

"You should go see your family," I told him, but he didn't move. "Go ahead. I will be there in a minute."

He gave me a kiss on the forehead before walking to the house to reunite with his family.

I walked over to a large oak tree in the yard beside the house and sat underneath it. It reminded me of summers when Becca, Seth, and I had been kids. We were always playing outside, climbing trees just like this one. I had never been as good at it though because I was so much shorter than they were.

"You're officially my hero," Seth said, pulling me out of the memory playing in my head. He sat down on the grass next to me. "You said you could do some unusual stuff, but I had no idea you could do all of that."

I let out a small laugh. "Neither did I," I admitted. "Some of it came as much of a surprise to me as it did to you."

"I think this goes without saying, but I'm quitting my job," Seth said, looking down at the ground.

"I'm sorry about your dad, Seth."

"Do you think your dad knows mine was working with Henley?" he asked.

I shook my head. "I don't think so, but I'm not sure about anything anymore."

I never would have predicted that Seth's dad had been working with Henley. I felt betrayed by Seth's dad, but I was careful to keep it to myself. Whatever betrayal I was feeling was nothing compared to what Seth must be feeling.

"So, what happens next?" he asked. "Do we just go home like nothing happened?"

"Honestly, I don't know," I replied with a sigh.

"I was afraid you were going to say that." He leaned his head back against the tree trunk.

"I think you and Jen can go home once Henley knows the rest of us are far away. Maybe go on a vacation first and let things simmer down," I told him as I thought it through. "Henley doesn't have any reason to suspect that Jen's involved in any of this, and he would only come after you if he thought you could lead him to what he wanted."

He lifted his head, fully prepared to debate on what I was about to tell him.

"Once Henley knows you don't have any contact with the rest of us, I think he will leave you alone. He's not after you," I explained.

Seth's forehead creased. "You're not doing this." There was a hint of anger in his voice. "You're not shutting me out again."

"Seth, I have to. It's not that I want to. I have no choice. It's the only way for you and Jen to move on and have a normal life." As the words came out of my mouth, I had a new appreciation for the sacrifice Michael had been willing to make for me. Even though I hadn't wanted him to leave, he had done it for the same reasons. He had done it to protect me, and I would do the same for Seth and Jen.

"Where will the rest of you go?"

It was a good question that I didn't necessarily know the answer to. "Well, I'll probably go back to where I was before I called you to

meet me here, and Michael and his family will go somewhere new."
My heart ached as I said it, realizing that, soon, I'd be saying good-bye to Michael all over again.

"You aren't going with them?" Seth blankly stared at me, unable to fathom that I was willing to walk away from Michael after all we had gone through to get him back.

I could hear Henley's thought repeating in my head, telling me he would see me soon. Now that Henley knew about my abilities, he would surely be looking for me too. Even if Michael and his family let me come with them, I would pose an even greater risk to their safety. Just when I'd thought I'd made progress in controlling my abilities, today was a reminder that there was still so much I didn't know. My abilities were much more unpredictable and powerful than I'd ever imagined. And that was dangerous.

"I don't think that's an option," I replied, unable to shake the look in Henley's eyes as we had left. It was like he had known something I didn't, like he had known he had an advantage over me.

"What is it?" Seth gently jabbed me with his elbow.

I hesitated, trying to put it into words. "I-I feel like something's off. Like we missed something. Or forgot something."

"What could we have possibly missed?" he asked. "We left with Michael and with our lives. Sounds like success to me."

I quietly sat there, trying to figure it out.

"Do you want to know what I think?" he said. "I think you're in shock by what happened. And who could blame you? You almost died today."

I opened my mouth, about to protest, when Jen opened the front door to check on us.

Seth waved to her and stood up. "We should go in. Everyone is anxious to see you. Even Raina asked about you." He offered me his hand.

"Okay, *now*, I'm in shock," I replied with a laugh, allowing Seth to help me up.

Seth put an arm around my shoulders as we walked to the house.

Jen squealed with excitement as I greeted her. "I'm so glad you're okay," she said, hugging me so tightly that I could barely breathe. She was a lot stronger than she looked.

Once we entered the living room, Lorena was also waiting to greet me with a hug. Raina didn't attempt to hug me but did give me a single nod, which was a nice step up from the usual scowl.

"Michael said that you were shot," Alexander said as Lorena released me. "If you are comfortable with it, I'd like to examine you to make sure you are okay."

I felt completely fine but sensed the concern in the room, so I agreed to let him examine me. Lorena summoned everyone to the kitchen to help her make dinner in order to give me and Alexander some privacy.

"Mind if I stay?" Michael asked.

Alexander looked at me.

"Sure," I replied.

With his black medicine bag in hand, Alexander motioned for me to sit down on the couch. I obeyed, and he sat next to me. Michael leaned against an armchair, folding his arms across his chest but didn't sit.

Alexander pulled a stethoscope from the medicine bag and asked me to take several deep breaths, so he could check my lungs. He listened to my heart and then pulled out a blood pressure cuff and checked my blood pressure.

"Your vitals are good," he said. "You were shot in the stomach, correct?"

"Yes," I replied. Out of the corner of my eye, I noticed Michael shift his feet.

"Do you mind if I take a look?" Alexander asked.

"Sure." I lifted my shirt just above my belly button and pointed to the spot where I had been shot. "I was shot here."

Alexander carefully pressed on the spot and around it. "Any pain?"

"No." I didn't feel any pain at all.

"Any light-headedness or dizziness?" he asked.

"No, I feel fine," I assured Alexander as he examined my back.

Alexander lowered my shirt and gave me a small pat on the shoulder. "You have some minimal scarring, but other than that, I think you are in perfect health. There is a small scar on your back, which is good because it means the bullet exited your body."

I glanced down at my stomach and saw a very faint scar where I had been shot.

I looked over at Michael, his jaw set and lips tight.

"Have you checked out Michael?" I asked. "He was pretty out of it when we found him."

"They gave him a sedative to suppress his strength," Alexander said. "They have various drugs capable of suppressing or enhancing Michael's and Raina's abilities, but the effects have worn off."

I noticed the bloody bandages on his arms were gone. All that remained were the same scars as before.

Michael followed my gaze and said, "They were already healed when my dad removed the bandages."

Alexander stiffened. "You weren't given the test drug, were you?"

Michael looked thoughtful and then shook his head. "No. Not that I recall anyway. I think it was Natalie that healed me."

I hadn't thought of that. I must have healed him without realizing it when I was trying to wake him up in the hospital bed.

"What test drug are you talking about?" I asked.

Alexander and Michael exchanged a look.

"Henley is testing a new healing drug," Michael told me.

"Does it work?" I asked.

Michael shrugged. "I don't know."

He made it sound like it wasn't a big deal, but I could feel the tension from both him and Alexander, which made me think there was more to the story than he was letting on.

Lorena announced that dinner was ready. Without another word about the test drug, we joined the others in the dining room for shepherd's pie made with sweet potatoes, which was apparently Michael's and Raina's favorite dish. Lorena said she'd planned to prepare it to celebrate, confident that Michael would be returning to them. I was a little skeptical at first of the sweet and savory combination, but after I tried it, I decided I liked it.

After dinner, Jen and Seth announced that they had booked a late flight to Hawaii and would be leaving. I smiled at Seth, excited for them to get away for a while and eventually be able to return home to start their life together. It would also be good for him to take his mind off of his dad's involvement with Henley.

I could tell Seth was still torn about leaving me as we said good-bye, so I assured him one more time that he was doing the right thing.

"This sucks," Seth said.

"Yes, it does," I agreed. "But it's for the best. You deserve to be happy. If anyone deserves to be happy, it's you."

"I'm here for you if you ever need me," he said as he climbed into the driver's seat of a car Stan had arranged in exchange for my rental car.

I'd insisted that they take it, eager for them to move on to somewhere safe. When the time came for me to leave, I would just take a taxi to the airport.

"I know. You always have been," I replied, starting to feel a little choked up. I couldn't have asked for a better best friend than Seth.

"I refuse to say good-bye," Jen said through the open window of the car as she fastened her seat belt. "I know I will see you again. You'll find a way out of this."

I smiled back at Jen but was unable to offer her the reassurance she wanted. Michael and his family had been living on the run for so many years and were nowhere closer to being free from Henley. In fact, the situation was grimmer now more than ever, thanks to me.

I let out a yawn as their car disappeared out of sight. I'd never used my abilities to the extent I used them today, and I had nothing left, physically or emotionally.

"Is it safe to stay here tonight?" I asked Michael.

We hadn't discussed our plans yet.

"Alexander thinks we can wait and leave in the morning," Michael replied. "Henley will want to make a move at some point but not until he knows how to regain control of the situation."

I yawned again.

"Why don't you go upstairs and get ready for bed? I'll be up in a few to say good night," Michael suggested.

"A shower would be nice," I agreed.

I went upstairs, took off my disguise, and stepped into the shower. I washed away most of the temporary hair dye that Jen had used to conceal my identity. If only I could wash away this feeling of uneasiness.

My mind continued to drift back to my last exchange with Henley. *What could he know that I don't that made him so confident that he could find me?* The thought made me feel unsafe, as if he could show up at any moment.

I needed to leave first thing in the morning and put as much distance as I could between myself and Michael. If Henley was coming for me, I didn't want to risk putting Michael back in danger.

Maybe going back to Kentucky wasn't such a great idea either. *If I go back there, will I be putting Aunt Gael in danger?* I wasn't sure where I was going to go, but it needed to be somewhere far from those I loved.

As I dried myself off, I caught a glimpse of the scar above my belly button in the mirror. I turned to look at my back in the mirror and saw the faint scar where the bullet had exited my body. It was hard to imagine that I had been shot earlier today and succeeded in healing my own bullet wound.

I had somehow managed to escape death three times within only a few months. The first was the car accident, the second was leaping from the bridge, and the third was today. I hadn't healed myself from the car accident, but it was possible that I'd healed myself from my injuries from jumping off the bridge. I recalled how my ribs had felt broken, but by the time I'd reached Michael at the safe house, the pain had left. It proved Alexander's theory that something dormant in me had been awakened when Michael healed me.

I put on my pajamas and returned to the bedroom Lorena had assigned me. As I pulled a pair of socks out of my suitcase, I heard a light tap on the half-open door. It was Lorena.

"Mind if I come in?" she asked.

"Of course," I replied as I sat on the bed and pulled the socks onto my feet.

"Alexander said your body has healed well, but I wanted to check on you to see how you were *really* doing after everything that happened today," she said.

"I'm okay." I forced a small smile. Truth was, I wasn't sure if I was okay or not. "I mean, it was scary, but I'm just glad we got Michael back. That's all that matters."

Lorena sat next to me, folding her hands into her lap. "This might come as a surprise to you, but I never wanted to be a mother. Alexander and I had an agreement when we got married that it would just be the two of us and maybe a cat someday."

"What changed your mind?"

Lorena seemed like such a loving mother to Michael and Raina that I'd never considered that she hadn't wanted children.

"One day, he forgot his lunch, and I decided to bring it up to him. Security wasn't quite as tight back then as it is now, so they allowed me to bring it to his office. When I got there, he was treating the cutest little boy who had cuts on his arm."

"Michael," I acknowledged.

Lorena smiled thoughtfully. "I know this sounds crazy, but it was like I became a mother that day. I began to worry about that sweet little boy when Alexander would come home and tell me all of these horrific things that were happening at work. I worried about Raina, too, when I found out about her even though I'd never even met her. Alexander was so conflicted by his part in it. At first, he thought he would just quit, but then he realized that if he wasn't there to look after Michael and Raina, no one would. That's when I told him we needed to get them out of there."

"So, breaking them out was your idea?" I asked.

"Yes, not that it took much to convince Alexander. He loves both of them so much." She put her hand on top of mine. "Love gives you the strength to do impossible things, not that I have to tell you that. Thank you for saving my son. You are truly an extraordinary young lady."

I blushed, not sure how to respond to her. I certainly didn't feel extraordinary. In fact, I felt like a borderline monster for how out of control my abilities had been earlier.

"Mind if I interrupt?" Michael said from the doorway.

Lorena gave my hand a quick squeeze before letting it go. She stood up. "I was just going to bed anyway. Don't stay up too late. You need to rest," Lorena told Michael as she passed him.

Michael came into my room, closing the door behind him. "Feel better?" he asked.

"I'm better now that you're here," I told him with a smile.

He didn't return the smile as he sat down in an armchair in the corner of the room. He put his head in his hands, roughly raking his hair.

"What's wrong?" I asked.

"I can't believe you put yourself in danger like that to save me," he replied. I couldn't tell if he was angry or frustrated or both. "What were you thinking?"

I walked over and stood in front of him, placing my hands on his shoulders. "A simple thank-you would suffice."

He looked up at me, no trace of amusement on his face. "I'm grateful, Natalie, but you have to promise me that you will never, ever do something like that again." He rested his hands on my hips. "If Henley ever gets close to you again, he's never going to let you go. Now that he knows what you are able to do, he's going to do everything he can to find you."

I contemplated telling him how I'd heard Henley's thought earlier when we were leaving and how I couldn't shake this feeling that we'd missed something, but I decided against it. Michael had been through so much the past couple of days. He needed time to digest it all before I added more stress to the situation.

"I can't do that," I said. "I would do it again in a heartbeat."

"That's what scares the hell out of me," he replied, swallowing hard. "When Henley shot you today, I thought that was it. I thought you were gone."

"But I'm still here," I gently told him, but he avoided my eyes.

He looked tormented, and it broke my heart.

"Please look at me," I begged.

He looked up, his eyes sad and haunted, but beneath it, I could still see strength. Despite everything he'd been through, he was determined to overcome this. His strength awed me.

"I'm still here," I repeated, hoping he understood my perspective.

I loved him and would risk myself all over again to keep him safe. And I believed he would do the same for me.

"Raina told me how you found her," he said, referring to the dream visitation. "I didn't know you could do that."

"Neither did I," I replied. "It's something I was just learning to do, and it worked."

He creased his brows together.

"What's wrong?"

"We have a new threat at Henley," he said. "When I was there, I was pretty out of it, but I overheard a conversation between my doctor and one of the scientists. They were referring to a raven."

"A raven? Like a bird?" I asked, immediately recalling the one from my accident.

"It's not a bird," he replied. "Not in this context anyway. They were referring to a person who has seeing abilities similar to yours. Henley has someone he's using to try to locate me and Raina. One tactic their raven has been attempting to use is dream invasion. They were testing it when Alexander was still there, hoping they could re-create it and sell it as an espionage technique, but they were never successful. But they also didn't have someone who naturally had the ability to try to mimic it. They were looking for someone who did, and apparently, they found them."

I recalled how Alexander had been afraid I was trying to trap Michael somehow by appearing in his dreams. I realized now that his theory wasn't paranoia. He was worried that Henley had found a way to do it.

"If they figure out how to do it successfully, hiding from them will become almost impossible," I said, stating what we both knew to be true.

"Alexander told me that you tried to contact me while I was captured, but it didn't work. He thinks maybe it was because of the sedation. He's going to try to work on a remedy, a way to block it, in case their raven is able to figure out how to make contact. He's going to ask you to help him test it out."

I nodded, thinking about how awful it would be if even our dreams weren't safe from Henley.

He moved his hands from my hips to my stomach. He lifted my T-shirt above the waistband of my pajama pants, exposing my scar. He lightly ran his fingers over it. My skin tingled beneath his touch.

"Where do we go from here?" I asked.

He stood up, his hands returning to my hips. "Where do you want to go?"

I could feel his heart beating steadily beneath his shirt as I rested my hands on his chest.

"I want to be with you," I confessed. "But I know you have to leave again. If I was a risk to you and your family before, I'm an even bigger risk now." The words made sense, but my heart screamed at me to shut up. *How am I ever going to survive losing him again?*

He sighed and studied my face. "I'm never leaving you again. Not unless you want me to. Leaving you was the hardest thing I'd ever had to do. I don't think I could do it again if I tried."

I ran my hands up the back of his neck, pulling his face to mine until our lips met. As much as I knew it was dangerous for us to be together, I didn't know if I'd have the strength to let him go again. Especially if he wasn't going to insist on leaving.

He kissed me back, wrapping his arms all the way around my waist, holding me tight against his body. His hands moved to my back, under my shirt. When his fingertips grazed the scar on my lower back, he pulled away.

"You should get some rest. Your body has been through a lot of trauma today," he said. Before I could protest, he added, "I'll be here when you wake up in the morning."

"Promise?"

"I promise," he replied, lightly kissing me on the lips. "I'm not going anywhere without you."

"Okay."

After everything we'd been through and our time apart, all I wanted to do was spend time with him, but he was right. We needed our rest. And despite how tired I was feeling, he was probably even more exhausted. He had been taken back to Henley to face his worst fears, not to mention the physical torture that he'd endured while he was there.

"What's wrong?" he asked.

I shook my head. "Nothing. Just tired."

"I love you, Natalie." He kissed me one more time. "Whatever happens next, we'll face it. Together."

"Together," I echoed in agreement.

Michael walked to the bedroom door and turned to look at me one more time before leaving.

I climbed into bed and turned off the lamp resting on the nightstand. I lay there in the dark, taking in the peaceful silence, allowing myself to be comforted by the fact that not only was Michael in the next room, but he'd also be there when I woke up in the morning. Even if we had to be on the run from Henley, at least we would be together.

I didn't recall closing my eyes, but one minute, I was lying in bed, and the next minute, I was back in the woods, looking at the wreckage from my car accident. This was exactly the same dream I'd had when I realized Michael had been taken by Henley.

Michael is safe now, so why am I dreaming about this again?

The faceless man appeared from behind one of the trees. I braced myself, waiting for the additional men to appear like last time but they didn't. Instead, the man just stood there, and I felt the urge to approach him. This wasn't the same dream after all. This one was different.

My body moved toward the man, almost as if it were floating. It was as if I had to approach him whether I wanted to or not. As I drew closer, I imagined that the man was Henley, forcing me back to him.

Right on cue, I heard Chad Henley say, "I'll see you soon, Natalie." His voice wasn't coming from the person in front of me though. It was as if it were playing from a loud speaker in the trees.

A knot formed in my stomach as I stopped directly in front of the man. He'd never had a face before, but I could see the outline of one in the moonlight.

Thunder rumbled in the distance.

Lightning struck the wreckage behind me, causing me to jump. Sparks began to fly off the mangled car, illuminating the woods all around me. I turned back to the man in front of me and gasped. It wasn't the faceless man at all.

It was Becca.

"You missed it," Becca said. Her tone was robotic, her expression cold. It wasn't like her at all. It was like a dead version of her.

"Becca, what are you talking about? Missed what?" I asked.

My heart began to beat wildly. Something was terribly wrong. Is Becca trying to tell me that she's dead?

"You missed it," Becca repeated.

"Missed what?" I asked, desperate.

She looked past me, and I felt a presence behind me. The knot grew more intense, warning me that danger was close. Shaking, I forced myself to turn around to face who was behind me.

I knew it was Chad Henley before I even laid eyes on him. He was wearing the same clothing he'd had on earlier today, and he was smiling at me. The moment our eyes met, his smile diminished, and his eyes grew dark. The charm was gone, and the real evil that was within him was exposed.

"I'll deal with you later for your mistake," Henley said.

I recalled how Henley had thought that earlier today, and it was directed at Mr. Weber. I didn't understand it then, and I didn't understand it now.

What is my dream trying to tell me?

Just as in previous dreams, the raven cried out to me from up in the tree. This time, its sound pierced through me like a thousand knives. Its cry was urgent, refusing to be ignored.

I startled awake and sat straight up in bed.

My eyes darted around the room, looking for danger, but everything was quiet. The knot in my stomach continued to ache, insistent that even if danger wasn't here now, it was certainly looming. My dream was trying to reconcile it.

I contemplated waking Michael, but I also feared that I'd lose the precious details of the dream if I started trying to describe it to him. Instead, I sat in the dark, carefully replaying the dream in my head. The clues were there; I just needed to piece it together. I felt close to figuring it out, whatever it was trying to tell me.

Somewhere in this dream was Henley's hidden advantage, but what could it be?

And then, it suddenly clicked. My body turned to ice.

It can't be.

I threw back the covers and sprinted across the room.

I grabbed my purse and dumped the contents out onto the bed. My cell phone fell out, and I picked it up, immediately thumbing through my saved pictures.

I stopped when I landed on it—the picture of me, Seth, and Becca outside his house with his new car. The knot in my stomach twisted, confirming I was on the right track. There it was. In the picture, behind us in the background, at the end of Seth's driveway, at the front gate, were two raven gargoyle statues.

My legs gave out as I sank down to the floor. She was right. I had missed it. I hadn't just missed it today at Henley. I'd missed it since Becca disappeared.

I closed my eyes and began to relive the details of the night Becca had been taken. As much as I hated thinking about it, I had to do this. I made myself recall how I'd walked down the hall to her room, terrified of what I might find. I remembered seeing her lying in her bed, the moon casting a soft glow on her sleeping face. I remembered the intruder appearing out of nowhere and catching me by surprise. Although it'd all happened so fast that night, I forced myself to slow down the memory.

Focus, Natalie. Focus. It's someone who had access to your home. Someone who knew your parents wouldn't be home that night. Someone who knew where Becca's room was. You know who it is.

Eyes still closed, I pictured the faceless man reaching up and grabbing my head. As if in slow motion, I looked between my assailant's fingers as my head fell backward. I finally made myself see what I couldn't see before.

I saw William Weber.

I opened my eyes. The knot in my stomach began to subside. It all fit together, like a perfectly carved puzzle.

Becca had never hidden her abilities the way I had, and Seth's dad knew of them. He'd even had her journal. He had taken her because of her abilities and given her to Henley to help him track down Michael and Raina. Becca was the raven.

The dreams hadn't been a coincidence at all. Instead of hunting us down, Becca had been warning us about Henley all along. She'd even warned Michael about my accident. She'd warned me about Henley the night at my parents' house to make sure we got out in time.

Becca was *alive*.

A shiver ran down my spine as I recalled the strange look in Henley's eye as we'd left earlier today. He had been so confident that he would see me again soon. This was his advantage. Henley had known he wouldn't have to come for me. He had known I'd be back for Becca—and he was right.

I fixed my gaze on the darkness before me. I was no longer the scared, helpless little girl who was afraid of the faceless man who had taken Becca. I knew who he was, and I could defeat him. I could get her back. I *would* get her back—at any cost.

Yes, Henley, I will see you soon.

THE END

ACKNOWLEDGMENTS

Completion of this book would not have been possible without acknowledging the following people:

My amazing husband, Dran—Thank you for encouraging me to follow my dreams and for always finding a way to make me laugh. I love doing life with you.

My mom, Catherine Metzger, and dear friends, Melissa Henry and Brande Wester—Thank you for reading my book, giving me your unbiased feedback, and for listening to me talk about this book and the publishing process nonstop for more than a year. I would not have had the courage to publish this book without your love and support.

My friend, Mary Ashbaugh Skinner, who has encouraged and supported my writing since high school—I appreciate how you've always gently nudged me to follow my heart in all areas of life.

My talented editor, Jovana Shirley—You are truly amazing, and I could not have done this without you!

Tim Barber of Dissect Designs—Thank you for creating such a wonderful cover for my book. I'm still amazed at how perfectly you were able to capture the essence of the story in one picture.

And last but certainly not least, thank you to all of my friends and family who have cheered me on throughout this process.

ABOUT THE AUTHOR

Laurie Harrison graduated from the University of Central Florida with a degree in Interdisciplinary Studies, majoring in both Letters and Modern Languages, and Social Sciences. She has since found her niche writing young adult and new adult fiction. When she's not writing, Laurie enjoys spending time with her husband, traveling, and getting lost in a good book. You can visit her website at www.laurieharrisonauthor.com.